I0777242

Smoke

A Thriller

P.J. Parker

Paperback ISBN: 979-8-218-52049-6
E-book ISBN: 978-0-9986856-9-4

Edited by Hayley German Fisher.

Cover Design & photo modification by P.J. Parker
Original: London Photographer | András Stefuca
Man Running along Road Through Forest in Summer Sunlight
pexels-andras-stefuca-17843096

Dedication

This is for Steven.
Because he's always been the one.

2 ounces rye whiskey
1 ounce sweet vermouth
2 dashes Angostura bitters
Garnish: brandied cherry

— Classic Manhattan

Chapter One

Thomas Smoke had been inside twenty-three people in the moments before each was dead. There'd be two more before the day was over.

He slowed to a stop beside a twisted maple to catch his breath. The ten-mile run through the streets of Riverdale was not as gentle as his usual route down the west side of Manhattan. Sweat slicked his bare chest and saturated his running shorts, making them cling, nothing left to speculation. He breathed the sweet suburban air deep into his lungs and sluiced the perspiration from his flesh as he ran, before dropping to tighten his laces, then continuing along Palisades Avenue. This was his favorite part of New York City. His favorite avenue. It was cool beneath the broad canopy of trees, with glimpses of the Hudson River glistening through the dense undergrowth. Stately homes hid behind manicured foliage.

His stride was easy, his legs honed by a decade of marathons, every muscle in his frame toned and strong, but built more for endurance than speed. With short buzzed hair topped with a thatch of blonde curls he had to grease down for work, he was considered boy-next-door handsome by those who knew him—and those who wanted to. A man with a ready smile, who loved to kiss, and who did it often and well.

Excitement shivered down his spine as he approached the *Taylor* tree. It had grown majestic since his teenage years. Great boughs extended out over the pavement, leaves green, almost to the far side of the avenue. His heart thumped, and an intense heat burned through him. He felt light-headed. Euphoric.

He'd been barely seventeen, not yet able to grow a beard when he had scratched out the sod with his bare hands and buried Taylor there, the body to be embraced within the maple's roots. It had followed an unexpected and passionate weekend spent on the dance floors of subterranean and rooftop Manhattan clubs, and amongst the ripped and rumpled sheets of Taylor's bed in a Spuyten Duyvil studio. Thoughts of their time together still made him hard. He pushed the growing bulge in his shorts to the side and continued along the pavement, passing the tree without slowing his pace.

Another two blocks and he passed the *Hayden* tree, and then the one whose roots cradled the bones of Morgan—a poetry major he'd picked up in a dive bar near NYU in his early twenties. They'd both been enamored by the words of Emily Dickinson. *"Hope" is the thing with feathers*. Over a decade had passed since their encounter, yet he could still envision the rapture on Morgan's face as the blood gushed from the gaping slash across the neck.

Such a beautiful human being.
Such a beautiful experience.

Chapter Two

Smoke slowed as he ran up the incline of Spaulding Lane, but returned to full speed before veering north onto the familiar stretch of Independence Avenue. A schnauzer barked at him through a white picket fence, its muzzle tight between the palings. Otherwise, the street with its morning breeze was quiet. By his reckoning, he was exactly where he needed to be. In less than a minute, he'd be at his destination.

It was a home belonging to a couple; he'd observed the husband several times, stepping into a midnight-blue Mercedes convertible to drive the three blocks down the steep road to the Riverdale Metro-North train station. A Wall Street type. Martinis and cocaine. Both with a twist. His suits were expensive, and he filled them well. They'd exchanged glances twice, each time with a nod and a knowing smile. Smoke had glimpsed the wife only once, but it was enough to take his breath and confirm they were the ones. Today was Sunday. They'd be on their broad front verandah, finishing breakfast. Croissants and scrambled eggs seemed to be their go-to.

He slackened his pace as he neared the hand-stacked, dry-stone wall fronting their single-story home, stopping to stretch at the entrance to their gravel drive. The grit crunched beneath his runners as he lunged deep, reaching down to grip his ankle.

And there they were, watching him in silence over the last of their breakfast.

"That coffee sure smells good," he called across the hedgerow.

The woman laughed. "You look like you need a shower more than a coffee."

Her husband stood and leaned against a pillar, his mouth spreading into an appreciative smile framed by rusty designer stubble. He wore a robe, loosely sashed at the waist, an open invitation to gaze upon the clipped hair of his chest.

"That sounds pretty good, too," Smoke said.

He wondered which one of them, husband, or wife, was the strongest. Which one would help him kill the other.

Chapter Three

Standing beneath the rain shower, the water cold and stinging, Smoke's skin was still hot and flushed. He ran a handful of body wash across his chest and abdomen, under his pits. Angi and Daan had a luxurious bathroom.

Veined white marble covered the walls and floor, and the entire outer wall was a set of wrought-iron and beveled-glass French doors opening onto a stone courtyard where at least a dozen fat koi were splashing in a lilied pond. A chandelier in the center of the vaulted bathroom ceiling shimmered with droplets of crimson crystals. Smoke chuckled when he realized it wasn't blood.

He luxuriated under the flow of water, his thoughts lost in the pleasant morning he'd spent with the couple in their lounge, their kitchen, their hallway, and bedroom, and now their bathroom. The taste of their mouths was something he'd not soon forget.

The blood washed easily from the muscled length of his body, pooling about his feet before slipping down the drain. He wiped a swathe of condensation from the shower wall and smiled at what he saw through the glass. Angi, lounging in the carved, white onyx bath, gloriously naked, one leg up on the rim of the tub. She held his gaze, a genuine lover's bond, her smudged lipstick almost as garish as the seeping gash across her throat, and the blood glazing her perfect, eight-thousand-dollar breasts. A lump rose in Smoke's throat as he relished how stunning she was.

Enigmatic.

Shampooing his hair, the water ran pink, then clear.

He skimmed the soap over his buttocks and thighs, then scrubbed his groin, legs, and feet with a surgeon's efficiency. Hunkering down on the marble, he scraped stubborn remnants of blood from beneath the smooth front edges of his toenails.

Huddled on the floor beside him, naked and shaking, was Daan. He stared at his wife through the rivulets of water cascading over his face, holding a cut-throat razor in his lap.

Smoke touched the tips of his fingers to Daan's chin and turned his face toward him. They were alike, the two of them, though Daan would never have known it if he hadn't caught Smoke's eye. Smoke rubbed the pad of his thumb over Daan's fleshy lower lip.

"It's all right, baby. Just one more thing we need to do. Okay?"

Resting back on his haunches, Smoke tenderly laced his fingers with Daan's so they both were holding the blade. Daan's eyes hovered close to lifeless and he put up no resistance as together they sliced deep into the flesh of his throat, hesitated, then dragged it further through the muscle and sinew. Daan's blood pumped a brilliant crimson across the glass, across the marble, across their naked flesh. It was warm and pungent. Salty on Smoke's lips and tongue.

Intoxicating.

Chapter Four

He tipped the shell and slid the oyster onto his tongue, savoring the sweet brininess of plump flesh in his mouth before swallowing. Attuned to the dim light of the room, Smoke peered out the windows of Bar SixtyFive and drained the last of his chilled Manhattan. The vista from the Rainbow Room and its well appointed watering hole atop Rockefeller Center was improbably spectacular, lifted further by the dramatic strains of Gershwin's "Rhapsody in Blue." The Empire State Building rose squarely in his view, its upper tiers cascading through the spectrum from red to violet, as the rest of New York City shimmered behind and below the imposing skyscraper, indistinct pin-pricks of silvered light in the late evening. He wiped at his eyes and checked his watch. It was almost eleven.

"Sir," the waiter said as he slid a fresh Manhattan onto the crisp white tablecloth toward Smoke's knuckle. "The lady at the bar has paid your bill and recommended I refresh your glass."

"Thank you." Smoke glanced up at the waiter and then past him toward the bar.

Tall and ebony-skinned, her dark hair in a pixie cut, and her bearing worthy of the waiter's honorific, a lady was weaving around the tables, her movement feline in a body-hugging illusion dress. Givenchy couture and confidence attracted the attention of many in the room. He stood as she approached, appreciative of her slender strength and poise beneath the play of barely-there gauze and crystal. A killer in every way. Her perfume was recognizably Chanel. She pressed her cheek to his in greeting, placing her hand firmly at the back of his hip.

"Raw silk," she said, impressed, skimming her fingers down the blue fabric that hugged the tight curve of his glutes.

"Tom Ford's summer collection."

"And no undergarments?"

"Why ruin the cut of a good suit?"

"Why indeed?" She nodded. "May I join you?"

"It'd be my pleasure." He pulled a chair from beneath the table as the waiter positioned a dirty martini.

"Do you often dine alone?" she asked.

"I appreciate my own company. More so when agreeably interrupted," he said.

She tilted her head and smiled. Smoke considered the crooked arch of her lips and thought it beguiling.

"Thank you for dinner. And this," he said, lifting and sipping the Manhattan. The sparkle of decolletage distracted him before he settled his gaze on the soft caramel of her eyes. "Are you going somewhere?"

"A private salon at the Peninsula. A stuffy work affair, really. Paunch-stretched suits and age-spotted wrists dripping with unapologetic blood diamonds." Again, that crooked smile.

"Then why are you here?" he asked.

She reached across the table and placed her hand on his. Her nails were champagne polished, their length lethal compared to the trim, manicured buff of his own.

"An Aperitivo. And..." She stirred the skewer of olives through the shimmer of Grey Goose and vermouth.

"And?" Smoke beckoned.

She drew in a deep breath before slowly blowing it out through pursed lips. She glanced at the room in the window's reflection, palpably collecting her thoughts, then returned her attention to him.

"Okay." She smiled softly. "The medical examiner has determined the Stuyvesants' deaths as a murder-suicide. All good on that account. She signed off the paperwork twenty minutes ago. NYPD Homicide still has several administrative hoops to jump through, but they should close the case without further incident or lines of inquiry."

Smoke recalled the gentle pleasure of Angi pressing into his nakedness, the fullness and warmth of her breasts against his chest, and the tender love and wonder on Daan's face as he kissed her. One last time.

"Media attention should be minimal since few would be aware of the Stuyvesants' connection to the House or Family, which is tenuous at best. The story should disappear by the next news cycle."

Smoke nodded, pulling his hand from beneath hers.

"Why are you here?" he asked again.

She managed a quick taste of her martini, barely a touch of her upper lip to the liquor. Revlon's *Fire & Ice* imprinted the edge of the glass.

"I wanted to tell you myself." She hesitated, then locked her gaze on his. "There was a discrepancy. A mistake. They were the wrong target." She watched him, searching for his reaction, no doubt.

Smoke held himself steady, though the room and his handler became hazy, his thoughts obscuring. The perfume of Angi's skin, the perspiration and stickiness of gratified thirst, the tender caress of her lover as he sliced the blade across her neck. He breathed in, Bar SixtyFive snapping back into sharp focus, pulling him from something that had once been wonderful.

"How is that possible? The brief gave the exact address. It included photos of…" He hesitated for a single beat of his heart. "It included photos of them. They were the ones."

"The House has assured me it won't happen again."

Smoke took a long draught of his cocktail, emptying the glass down to the rocks.

She stood, and he followed, reaching to lightly grasp her wrist with the tips of his fingers. "Gabrielle, how do we know it won't happen again?"

"I told you. The House has assured me." She touched her hand to his jawline. "I like the new look. The stubble suits you." She flicked her attention toward the bar. "Your contact is here to pass the peripheral containing the next assignment. This one's a slow burner. No rush. I'd have delivered the documents myself, but…" Gabrielle motioned toward her curve-hugging couture. "No pockets. Of course."

That crooked smile again. She turned and made her way out of Bar SixtyFive toward the elevator lobby, and Smoke's gaze followed in her wake. His vision was a blur as his thoughts drifted not to the hours and days to come, but to the veined white marble of the Stuyvesants' bathroom, and the blood cast across it.

Chapter Five

Sitting on the steps of the Metropolitan Art Museum, Smoke chewed on a Nathan's famous hotdog from a nearby food truck. Waiting. The noise, heat, and stink of Manhattan were pervasive, hardly subdued by a fragrant breeze that crept around the museum from Central Park. He picked up and sipped his Coca-Cola. It was nice and sweet. Nice and cold in the heat.

Traffic crawled and honked along Fifth Avenue in front of him. This was always a decent location to read people and hone his observation skills. A confluence of Midtown suits, Upper East Side socialites, dog walkers, school groups, and tourists. Thousands of tourists. Locals pushed swiftly along the sidewalk in their sensible shoes, palpably aware of their surroundings and any slight opportunity to sidestep and outpace any idlers in their path. Tourists, on the other hand, gaped, pointed, and dawdled or stopped outright for selfies, or no apparent reason. The very best New Yorker vocabulary and brazen attitude invariably countered any obstruction or delay by the out-of-towners. To Smoke, the only thing that defined the greatest city on Earth more than that attitude was a Manhattan rat dragging a slice of 2 Bros cheese pizza pie down the steps into the subway.

He licked mustard off the side of his thumb and took another slug of Coke.

The hot afternoon sun felt good as he leaned back onto the steps. Still, he rolled the sleeves of his collared shirt up to his elbows and tugged the linen hem loose from his jeans to catch the breeze.

A black Lincoln SUV pulled to the curb almost directly in front of him, and his target stepped out. A socialite in her late fifties, or early sixties. Well over twenty years Smoke's senior, with dark hair piled high over Chopard De Rigo sunglasses. Smoke savored the last of the dog, intent on the handsome arch of his target's calves, the swing of her toned arms as she climbed the stairs to the main entrance of the Met with the bounce of a much younger woman.

Punting his trash into a nearby can, Smoke pulled his Culture Pass from his pocket and followed Eleonora di Toledo into the museum. He glanced after her as she turned to wander amongst the monolithic statues of the Egyptian wing, but he headed straight through the Great Hall's ionic colonnade and leaped up the broad marble steps, two at a time, toward the European art collection on the second floor. He took his position on a bench in front of a Bronzino portrait, sliding to the far end so Eleonora could perch where she had every afternoon for the past week.

The painting was of a woman in Renaissance couture. Silk a brilliant vermillion. Elaborately braided coiffure. Jewelry understated.

Resting his elbows on his knees, his chin on lightly clenched fists, Smoke sat mesmerized—not by the painting's aesthetic but by the palpable authority behind every brushstroke. The positioning of hands. The regal gaze toward those who dared observe. He wondered what attracted him to strong women. Always so much more interesting.

Eleonora sat down on the bench beside him at 4:35, arching her neck as she, too, studied the painting. She hardly breathed, her posture mimicking that of the portrait's subject, touching her hand to her abdomen. Slipping into an attentive reverie.

Smoke maintained silent focus on the artwork for twenty full minutes, slowly altering his posture and the cadence of his breathing to perfectly match Eleonora's.

"Do you think she's beautiful?" he eventually whispered, without turning from the portrait, loud enough so only Eleonora could hear him above the echo of others in the gallery.

She dropped her gaze to the floor. "Perhaps physically beautiful in the painted light of the artist."

Smoke noted the crack in her voice, the glisten in her eyes, the slight tremor in her hand, curling toward a fist at the edge of his vision. He segued by instinct.

"She reminds me of one of my foster mothers," he said. "A brutal woman, adept at weaponizing kindness. At utilizing sincere motherly affection to deliver only uncertainty and heartache."

Eleonora looked at him. "As only a mother can," she said.

He nodded. "I've no doubt the painting's purpose was to project power and status. To convey a cultural refinement. Perhaps to assert a family superiority or dynasty. But I think Bronzino captured more than that with the strokes of his oils."

Eleonora's attention was now fixated solely on him. "The heartache she caused—knowingly or unknowingly. What gives it away?" she asked.

Smoke pulled his knee up onto the bench between them, jeans stretched tight, wisps of blonde leg hair curling through the ragged threads of a stylish rip at his inner thigh. "I can't decide whether it's her smug expression or the fear in the eyes of her lapdog." He smiled. It was the smile he couldn't fake when someone genuinely piqued his interest.

"I think it's both," she said as she stood. "Come on. You look like you need a drink. I know I do."

"Well," Smoke said. "Are you certain it's safe to pick up a random stranger in front of a Bronzino?"

It was her turn to smile. "I guess you'll find out."

* * *

The tables of the Italian restaurant near Madison Avenue spilled out across the footpath and into the gutter, its clientele defined by the red-soled Louboutins, Jimmy Choo slingbacks, Chanel pumps, and Valentino boots showcased at the curb below the hang of pristine white tablecloths.

They didn't need to order. A waiter delivered two brandy balloons of Hugo Spritz and a platter of grilled artichokes, the distinct aroma of herby lemon aioli swirling between them.

"*Grazie*, Federico." Eleonora smiled fondly, brushing her fingers across the back of Federico's hand.

"Signorina di Toledo," the waiter said with a slight nod before briskly stepping back into the restaurant.

Smoke rotated the stem of the glass between his thumb and index finger, his gaze hovering from Eleonora's lips to her cheeks, brows, eyes. "You're beautiful," he said, barely realizing he'd shared his inner thoughts aloud.

"To Bronzino." She clinked her glass against his.

"To Bronzino." The sparkling cocktail was refreshing, with a gentle, floral flavor. A hint of herbaceous mint. He smacked his lips and smiled. "Do you have any plans for this evening?" he asked.

"I may." Eleonora studied him from across the rim of her balloon. "I'm not certain yet. First, I think I need to see how you get that gorgeous mouth of yours around a wild boar pappardelle and a bottle of Chianti."

Chapter Six

Freshly showered and dressed, and cradling a piccolo espresso, Smoke thumbed his acknowledgment of a message on his phone before slipping the device into the inside pocket of his suit jacket. Eleonora approached him across the opulent lobby of the Plaza Residences, the sought-after condominiums within the Plaza Hotel.

"You clean up well, darling boy." Eleonora held out her open hands toward him. Vermillion silk—reminiscent of the Bronzino portrait under which they'd met the week before—draped below her bare shoulders, cinched tight at the waist by gray couture slacks.

"And you grow more stunning with every encounter," he said. Standing, he lightly grasped her fingers and pressed his cheeks to each of hers in greeting, breathing in her innate perfume, heady and enchanting. Natural. Unrecognizable. "You always smell so good," he whispered in her ear. "As good as you taste." He leaned in close, enamored by the precise line of her lipstick, the blush of her unblemished cheeks, the curl of her lashes. He gently kissed her neck, barely a touch of his lips where an artery pulsed strong beneath her olive skin. Imagining their last moments together sent a delightful frisson along the most intimate lengths of his body.

"I've booked a table at a nearby roof bar to start the evening," he said. "But we don't need to venture far, or long, from your condo tonight if you don't wish to." He lifted her hand to his lips, his gaze tight to hers.

"Cheeky boy," she said as his lips lingered on her skin. "I've been invited to a small soirée on West 44th later tonight and I have to go. A mix of intelligentsia, Broadway royalty, and old souls. Plus, the usual beautiful riff-raff. It should be easygoing and pretty fluid. I'm sure you'll find it of interest."

"It does sound intriguing." He held out his arm and gripped her hand tight when she placed it on his sleeve.

They settled at an outside high top, forty-seven stories above 59th Street. The early evening view of Central Park stretched north toward the awakening luminosity of Harlem.

"You've avoided answering my question from the other evening," she said.

"Which one?" he asked.

She arched an exquisitely groomed eyebrow. "Tommy, I've noticed the way people look at you. Both men and women. How could I not? You're a desirable young man in a city overpopulated by those seeking companionship. Who don't wish to be alone."

"You find me desirable?" he asked, lifting his cocktail to his lips.

"Don't change the subject," she said.

"I don't believe I have." He smirked and took a sip.

"You know what I mean."

"I do," he said quietly. He stared thoughtfully into the depths of Central Park, the incongruous roar of a beast echoing through the darkness from the zoo. It was unexpected and enigmatic, punctuating the incessant drone of the traffic gridlocked around the greenery. "But it's really not that simple. Random hookups and sex in this city are all too easily orchestrated. At any time of day or night. A dimension of Manhattan life I appreciate and employ not infrequently.

"But those liaisons are rarely more than anonymous. Rarely employed beyond the tacit understanding they will never evolve into anything more. Anything real." He wiped his thumb across his lips. "Not friendship. Not love. And not to build the type of connection you could actually depend upon, with someone you could ask for help when you truly needed it."

He stopped to collect his thoughts, wanting to get it right. Even if only for his own understanding of how he felt. "Relationships, genuine relationships, are rare. Especially in this city, where people can be reckless with others' emotions, and their own. Let's just say I'm reticent to have my heart broken again and leave it at that. By friends *or* lovers. No more strings. No more misplaced reliance. Ever."

"Ever?" She looked thoughtful, and then nodded, seeming to understand.

"Remember the day we met?" he asked.

"Your breath smelled like hot dog," she said.

He chuckled. "That didn't stop you from kissing me."

"No, it didn't. What can I say? I'm an all-American girl."

He reached for her hand; it was soft and warm. "I followed you into the Met that day."

"You were already at the Bronzino when I entered the exhibition."

He shook his head. "I first saw you studying that portrait the Monday before. I was mesmerized by it and by you. By the intensity of your contemplation. I saw you there again on Tuesday, and again on Wednesday. You say you've seen people looking at me, when the whole time I've been looking at no one but you."

Eleonora leaned in and placed her hand on his upper thigh. Smoke shivered at the touch, his breath catching in the back of his throat.

"I know you have," she said, quietly. "And I do appreciate your candor and deliberation."

Dinner that evening was Vietnamese. A hole-in-the-wall concealed along 6½ Avenue. Eleonora advised it involved a three-month waiting list for patrons of pre-verified economic and social status. Its tiny neon sign, less than one inch by four, was like a surreptitious whisper of its name— *Pho-Q*. It was the personification of Manhattan decorum and ironic hospitality.

Just shy of midnight, they climbed the stairs to a fifth-floor walk-up in the middle of Hell's Kitchen. In one hand, Smoke gripped a bottle of merlot from the bodega downstairs, his other hand flat against the small of Eleonora's back to steady her, lest her Manolo Blahnik stilettos catch in the shag tacked to the steps sometime last century.

"Reminds me of my first Manhattan studio apartment," he said. "Well, not mine. A college buddy's rental. I paid her a hundred bucks a week for the pleasure of crashing on her Murphy bed while she was at work."

"Sounds like the two of you were close," Eleonora said.

"Ships in the night, so to speak. But, yes, there was some overlap, both with the bed and who we shared it with. We were pretty tight until I found my footing."

"Are you still in touch?"

"Looks like this is the top," he said, as they reached the landing.

The top-floor studio was a comfortable size for two, though Smoke surmised its occupants would need to be very much in love, at all times, to survive in such a small space. Tonight, the tony crowd made it tight—no room for modesty—with every opportunity to know intimately those pressed in around you. He couldn't differentiate between the conflicting perfumes in the apartment but found the overall odor pleasant, with a subtle hint of high-end weed mixed with bergamot.

They made it as far as the refrigerator, two feet in from the entrance, but with a clear view of the entire room. Nearby, a man stood before an upright piano playing Sondheim, his dance-toned butt cheeks displayed in assless chaps. A tune from *Assassins*. Two Broadway divos lounged on the crowded sectional, belting along, intermittently sipping Miraval Côtes de Provence Rosé. Smoke recognized all three men from posters plastered along 42nd Street and Shubert Alley through the years. He was certain the guy in chaps had headlined with Chita at Carnegie Hall, with its thirty-dollar gin and tonics that had to be gulped down before the ancient ushers locked the theater doors.

Smoke leaned his back against the refrigerator, twisted the cap off the merlot, and reached for two stemmed glasses on a shelf above the sink. He poured the wine as Eleonora settled against his chest. She lifted her chin and he bent to hear her over the whole room singing along with the chorus.

"We won't stay long, Tommy. I just need to be seen by our hostess. A second cousin of sorts. Besides, these soirées invariably devolve into die-hard debauchery by two in the morning."

Smoke checked his watch. "Hmm, that's a shame. Leaving, I mean. I had high hopes for tonight." He sipped the wine and placed a hand flat against her abdomen, bracing her against his bulk in the swaying movement of those in the tightly crowded galley kitchen. He'd no doubt the couple nearest the dishwasher had already raised the curtain on the third act of promised hedonism.

The studio lighting dimmed almost to black.

A woman stepped around the sofa and sidled to center stage in front of the studio's sleeping platform. She held a candle that sent flickering light across her face. Her skin was pale and freckled, her faded red hair pulled tight in a long Ariana Grande ponytail. She twisted her mouth dramatically and began soliloquizing in a deep, guttural voice.

"German," Smoke whispered at Eleonora's ear. "Goethe, I believe. Yes. *Wanderer's Nightsong.* The first one. Though spoken with an intensity, I doubt the poet intended."

A petite ballerina in a pancake tutu rose from the sofa to plie and pirouette to the rhythm of the Germanic verse. She shifted effortlessly from adagio to allegro in the space between pianoforte and coffee table.

"Wretched hearts. Pain and desire," Smoke translated.

The ballerina tugged down her bodice at these words. Her abdomen and breasts were flat and tight, areolas dark and dominant against porcelain flesh. The orator looked on hungrily, biting her lower lip between each stanza, a desperate urgency in her countenance.

"…come into my breast." Smoke nuzzled into Eleonora's upswept hair.

"You seem to like this merlot," she said.

"It definitely likes me." He chuckled and brushed his lips against the helix of her ear. It always felt good to let his guard down, to relax and enjoy the varied moments leading up to a kill. It made him feel alive.

"You're incorrigible. The charming bad boy." She slid her hand into the warmth between the small of her back and his lower abdomen.

A woman closer to Smoke's age than Eleonora's roughly pushed into the crowded kitchen and bumped against them. Her face was pretty but smothered in too much makeup. "Eleonora!" she said too brashly, with a downturn of mouth, a flare of nostrils, and a condescending tone that announced her true nature. Smoke, attuned to reading people, their mannerisms, and words, instantly thought of her as hideous. A characterization he seldom attributed to anyone or anything. But in this case, he held no doubt.

"Rafaella," Eleonora said.

"Well, you came. I saw. Now you can leave. I'll pass your condolences to Uncle." Rafaella glared at Smoke before turning and pushing off into the crowd.

"Charming," Smoke said with a raised eyebrow.

Sondheim swelled again, dark baritones and contraltos issuing from the now velvet black submerging the studio. The melodies and harmonies of *Assassins* swam within the subtle movement, touch, and whispers of the crowd, utterly obscured in the dark. The Third Act had officially begun.

Smoke kissed Eleonora's ear, and whispered: "Would you die for me tonight, my darling Bronzino?" He turned her within his embrace. "*La petite mort.*"

"Silly boy. No more wine for you."

* * *

He rubbed the sleep from his eyes, yawning into the back of his hand as he luxuriated in Eleonora's Caesar bed, his head at the footboard, his naked bulk stretched along the silk, his bare feet buried deep beneath a deluge of pillows and brocaded cushions at the upholstered headboard. The domed ceiling of a turret soared twenty-three feet above him. The mirrored baubles of an elaborate Italianate luminaire reflected the traces of spent carnality beneath it—a multi-spherical distortion of their nudity, of the rouge-colored splatter across the sheets between them, of the vivid crimson stain along the length of his thigh, across the corrugation of his stomach.

He rolled onto his side, the sheets still wet and aromatically sweet, and pressed his lips to Eleonora's *boudoir* Manolo Blahnik stilettos. She'd worn them throughout the night, an adventuress of unexpected delight. He licked his tongue across the blood-red leather, then over the bridge of her foot, before traversing the smooth skin of her calf and thigh. He could smell and taste himself upon her, relishing the curve and dip of flesh, the umami of their shared passion. She was still slightly warm to the touch, but only just, and he wondered how long he'd been asleep beside her cooling body. He reached for the eiderdown and pulled it up over them, cuddling into her side, his cheek and lips pressed to the curve of her breast.

"I have to go soon," he said, peering at his watch on the side table. He didn't expect her to answer, but was glad when she did.

"That *was* an excellent red wine, wasn't it?" she said. "Shame about the sheets." She ran her fingers through his hair, gently scratching his scalp with her nails. "Are you certain you have to leave, darling boy?"

Smoke savored the touch, considering her words before squinting a second time at his watch. "Twenty minutes is nowhere near enough time for what I want to, *have to*, do with you." He pushed up onto his elbow and leaned in to kiss her on the mouth. He closed his eyes, intent on the pleasure of her tongue against his. "Fuck," he breathed as he pulled his lips from hers. He couldn't help but smile. "Fuck," he said again, shaking his head.

Eleonora's eye makeup was immaculate despite the night, though her lips were made bare by his mouth and tongue. Her pile of hair lay a sexy dishevelment about her shoulders—more reminiscent of Fellini than Bronzino.

"I've several errands to run this weekend," he said. "But I'll drop by that bodega if you're up for another bottle of that merlot through the week."

Chapter Seven

Smoke left the Residences through the connecting door into the Plaza Hotel's grand lobby, to jog down the main steps and across the street. He wove through an armada of taxis and horse-drawn carriages toward Gabrielle, who was sitting on the surround of the Pulitzer Fountain, two bikes at her side.

"The Sheep Meadow?" he asked.

"Too easy. Great Hill in the North Woods, and then you are buying me breakfast in Harlem," she said.

"Deal." He threw his leg over a bike saddle and daredevilled it through the street traffic into the verdant early morning shadows of Central Park. They kept an even pace on the East Drive, skirting the zoo, lakes, meadows, and baseball fields. Passing over and under century-old bridges and beneath vast mottled canopies. Once they leaned into the long stretch of blacktop beside the reservoir, Gabrielle came into her own, her slim profile held low, increasing her speed beyond Smoke's capacity with his heavier bulk.

By the time Smoke was pumping his pedals up the last incline toward the top of Great Hill in the northern section of the park, Gabrielle was already lying on the grass, checking her phone for messages. He dropped his bike and fell to the ground beside her, rolling onto his back, trying to catch his breath. She'd chosen a spot where all they could see was grass, trees, and sky. No sign of the city surrounding them. No sign of concrete, or granite, or glass.

"Fifteen minutes," he said, panting. "That has to be a record for us."

"For you, maybe. I've done eight at night with no runners and tourists to evade," she said.

"You must have run a few red lights through the park," he said, snickering

"A few." She handed her phone to him. "No peripherals or hard copy dossiers for these next three cases. All are time-sensitive with no leeway for errors. And all supersede di Toledo in priority. I've confirmed and reconfirmed *all* as valid targets requiring immediate retirement."

"Valid targets…" Smoke echoed, his voice hoarse. He scanned through the two dozen photographs and pages of text. "Why the rush?"

"You know I couldn't tell you, even if I knew, which I don't. Neither of us has the clearance for that data."

"Three kills in three days," he muttered. "On top of those I've already completed this month." He whistled low through his teeth. "That's more than my count for the last four years. And in such quick succession."

"Do you have doubts?" she asked.

"No," he said, clicking off the phone.

He handed Gabrielle's phone back and sighed, staring up into the sky, his thoughts drifting to the hours spent last night tangled in Eleonora's sheets, intimately exploring her body with his lips, tongue, fingertips, and cock. "And di Toledo?" he asked.

"That brief has not changed. Deadline still by New Year's Eve. The moment and method still entirely at your discretion."

Smoke

Smoke continued studying the clouds hanging in the sky above them. *Fuck*, he thought.

Chapter Eight

Straddling a stool in the Carlyle Hotel's piano bar, Smoke sipped a glass of water even as he stared into the depths of an untouched martini. The shimmer of alcohol in the dim light reflected the gold-leafed ceiling. The walls of the legendary bar were covered in a fanciful mural of Central Park throughout the seasons. An eccentric elephant holding a parasol. A dapper bunny with a boater. Another rabbit chomping on a cigar. Smoke speculated whether the quirkiness of each character, every giraffe and gamboling animal, held any implied commentary on the well-heeled locals slurping cocktails and chatting beneath them. The room was teeming with Gen Zs with disposable cash, attitude, and friends, mixing with the faded class of billionaire boomers. He decided it didn't, that the mural was whimsy for whimsy's sake, a sharp contrast to the vibrating city outside the comfort of these gilded walls.

Waiting for his antipasti, he munched on a bowl of salty, sweet, and spicy nuts, his attention drifting around the room. He hadn't been to the Carlyle in a while. Not since he'd tripped and fallen down the lobby steps onto the reception area's marble floor. It was more embarrassing for him than for the young lady he'd been chaperoning and would later kill in the Royal Suite upstairs. More fortunate for him as the downward movement shielded his face from the single lobby security camera.

The young lady's overdose was not the first scandal at the luxurious hotel, and it was certainly more easily mitigated than the rumors of Marilyn's service elevator entrance and whispered escapades up in JFK's duplex in the sixties. One could never underestimate the value and integrity of a dedicated night manager. Particularly in Manhattan, where high-end clientele relied on personable hospitality with uncompromising discretion.

Smoke took the sliver of lemon rind from his martini glass and bit into it, relishing its sourness on his tongue. The melody from the bar's Steinway was little more than subliminal under the gentle chatter of the room, intimating more than dominating the quiet lulls between conversations. Varying melodies of Broadway interspersed with moments of pure *Birdland* jazz. Smoke considered it reassuring and delightful in every way.

Gabrielle strode into the bar, her features unknown and unrecognizable to anyone but Smoke. Black latex sculpted the contours of her body. Seven-inch heels designated her more than a match for any man or woman game enough to approach her. Even the piano quieted with her entrance. Smoke scanned the room, knowing the question on everybody's minds. *Where's the whip?*

And then, in he came. Five foot nine on a good day, the sleeves of his Hermès suit rolled up to the elbows, exposing detailed forearm and hand tattoos. His pink silk shirt was unbuttoned for the full depth of his breastbone, highlighting further tats across his smooth, hairless chest. Smoke didn't know him, and he wondered if the tats were real or applied just for this diversion. They were definitely sexy. Intriguing. Lickable.

Gabrielle turned and slapped the guy across the face, hard. And then, spewing words in French, she slapped him in the other direction. Her accent was pure Parisian 7th arrondissement, and the extent of her choice of vocabulary both surprised Smoke and enhanced his admiration. Gabrielle leaned in and kissed the guy on the lips, long and passionate, their audience captivated, and then she slapped him again before striding out of the bar. He followed in her wake without uttering a word. The two of them would be the subject of cocktail talk for the rest of the evening, etching into the bargoer's minds a fond memory of a night at the Carlyle. Anyone else they had seen or would see tonight would fade into utter anonymity, beneath relevance or recall.

The pianist segued into the blues theme from *An American in Paris*. A real pro.

Smoke raised the martini to his lips as he caught the eye of two women in the booth below a Bemelmans hand-painted lampshade. He lowered his gaze and raked his fingers through his hair before glancing at them a second time. One woman subtly flicked her hand, and the other nodded.

He was in.

This was exactly the scenario he'd alluded to the previous evening with Eleonora. The ease of obtaining sexual adventure and gratification in the city without accountability or intended consequence. He already knew these women were not interested in him as a person. The conversation would be pleasant. They might inquire whether he was Uptown, Midtown, Downtown, or out-of-town, but they'd already made their decision as to how the evening would end based on his suit, his haircut, and his quiet demeanor. He knew they all would enjoy the evening. But the women had no plans for a relationship beyond a five-hundred-dollar multi-course dinner followed by sex on their terms. Entirely on their terms. Smoke was only too content to oblige, to allow them the absolute control they desired. But in the end, when both he and his intended target were ready to have the illusion shattered, it would be. And he and his target would both understand and accept why.

He slipped a twenty into the hand of his waiter. "Please have my antipasti delivered to the booth. It appears I'll be sharing it as our first course."

By the second course, he was comfortable between the two women on the plush leather banquette, each with her hand resting atop his thigh. Liz and Julianne. Liz was a hedge fund manager with a multibillion-dollar portfolio, and Julianne was the CFO of a tech firm down in Tribeca.

He only needed to kill one of them.

"Coffee? Drambuie?" he asked, once the waiter took away the remnants of a New York cheesecake with its passion fruit vanilla coulis.

"Not for me." Liz slid her hand deep into the warmth of his inner thigh, his flesh resolutely responding to her touch.

"Did you have something else in mind?" he asked.

"A subway ride downtown. Do you think you can wrangle an empty car?"

"The 6 train or the 4?" he asked.

Two blocks over and down the steps of the 77th Street Station, Julianne had already unbuttoned Smoke's shirt down to his belt by the time the 4 train shuddered to a halt at the platform. The last car was vacant. And surprisingly clean. By Smoke's reckoning, it was over one hundred blocks from 77th to Wall Street. At least thirty, maybe forty, minutes of pleasure on all accounts.

The women were not shy. Definitely not transplants from Minnesota or Iowa. They were true New Yorkers through and through. Well practiced and in tune with the sway and vibration of the carriage. *They've done this before*, he thought as Liz selected condoms in his size from her Kate Spade shoulder bag. Julianne was voracious, agreeably mean, and unafraid to draw blood, while Liz was sweet as honey, asking if he was okay, and what he liked. Her mouth was wet and hot as she lifted her skirt and urged him into her.

They left him spent, legs weak and shaking, leaning against the glossy white subway tiles of the Wall Street Station and thumbing the buttons of his shirt closed. They each kissed him good night before Julianne whipped the belt from the loops of his pants and clasped it around her waist.

"A trophy," she said, the words echoing along the deserted platform as both girls walked away.

Smoke shoved his shirttails back into his pants as he caught his breath. "How can you not love New York City?" he muttered. He heard the reverberating double clack of the turnstile, followed by the distant click of heels climbing the stairs, and he nudged himself from the tiles to follow. As he emerged into the shadows of the sidewalk, Julianne slid into a yellow cab on Broadway. Liz trod toward the cobbles of Wall Street, fearless of her surroundings. He followed her.

He had often pondered why New York was called "the city that never sleeps." Here he was on Wall Street, the center of the financial universe, and yet there wasn't a soul other than himself and Liz up ahead. The soft leather of his brogues made for an easy approach, his footsteps indistinguishable beneath the echoing clip of Liz's stilettos.

"Hey, Liz?" he called along the street, his voice and temperament friendly. Good-natured. "Wait up."

She reached for his hand as he stepped to her side. "Come on. I guess I owe you a coffee. What did you say your name was again?"

"I didn't. Does that matter?"

She smiled. "No."

Liz was dead within the hour. Her apartment had a glorious glimpsing view of the moon shining on the Brooklyn Bridge. An overflowing sink. A toppled electronic coffee maker. The overhead lights flickering.

Smoke walked out and took in the night sky, drinking the calming silence of the city as he walked home. He still had time for a good ten hours' sleep, maybe a workout, and a quick pantry run through the aisles of his local D'Agostino grocery. Then he'd pick up his tux from the cleaners and head off for the second job.

Strolling along the emptiness of Greenwich Street toward the West Village, he again pondered the quick succession of jobs before pushing the thoughts from his mind.

The House must have good reason.

Chapter Nine

The bride and groom arrived by gondola.

Central Park's Boathouse restaurant was a beacon within the Manhattan twilight, scattering light across the lake and surrounding foliage, both rippling in the evening's warm breeze. The winged angel touching down upon the nearby Bethesda Terrace fountain was aglow; her face turned away. The gondolier twisted his rowing oar and skimmed his Venetian pride and joy across the lake, pulling in alongside the dock as the Boathouse resonated with the sirens and riffs of Madonna's "I Love New York."

Adorned in his tuxedo with his blonde hair slicked back, Smoke mingled amongst hundreds of guests, picking up pleasant dialog from one topic to another in the restaurant's opulent dining room and colonnaded waterside loggia. Handshakes and celebratory air kisses buffeted him through the well-heeled crowd, making acquaintance and moving on. Blending in. Canapés of duck, lobster, caviar, carpaccio, and truffle punctuated the tête-à-tête. He knew none of these people and none of them knew him, or his relation to either family in the wedding. Moët & Chandon lubricated the pleasantries as Smoke accepted business cards and furtive looks from those who believed his cover. Those who imagined opportunity, either for business or just for tonight.

A champagne saucer to his lips, Smoke surveilled his target at a waterside table. The striped canvas awning of the loggia cast a distinct moon shadow across his target's torso, the features of his face almost indiscernible.

"Bride or groom?" asked a young woman at Smoke's side, placing her hand on his forearm.

"Bride. Isn't she beautiful?" he said without hesitation, motioning across the room toward the woman in white satin with feigned affection.

Smoke settled his attention on the woman beside him. She wore her hair high, dark ringlets curling around her ears, her shoulders bare above a black cocktail dress, cut low at the back. Her eyes were a deep sapphiric blue.

"Lucy," she said.

"Tommy," Smoke said, speaking his name for the first time that evening. He flushed and the physical reaction surprised him. "Would you like to dance, Lucy?"

"That'd be a promising start." A smirk dimpled her cheeks. She gripped his hand and pulled him away from the dancefloor.

"Where're we going?" he asked as they weaved through the crowd. The delicate line of her backbone was a beautiful distraction.

She led him along the loggia and out onto the flagstone terrace that stepped down into the lake. It was deserted except for the docked gondola, rocking in the water.

Out here the music was a quiet echo against the lap of water, providing a gentler, more personable ambiance and rhythm. He touched his hand to her back, her skin as warm as his own as they fell into an effortless sway together. He glanced past her; his target still within view toward the other end of the loggia.

"Who are you really?" Lucy slid her hand up onto his shoulder, the backs of her curled fingers brushing his neck. "I bet you don't even know the bride's name."

He breathed in her innate scent: clean skin without some overpriced artisan *parfum* from Bergdorf Goodman.

"I'm just a guy from Manhattan," he said. "And you?"

She smiled. "Just a girl from Staten Island. Proud to follow my dad and granddad's footsteps into law enforcement."

Smoke was thoughtful. He knew better than to believe this was a coincidence. Or fate. "Uniform or detective?" he asked.

"Neither," she said, pulling him closer.

Something in her manner and confidence intrigued him. "You're strong," he said.

"I bench press above my weight," she said.

It wasn't what he meant, but it made him smile. "Good to know. What *is* the bride's name?" he asked.

Lucy shrugged. "She is beautiful, though."

Their slow dance continued as the music from the Boathouse shifted through the decades, settling into the smooth vocals of Hoboken's own, Sinatra. It went almost unnoticed beyond their deepening conversation.

They held the same passion for art. For reading. For theater and fine dining. And double cheeseburgers. For scummy dive bars and all-night dance parties. For falling asleep in the sun-drenched Sheep Meadow after a bottle of wine. For happily tripping into the gutter following a boisterous night of Broadway by the talented waitstaff at Don't Tell Mama. For being New Yorkers.

They'd been within a block of each other when the second plane hit.

Smoke felt no need to lie about the broader aspects of his life though he skirted any subject remotely veering toward occupation. There was a moment when the music stopped, but still they held each other close, only the fine weave of raw silk between them. Smoke was suddenly excruciatingly aware of his body. And Lucy's. And a familiarity that until this past week, he'd not felt for a very long time. Not until he'd spent intimate conversational moments with Eleonora. And not until right here, right now with Lucy.

A shiver of confusion went through him, and he attempted to shake it off. Aware he was not ready. For whatever these relationships were. Whatever they might or might not become. What they couldn't become because of who he was.

Smoke stepped back from Lucy, checked his watch, and peered through the door inside the Boathouse. His target was now lounging at the bar in conversation with an elderly woman.

"Hey, I might have to leave in a hurry," he said. "I promised to take care of my cousin tonight. He's not very good when it comes to alcohol."

Lucy tilted her head and smiled. "You are a curious one, aren't you?"

Smoke cleared his throat. "I'd like to see you again. If you'd like. Lucy." The feel of her name in his mouth was satisfying. More so than he expected.

"Best we keep dancing while we can, then," she said, pulling him tight against her.

Chapter Ten

Smoke glanced at his wrist to check the time on his Patek Philippe, before focusing on his target, reclining alone at the wood-paneled bar across the Boathouse dining room.

His name was Jameson De Vries, and he sat with a glass half filled with his namesake and a melancholy smile on his face. With dark vibrant eyes below thick lashes and brows, Jameson was substantially beefier in build than Smoke was. He was well-defined muscle. A football tight end for sure, back in his college days.

Jameson looked up from his whiskey and immediately honed in on Smoke. They held each other's gaze, neither shying from the connection. It was an intimacy devoid of ambiguity, each scrutinizing and reading the subtle insinuations of the other. Wedding guests crossed their line of sight but the link between predator and prey remained firm. Smoke wondered if Jameson knew which he was. He sensed his target's conclusion by the subtle machinations playing across his whiskey-softened face. By the way he gripped his chunky glass. How his other hand hung loose, his forefinger caressing the sharp crease of his pants. And by the way his attention slid leisurely down the length of Smoke's body, taking him in. There was admiration and a glimmer of something else. Triumph?

After a subtle smile and nod, Jameson downed the last of his drink and strode toward the far end of the room. Smoke followed him.

A corridor led to the men's restroom. Jameson nudged each of the stall doors open to confirm they were empty, before stopping at one of the five urinals, loosening his belt, and unzipping the fly of his tuxedo pants to urinate. Smoke unabashedly took position at the urinal immediately beside him, thumbing open the buttons of his pants. The belly of his cock was fleshy, smooth, and warm in the palm of his hand as he pissed.

The speakers piped in "Empire State of Mind," the words echoing in the dimly lit space. The tension that had been building in Smoke's back and shoulders relaxed as he hummed along with Alicia Keys. Deep and resonant.

"It's a beautiful night for a walk through the park," Jameson said.

Smoke perceived remnants of a Dutch accent almost hidden beneath the harsher Manhattan dialect. "That it is," he said.

"Smoke?" Jameson asked.

Smoke stared intent on the wall in front of him, reviewing everything he'd said over the last few hours to the other wedding guests. Had he told anyone his real name? Anyone other than Lucy? And even then, with her, he never uttered his surname.

"I've got cigars. A gesture from the groom," Jameson said.

"Ahh," Smoke said. "No, thank you. But I'm more than happy to keep you company."

Jameson changed grip and held out his hand.

Cheeky bastard, Smoke thought, appreciative of the easy familiarity as he also swapped his grip and shook hands with his target.

"I'll meet you out front," Jameson said. He shook and zipped his fly. "I promised the bride and groom one last kiss before I left."

One last kiss.

Smoke's thoughts abruptly fell into his final moments with Angi and Daan, the desire in their last kiss. The ensuing shared intimacy of their deaths. Deaths he'd believed were warranted, advocated by the House.

But something had changed within him since learning they were the wrong target. Something he had not yet determined, or started to come to terms with.

It won't happen again. That's what Gabrielle had said.

He had to believe that was true.

He took his time, emptying his bladder, washing his hands, and wiping down the marble counter where Jameson had flicked water instead of using the monogrammed hand towels.

They met outside beneath the Boathouse's awning, and set off into the Ramble. With thirty-eight acres of winding wooded paths, it was easy to get lost within Central Park's dense, wild woodland—a circumstance Smoke had taken advantage of many times, either with a companion or looking for one.

Tight beside each other, he and Jameson wandered a circuitous path away from the echoing noise of celebration, both men content without small talk.

Jameson was a good two inches taller and broader shouldered than Smoke. And palpably stronger. Smoke respected his physicality, and he would need to account for it when the time came. While some targets quickly resigned to their fate, and a rare few even savored it, there were those who panicked and lashed out during their last gasps of life.

Their course took them in a roundabout way back to the Lake, to a large shard of granite protruding from the landscape at the water's edge. They stepped up onto it, a natural pew to worship the cityscape rising into the evening sky. They hunkered down, stretching their legs across the stone. Jameson pulled out a cigar, clipped off the end, and lit it.

"You sure you don't want one?"

"I'm not really a smoker," Smoke replied. "Not anymore, anyway. And that looks like a high-end cigar. I wouldn't want to waste it."

Jameson's face softened as he contemplated Smoke's eyes, his mouth, and then his eyes again. He reached to brush back a wayward curl from Smoke's forehead, his affable forwardness kindled by the several whiskeys consumed at the Boathouse bar. Jameson was so intent, he might recall every detail of Smoke's face, but Smoke was unconcerned. It would only be for the rest of his life.

"I know why you're here with me," Jameson said.

Nearer the end, they always knew, Smoke thought. Angi and Daan had known. Liz had known.

"I'm here to kill you," Smoke confirmed. "Or at least, to ensure you are dead, and discovered well before the last hour of the closing bell on Monday."

"Tomorrow…" Jameson nodded slowly, no change in his countenance. "I guess I finally overstepped the line. We should share this," he said, holding out the cigar. "I'd like that."

Smoke placed the cigar between his teeth, the leaf wet from Jameson's mouth, the taste of whiskey mingling with his own champagne. He took a puff and handed it back. "Are you married?" he asked, noting the band of gold on

Jameson's ring finger. There'd been nothing in Gabrielle's notes about a wife.

"I am. I mean, I was," Jameson said. "Giulia died last July. They said it was suicide, but that isn't true. It was an accident. She fell through the rusted pedestrian deck of the George Washington Bridge."

Smoke's ears pricked in recognition of the event on the GWB. He'd known her as Giulia Rossi. He nodded.

They smoked the cigar in silence, handing it back and forth, contemplating the skinny, super-tall condominium towers of Billionaires' Row.

"Do you live near here?" Jameson asked, placing a steady hand on Smoke's knee.

"West Village," Smoke said.

"I'm Tudor City. Just a short stroll, and we can stop by the Townhouse Bar for a whiskey on the way. I could sure use the walk to clear my head, anyway. And you're not the ugliest guy to hang with for a couple hours of mischief."

Smoke reached for the cigar. "Sure, Jameson. Whatever you need."

* * *

"Gentlemen," the Townhouse doorman said. Dark glossed curls and a Zorro mask enhanced his green, heavily lashed eyes. He pulled open the entrance doors at the top of the granite stoop. "Welcome back, sir," he mouthed as Smoke pressed a couple of Hamiltons into his gloved hand.

They settled at the corner of the bar furthest from the piano.

"The usual, Mr. De Vries?" the bartender asked.

Jameson glanced at Smoke, then nodded. "Make it two doubles, neat, for me and my friend."

"You holding up okay?" Smoke asked. He skimmed his open hand across Jameson's back to rest upon his shoulder and hold him stable on the barstool. The bartender placed two squat tumblers of Johnnie Walker Blue Label, and two glasses of chilled water on the mahogany bar before them.

Jameson gripped Smoke's hand in his at his shoulder. "Surprisingly well." He lifted the tumbler and breathed in the whiskey's heady aroma before taking a sip. Smoke did the same. "Is it easy for you to do what you do?" Jameson asked.

Smoke was thoughtful of the question, taking a few moments to recall each one of his kills over the last eighteen years, before locking his gaze with Jameson's once more. He noted the fleck of hazel in the darker chocolate of both irises. "Yes," he said.

A fleeting image of Eleonora crossed his mind.

So far.

He took a sip of water and another of Johnnie Walker. He welcomed the alcohol in his veins as it heightened his senses rather than numbed them.

Jameson glanced over his shoulder toward the piano where a *Real Housewife of Somewhere*, probably here, was monopolizing the microphone. He smirked. "She's pretty good. Kind of sexy and sultry." He fell silent for several moments contemplating the depths of his glass. "There are some things I won't miss about this city. This life," he said. "I miss Giulia. More than I can put into words." He rubbed his thumb back and forth along the side of Smoke's hand. "Do you fear for your own life… Ah, I don't know your name. Will you tell me?"

"No," Smoke said, even though at this point it really didn't matter how much Jameson knew.

"And no," he finished. He didn't fear for his life. But if it was in danger, he would never accept death so readily as some of those placed in his charge. He knew he would fight. He knew he would rather kill than allow himself to be killed.

At least, not without very good reason.

* * *

I guess I finally overstepped the line.

Jameson's words rang in Smoke's head as he buttoned his collar and re-knotted his tie into a full Windsor on the terrace of Jameson's Tudor City penthouse. Gargoyles crouched along the parapet amongst the topiaries. Just as they had done for almost a century. They and Smoke contemplated the thin sliver of the sun rising beyond the East River and Long Island, emboldened by the noises of the waking city echoing between the canyons of glass, stone, and steel. Smoke breathed in deep. The air was cool in his lungs after the ache and heat of the night. After too many puffs of Jameson's cigars. He ran his thumbs behind the waistband of his trousers and stepped back through the double doors into the elegantly appointed living room.

Morning light filtered through triple-height Gothic windows, dappling polished floorboards, furnishings, and a luxuriant rug, rich beneath Smoke's bare feet and toes. Jameson writhed and choked at the carpet's edge, naked except for his wedding ring, torturing his flesh in one last swan song of self-ingratiating pleasure. A silk was tied taut around his neck, the other end knotted to a doorknob. A full Windsor.

Smoke sank into a tufted club chair and poured himself another whiskey. There wasn't much left in the bottle after their night of unguarded conversation and acceptance. The reminiscent ramblings that seemed important to Jameson. It had ended as it sometimes did, with the prey choosing their demise. Smoke watched Jameson contort on the rug, his determined grip, the arch of his muscled back, the darkening hue of his face, his grunt for breath and satiation. From Smoke's experience, erotic asphyxiation rarely achieved the desired result. *His* desired result. But it placed the prey into an oxygen-deprived elation that Smoke could easily thrust over the edge. Jameson spasmed, gagged, and twisted sideways into semi-unconscious relief as semen splattered, puddled, and dripped across his abdomen, glistening in the broad shafts of light refracting through the beveled windows.

Setting his tumbler carefully in the center of a coaster, Smoke crossed the room, sidestepping the rumpled tuxedo, dress shirt, boxers, and shoes. Jameson was little more than a slack heap of muscle on the rug, his eyes rolled back beneath fluttering lids, saliva dribbling from his mouth. But he was far from dead.

"Just a few moments more, my friend," Smoke said softly, kneeling at Jameson's head. "Relax into it. Enjoy the calm. There's nothing more to worry about. I've got you from here."

He pressed the soles of his feet against the tops of Jameson's bare shoulders. Then he twisted the length of silk around his forearm, tightening the expensive noose into the flesh of Jameson's neck. Ropey veins and arteries bulged, fat and blue, on either side of the fabric. He held the tension as Jameson convulsed, a frantic torquing movement of his entire body that abruptly collapsed into a shivering quiver. Smoke maintained his grip, counting the rapid thumps of his own heart until the swell of Jameson's veins eventually contracted as the blood drained, no longer pressured by the pulse of a living heart. When he reached one hundred, he loosened his hold on the silk. A final breath escaped Jameson's lips as his body settled. Smoke uncurled his toes and exhaled a deep sigh of his own. The ache, the intimate conversation and familiarity of the night, and Jameson's retirement were all exhausting. Exhilarating and exhausting.

"What did you do to deserve this?" Smoke muttered. It was a question he wished he'd had sanction to ask during their bottle of Johnnie Walker. But he'd refrained, resigned that he would never know.

He stayed on the floor with Jameson as he cooled, as the anguish of losing his wife fell from his face, tension releasing from his eyes and mouth. Smoke's attention drifted down the length of Jameson's crumpled body, then scanned the room. His fingerprints would be discernible on the neck of the whiskey bottle, and his glass, but nowhere else. This would be an easy clean.

He returned to the tufted chair, pressed the power button on the TV remote with a knuckle rather than a fingertip—*Good Morning, America*—and settled in to pull on his socks and dress shoes. And finish his whiskey.

The news crawler at the bottom of the screen caught his attention. *Fuck!* The Stuyvesant's case had been reclassified as a homicide, one with a multi-agency task force. He shook his head in disbelief before checking his watch. There was no time for distraction. He had thirty minutes to get across town, the length of 42nd Street, and take his position for his next assignment.

Chapter Eleven

The subway station beneath 42nd and 8th was already overcrowded. Yet thousands of commuters continued to pour down the stairwells and through the subterranean passages onto its platforms. It was mostly suits from New Jersey who'd traveled into Manhattan by ferry, bus, or local jitney as the first leg of their office commute. The subway would take them further into the island's guts: Uptown, Downtown, Midtown East, and beyond.

Smoke never stood less than six or seven feet from the platform edge. He knew from experience, and duty, that any tightly packed crowd could heave without warning, lose balance, and push forward. Or sideways. Or backward. The sea of bodies could ripple until those at the end of the effect stumbled to the ground, or worse, were thrown onto the railway tracks. Intentional or not, it was best never to tempt fate beneath the streets of Manhattan, especially with no way of knowing when some random hammer-wielding belligerent might decide to take out their frustrations on society.

He loosened his tie, rolled it, and stuffed it in his tuxedo pants pocket before thumbing open the top buttons of his dress shirt to mitigate the heat of the accumulating bodies. He settled against a steel column by the north stairs to await the last target of the weekend triptych, scouring the faces of the descending crowd for the features only made familiar by a handful of photos on Gabrielle's cell.

The target was a man in his late forties whom Smoke considered more pretty than handsome. A well-aged Madison Avenue model type, no longer gripped by the uncertainty and desperation of youth, with a silvered fade rising from a cleanly shaved neck and jawline, his skin fair, and his eyes a pale baby blue.

The crowd lurched forward, and Smoke intuitively grabbed a young woman by the elbow, swinging her away from the four-foot drop and hard against him. Her face was pallid with shock as she mouthed her thanks, then hurried away, keeping her distance from the platform's edge.

When he returned his attention to the staircase, it was the brilliantly buffed Dior shoes he first noticed. They were bespoke and so was the suit, worn by one who did not need to work in an office, but did, anyway. One who could have easily commuted by a private town car, or helicopter, but chose otherwise. The leather laptop satchel hanging from his shoulder was of a far superior quality than any of the garish brands hawked along Fifth Avenue. It appeared to be lamb. Supple. Unblemished. The initials E.G. were embossed above a platinum and hickory buckle.

Elgan Glyndwr.

The brief had offered no information beyond the target's name, photos, daily travel routine, and life-threatening allergen. That was more than enough.

Smoke pushed off of the steel column and slid into the crowd of commuters, positioning himself immediately aside Elgan. The platform was over-packed, with still more travelers on the stairs, anxiously checking their watches as a warm breeze pushed into the station ahead of the oncoming train. The rushing air smelled metallic, mellowed by an underlying odor of mulled grease. The press of bodies on the platform intensified, and soon Smoke was forced against his target. They squinted at each other in the crush and nodded acknowledgment as the E Train shrieked in, already loaded up from Penn and the other stations further down the island. Several carriages passed before the train slowed and shuddered to a standstill. One of the eleven sets of double doors slid open before Elgan and Smoke, presenting a carriage already with standing room only.

"Stand back," Elgan called over his shoulder, his hand against Smoke's chest, to make way for the commuters exiting the carriage. Three disembarked. Twenty crammed into the space they vacated, including Elgan and Smoke.

Smoke had thought the tiny studio in Hell's Kitchen where he'd attended the soirée with Eleonora had been tight. But that was free range compared to the morning commute on the E. He was in direct physical contact with at least eight other suited commuters, gendered and genderless—an unavoidable and unacknowledged intimacy. Pressed tight against one another from shoulders to shoes, bonded by the mingling scents of fresh dry-cleaning, styling mousse, and cologne. He was hard against his suited target. Chest to chest, stomach to stomach, groin to groin.

"Apologies," Smoke said as the doors slid closed behind them, urging them tighter still.

"None required," Elgan said, his Welsh clip discernable.

They were the same height, each with their face turned to avoid staring eye to eye. The soft bristle of Smoke's stubbled jaw brushed against Elgan's clean shave as the train pulled forward, rocking side to side. The carriage's metal wheels made a two-note squeal that always reminded Smoke of the intro to the *Star Trek* theme, before lifting into the familiar vibrating shriek of New York's underground transit.

They maintained their intimate stance as the train headed uptown, the conductor's announcements an incoherent distortion that served only to frustrate, then curved east beneath 53rd Street. Smoke had nothing to hold onto as the weight of his bulk drifted with the turn, his leg muscles aching with the strain of flexing to remain upright within the pack. If he lost balance, he'd take several of his fellow commuters down to the sticky linoleum with him. He slid his arm around Elgan's waist to grip the chromed stanchion at his back. The posture instantly reminded him of Daan and Angi in their embrace, the heat of their bodies pressed together, sharing an intimacy only lovers or absolute strangers dared. He relaxed, heaved a deep breath, and nudged his jaw along Elgan's.

"Elgan," he said, his mouth at his target's ear. The single word went unheard by anyone else over the train's ambient noise and the commuter's disassociated attitudes.

Elgan flinched, turning to face Smoke. "Do I know you?" he asked, their eyes inches apart, his smile wavering between friendly and uncertain.

"No," Smoke said.

Elgan tensed against him as he glanced at the people around them. "What is this?" he asked.

"You don't know me, but I'm certain you know *of* me," Smoke said. "Those I acquaint with always do."

The blue of Elgan's eyes paled further, and his mouth went slack. He licked his lips and took in several slow, deep breaths, his chest expanding against Smoke's, the beat of his heart escalating.

"I'm not ready for this," Elgan said.

They held each other's gaze, Smoke studying the minuscule movement of Elgan's facial muscles as his target processed what was happening.

"How did they find out?" Elgan asked. "Can you tell me that?"

The lights of the carriage flickered, then extinguished, throwing them into absolute darkness. The echoing roar of the engine several carriages ahead died, and the train drifted to a standstill in the pitch black of the tunnel.

Seventy feet underground.

The passengers around them stood in resignation, only a few nervous giggles and expletive murmurs punctuating the silence. The ambient light of cell phones flicked on throughout the carriage, but there was no signal for them to ping. Not down here, beneath several stories of suffocating soil, concrete, and schist. Beneath confusing tangles of electrical, water, gas, and sewerage ducts. Beneath multiple north-south subway lines and the unheard growl of 53rd Street traffic, somewhere between Madison and Lex, amid the swaying weight of lofty skyscrapers.

"Will it happen here?" Elgan asked.

Smoke nodded. "You'll not be leaving this train alive." His stubble brushed Elgan's cheek with each muttered word.

"I'm not ready for this," Elgan said again, his voice little more than a whisper in the dim, their noses side by side, his breath a pleasant waft of marmalade and Earl Grey. His eyes shone with unexpected wetness in the subtle lighting emitted by the electronic devices around them.

"I understand, but it is going to occur." Smoke was thoughtful as the rapid thump of their hearts fell into alignment. "What can I do to assist you through this?" he asked.

Elgan held his attention for several beats, contemplating Smoke, attempting to read him, before squirming within the tight confinement to slip his arms inside the warmth of Smoke's tuxedo jacket, around his torso in a tight embrace. He tugged at the tails of Smoke's shirt until his open hand found bare flesh beneath Smoke's jacket. Then he buried his face in the crook of Smoke's shoulder and shuddered.

Smoke accepted and returned the embrace with equal intensity, his hand at the back of Elgan's neck, caressing the recently cut spike of his fade. They held their tender grip for uncounted minutes, and Smoke's collar was soaked when Elgan finally lifted his face from it to confront his assassin.

Two men.

A killer and his assenting victim.

Alone and unseen in the crowd.

Smoke whetted the tip of his forefinger and reached into his breast pocket. He pulled it out again, with a milky white capsule affixed to the sheen of spit above his nail. He held it between their lips.

"I'll look after you, Elgan. I promise you that." Smoke's voice was deep and gentle, the truth resonant at such close quarters.

Elgan nodded, acceptance steeling his features. He enveloped the tip of Smoke's finger with his mouth, drew the capsule from it, and swallowed. Then alarm lit over his face.

"My laptop," he said, pulling at the satchel on his shoulder. "You can't leave it for the authorities. Or anyone else. Take it. You'll need to destroy it."

"Understood," Smoke said.

Elgan embraced him tightly for several moments more, leaning heavily into him, his body shivering, until his grip slackened and his arms dropped to his sides. The final thump of his heart reverberated against Smoke's. Smoke tightened his grasp to compensate, holding Elgan's dead weight close, their chins upon each other's shoulders, their eyes closed to those around them.

Forty minutes later, the carriage lights flickered back on, and the E Train slowly squealed and lurched forward once more. At 53rd and Lexington, where most of the carriage emptied, Smoke lowered Elgan onto a now-vacant seat and sat with him, his arm around his shoulders, as they crossed beneath the East River into Queens.

Chapter Twelve

He could have reversed his course and taken the E Train back home to the West Village. Instead, Smoke strolled through Queens, crossed the bridge onto Roosevelt Island in the middle of the East River, and walked the island's length to the park at its southern point. With his tuxedo jacket draped over his shoulder, protecting the laptop satchel, he climbed the grand granite staircase to the vista of FDR's Four Freedoms Park. The inspiring simplicity of the groomed lawn stretched through an avenue of trees to frame the large bust of President Roosevelt. He passed the sculpture without catching its gaze and settled onto the steps at the tip of the headland. Water churned and slapped against the stones just a few inches beneath his dress shoes, but Smoke's thoughts were lost in the panoramic vista of bridge after bridge, suturing Brooklyn to Manhattan along the river's loud, dirty surge. He wondered how far upriver it was to the prison on Rikers Island—a detail he was more than happy not knowing, but one he thought he might eventually need to confront.

Three people in less than three days. Each had been genuine.

Personable.

Accepting.

People he might readily have had as friends if they'd traveled the same circles. And yet their paths *had* crossed. And now they were dead.

The United Nations buildings rose on the west bank of the river, a distance covered easily by an angry golf swing and a lost ball. The Tudor City Residences rose higher still behind them; he could just make out the gargoyles holding vigil on the penthouse terrace. The house staff would have found Jameson within the last hour, his face blue, his body sagging, releasing fluids to soak the $200,000 Kashmir rug.

As he buried his face in his hands, his fingers trembling, he wished he had one of Jameson's cigars and another tumbler of whiskey.

He didn't need to look back to read the words inscribed on the stone slab behind him. He'd long known them by heart.

And now, he couldn't help wondering which of the President's Four Freedoms warranted his following the orders of the House.

Freedom of speech?

Freedom of worship?

Freedom from want?

Freedom from fear?

He couldn't think how any of them justified what he had done.

Chapter Thirteen

He ruffled his hair, loosening the remnant hold of the previous evening's styling goop, and fingered his errant blonde curls, flopping them low over his mirrored aviators. Still wearing the tux, and with Elgan's laptop in a secure location farther up Manhattan, he sidestepped from his walk of shame into the petite French bistro on the corner of his street in the West Village. He settled at a window seat with a brioche and coffee as an NYPD cruiser, three black sedans and a non-descript van swerved to a halt in front of his townhouse. Uniformed officers hastily stretched crime-scene tape across his stoop.

"That won't make the neighbors happy," he said, more to himself than to the waitress who stood at his side, mesmerized by the activity blocking the street.

The nineteenth-century brownstone was long ago reconfigured into multiple condos, one on each level. He rented the second floor, the plantation shutters closed tight.

"What do you think is going on, *chérie*?" asked the plump young waitress.

Smoke shrugged. "Not sure, *mademoiselle*." He doubted his landlady operated a meth lab in the basement.

Then he spotted the high-intensity beams flaring through the slats of his second-floor shutters. Now, he was sure.

"Damn," he muttered beneath his breath.

He headed out and circled the block to the cobbles of Jane Street. Thumbing a code into the pin pad next to a double-wide weathered mahogany entrance door, he bypassed the caged freight elevator and ran up the stairs to the fourth floor. A second pin pad and a biometric thumb press and he entered the loft he actually called home. It was secure enough to make him feel safe. And it offered a view of the condo he'd registered with the House, which he treated as nothing other than a decoy.

He strode to the loft's large industrial windows and swung his telescope from Liberty, standing tall in the middle of New York Harbor, toward the second-floor condo at the back of the block. A magnolia partially hindered his sightline into the kitchen, but the views through the living room, primary bedroom, and bathroom windows were unobstructed. He could see a dozen or more NYPD inside. A few uniforms, four plainclothes, and several forensics suited up in disposable white coveralls. He wasn't concerned with what they'd find.

Smoke had never entered the condo in the years he'd been renting it. A Brooklyn Bohemian, a medical student he'd not met in person, dropped by once a week to check on the sole cactus and tidy up. And to Smoke's thoughtful distraction had left more than just fingerprints and epithelia on the sofa and ottoman. Amongst other surfaces throughout the space. Sexuality was always interesting to observe from a distance. Whether solo, in tandem, or otherwise. It's naivety or prowess. It's exploration and surprise, particularly with the pleasure heightened by the possibility of being caught mid-intimacy in an unauthorized location. It didn't bother Smoke what the Bohemian did in his condo. He was happy to contribute to the young man's NYU tuition fees, and bourgeoning sexual awakening so his decoy home would have that lived-in feel.

He swung the telescope back toward the living room. "Now, that's interesting," he muttered, sharpening the focus.

He nudged the burner from his pocket and punched in the phone number he'd recently memorized, his eye steady to the scope, squinting, as the cell chimed.

"Lucy O'Donnell."

"Hey," he said.

"Oh, hey." He watched Lucy step out from his second-floor living room onto the fire escape. "Where are you?" She leaned against the rail and peered back into the condo.

"At home."

Lucy waved to catch the attention of a plainclothes officer inside his condo, then motioned to her phone. She closed the door behind her and faced out into the depths of the magnolia. "I had fun last night."

"Me too. I've a couple of hours free. You want to catch up for coffee or something?"

"I can't, Tommy. Sorry." She glanced over her shoulder as the plainclothes officer opened the fire escape door, shook his head, and shrugged. "Just started a new, um, project. Maybe tomorrow. Definitely next Saturday if you're available."

"Sure thing," he said. "There's a new Harley Davidson exhibit at the Guggenheim. Looks like it might be fun. If not, we can hang amongst the Kandinsky artworks. My treat."

She peered through the branches of the magnolia as they said their goodbyes and she flipped her cell closed. She seemed to be looking directly at him, but he was confident she couldn't see him in the late-morning glare.

He kept his telescope trained on the activity of the NYPD throughout his condo, Lucy his primary focus. They slowly trickled out, and the last of them left several hours later. Smoke wasn't going to chance a snoop to determine any damage done, presuming they might have left an unmarked car out front to continue surveillance.

He showered and shaved and then sat cross-legged on the kitchen island with a bowl of cereal and a triple-shot espresso to watch the news.

The deaths of the Stuyvesants were the lead story. Developing details of the double homicide repeatedly broke into the programming. So much for dropping off the news cycle.

Footage showed externals of their home in Riverdale, before cutting to an ABC reporter, live, in front of his condo half a block away.

"What the hell?" How could they possibly draw a link?

He texted Gabrielle: "?"

The escalating threads of the story headlined the 5:00, 6:00, and 11:00 newscasts. It had gone national.

Chapter Fourteen

Little Island jutted into the Hudson River at Chelsea, rising from the water upon concrete tulip-shaped stilettos. Smoke jogged the circuitous route through the island then back onto the greenway south along the great river's parkland edge, Joni Mitchell's husky contralto in his ears. It was too early for most tourists in this section of Manhattan, the low morning sun glinting off the New Jersey waterfront high-rises on the far side of the river. Still, Smoke dodged hundreds of Manhattanites running off their daily burst of energy and physical fortitude geared toward their wellbeing, before pulling on suits and attitudes to maintain the island's churn of creative, intellectual, and financial wealth.

He wore his lucky camouflage tank top, unwashed, ripped, and sagging low. A favorite that had weathered many a weekend dance party at Rockbar, and the last three New York marathons, bettering his time each year. It stank, and he loved it. He pulled up the hem to wipe the sweat from his brow.

The cell phone strapped to his bicep chimed over the guitar chords of Joni's "Chelsea Morning." It was the distinctive double knell of the encrypted short-range radio channel. He tapped the Bluetooth bud at his ear to switch from the music.

"What do we know?" he asked, pacing himself with the runners in front of him. He craned his neck to see Gabrielle was about two blocks ahead of him, her gait smooth, her silhouette distinct and sleek in gray Fabletics as she ran.

"Forensics returned to resweep the Stuyvesant house, and the chief medical examiner's forensics team retested all autopsy samples. They isolated unidentified male DNA."

Smoke's brow furrowed. "Mine?"

"Unverified. You've nothing to worry about, though. Your prints and DNA sequence are secure. Even if they pulled them from the scene, there'd be no visible ping against any public or law enforcement records. And we'll ensure they lose their samples and documentation during due process."

"And yet they tied the deaths back to my West Village condo? The god damned NYPD? How could they possibly tie it to my property? Is the House cleaning up—"

"Don't go there, Smoke. It was a single family member, a relative of the Stuyvesants with enough influence in the mayor's office to have the case reassessed. One who is not kept in the loop. At this point, we are still gathering data. Still attempting to work out the breach. How they could have possibly tied anything to you."

"Okay, I got it." He closed the gap with the runners ahead, ready to pass where the pathway widened. He sidestepped and increased his speed.

"The House is putting you on hiatus until further notice. And best you don't go home for a while."

"Well, obviously not, as the cops have already ripped it apart."

"Smoke, you're not listening to me. You and I both know that location was only a decoy. I know where you actually live. And if I can determine your home address in Jane Street with my contacts, then so might the NYPD. Don't go home. Not until I've handled—"

There was a sharp echoing crack and Gabrielle fell to the ground ahead of him, a ribbon of blood spiraling sideways from her upper torso as she went down.

Smoke instinctively dropped to the pavement, just as the head of the runner he was passing exploded. The shattering fracture of the skull. The violent squelch and spray of blood and fatty cords of brain matter. The gagging repulsive stink of gore. Rolling to his knees, Smoke scurried low on all fours, glancing over his shoulder, scanning the surrounding buildings, ignoring the terror, and shrieking panic escalating all around him. The roof of The Hotel or the Whitney Museum were the most likely locations for a sniper's nest. A glint of movement from the top of the hotel and he knew to tumble sideways. He fell into the West Street gutter, a driverless Tesla swerving to avoid him as bullets impacted the sidewalk, scattering chunks of concrete and lifting dust into the air.

He lurched backward and hit the rolling wheel of a truck, the torque flipping him over and smashing him chest first into the tar. Disoriented, his vision an oscillating blur, he staggered to his feet, crouching amongst the traffic until he regained his bearings. Car and truck horns blared, an ugly dissonance compounding the rapidly escalating ache in his skull. But he hunkered alongside them with his head down, leaving their bulky protection only when he came close to where Gabrielle had been hit. A pool of blood swathed the path. Fellow runners had pulled her to safety behind a concrete road barrier. Firefighters, lugging large medical duffel bags emblazoned with a Red Cross, were shouting, and running toward them along Gansevoort Pier from FDNY Marine 1.

Smoke sprinted across the blood and skidded to Gabrielle's side behind the weathered block. She was a mess, blood soaking through her clothing. He ran his hands down both sides of her rib cage. The bullet had entered at the base of her neck, passing through her torso to blow her open at the armpit. Blood pumped from an artery hanging loose. "Pressure here!" he yelled, grabbing an onlooker by the hand to press it hard against the exit wound. He peeled off his tank and ripped it down the middle, tourniqueting Gabrielle's arm and shoulder as best he could, yanking it tight to reduce the flow. Sirens blared in the near distance, and the firefighters were quickly closing in on foot. He had to get out of there.

Smoke seized the runner who'd pulled his handler to safety, gripping him by the hair, forcefully clapping their foreheads together. He yelled over the increasing ruckus of people, cars, and sirens.

"Listen to me. Tell the cops this wasn't just a random drive-by. This woman was one of the shooter's prime targets. They'll come after her again." He stabbed a finger at Gabrielle. "They can't trust anyone. She needs to be protected. You got that? Have you got it?"

The runner nodded, terror in his wide eyes. "Who do they need to protect her from?"

Smoke loosened his grip and fell back, his mind blank.

He didn't know.

Chapter Fifteen

He needed to think. And the best way he knew to do that was to run. He ran into the depths of Manhattan, far from his usual training route along the Hudson. Far from the incident, which would no doubt already be on broadcast and online news.

Looping east, then south, he strode into the West 4th Street basketball courts, turning his back on a group of lanky kids who'd stopped shooting hoops when he'd entered their cage, their attention swinging toward him. He washed the blood from his hands and wrists at a drinking fountain. His chest and shoulder were bruising, broken blood vessels spidering across his flesh ahead of a swelling mottled blue. Every part of him was tender and painful to the touch. He'd definitely broken a finger when he'd hit West Street. He pulled it straight with an audible pop and thought it should be okay. At least he was alive. He wondered if Gabrielle was alive. Wondered who wanted them dead. Had they, too, overstepped that line Jameson had mentioned?

"Hey, mister," called a kid. Smoke ignored him.

He realized his phone was still strapped to his arm. He pulled it loose, hesitating as he considered the information it held, then threw it down against the concrete, wincing with the pain of the movement. The phone disintegrated when it hit the tar, but still he picked up the remnants and tossed them out onto 6th, for the Avenue of the Americas traffic to pulverize.

"You need help, mister?"

Do I need help? Smoke thought. He couldn't go home. That was clear. He checked himself over to ensure no missed blood and to account for what he actually had. Running shoes. Socks. Cotton Nike shorts shredded on one side by the pavement of West Street. He lifted his foot and patted his sock above the ankle. Amex Card and Chelsea Piers Fitness ID.

All good.

He trotted from the cage, slowly increasing his pace to stretch through the discomfort, to stop his muscles from seizing. He circumnavigated Washington Square Park twice, noting those on the sidewalk before and behind, cutting through the park, and dawdling at the fountain. He didn't sense he was being followed.

Confident he was on his own, Smoke ran beneath the park's grand marble arch, up Fifth Avenue to the Flatiron District, then west toward Chelsea Piers.

Chapter Sixteen

He stepped into the lobby of Chelsea Piers Fitness and scanned his ID card, flinching as the machine verified the barcode… and who he was. Pushing any concern from his thoughts, he jogged around the reception desk and through the double-height cafeteria, past the stairs rising to the main exercise floor. This gym was a second home to him. A safe space. Full of friendly people. It resonated with the metallic clank and screech of high-end strength and cardio fitness machinery, the cushioning squelch of runners' footsteps on the quarter-mile running track, and the grunts of the men and women training muscle. The salty-sweet smell of dedication and ambition. He headed into the locker room.

He passed two men, each at least five inches too short for his needs. Another too bulky. None of the guys in the changing alcoves or wet rooms matched his size. He had no choice but to wait. He shucked off his runners and socks, threw his shorts into the trash, grabbed a towel, and hit the showers. He wrenched on the water but left the frosted shower door ajar to monitor the movement of those passing his vantage point.

He was suddenly tired. Exhausted. His mind was numb. He pressed his hand against the wall, shoulders slumped, head beneath the steady stream of hot water. He breathed in and out, slow, and deep, relishing the steam, the echoes of men in the other stalls who didn't want to kill him. Probably. He pressed his fingers to his eyes to combat the ache behind them, then peered out the gap in the door, watching several guys pass through the locker room, to and from their workouts.

Twenty minutes passed before someone suitable came into view and dropped a gym duffle onto the floor, a Gucci suit bag slung over his shoulder. He was maybe six foot three, 210 pounds, give or take. Feet not as large as Smoke's but that was okay. Smoke still had his runners.

He turned off the shower faucet and started wiping his torso dry as he padded toward the locker room. He reached for another towel and tied it around his waist.

"Jeepers, bud. Looks like a rough workout," the guy said.

In the mirror, Smoke took in the bruising on his shoulder and chest, and the guy behind him in reflection. "Yeah, my trainer has issues."

"I'd be more than happy to spot you." The guy peeled off his T-shirt and pushed off his sweats and boxers to kick them into the open locker.

Yep. An impressive six foot three, 210 pounds. Ripped.

"That'd be great. Looks like we have a similar regimen, or should," Smoke said. "And I'd be glad to take you to brunch at Elmo's anytime in exchange."

"Sweet. We'll go Dutch on the martinis and I'll cover the tip. I already know what I want for dessert."

His name was Hugh.

They kept talking, back-to-back as Smoke dried off and finger-combed his hair in the mirror. Hugh tugged on his gym clothes, ensured his Gucci wouldn't scrunch where it hung in his locker, and flicked the wheels on his combo lock: 1-4-9-4.

"See you next weekend, Tom," he said, throwing a towel over his shoulder and heading for the machines.

Smoke waited several minutes after Hugh left before flicking the lock back to 1-4-9-4. He unzipped the suit bag and ran his fingers across the lapel. "Nice. Hugh has style." He re-zipped the bag and bent to check the duffle. Three pairs of dark jeans. Four charcoal-colored T-shirts. All new. A Prada wallet held six credit cards, a New York driver's license for Hugh Danvers—thirty-six, a Greenwich Street address, flawless black skin, and ruggedly striking features in his DMV mug shot—and $200 in bills. Enough cash to last a typical day with a long lunch in Downtown Manhattan, chased by an early evening drink.

He drew on a pair of Hugh's jeans and one of his T-shirts before slipping on his own socks and runners. He nudged the wallet back into the duffle, secured it, and the rest of Hugh's gear in the locker, and scrambled the numbers on the lock.

Chapter Seventeen

Smoke believed in karma.

And this time it was almost instant.

Two suits were standing in the gym reception. Young men. In their early twenties, if that. They were not NYPD. By their stance, and the skinny cut of their jackets and ties, they didn't even look American.

They made him as soon as he exited the locker room. He pivoted on the ball of his foot and took off at speed. The suits immediately gave chase, drawing weapons—stainless steel Walther PPKs, by Smoke's backward glance. Smoke leaped up the stairs, three at a time, grabbing the handrail at the top landing to make the sharp turn and swing back toward the land end of Chelsea Pier 60, as the first report of bullets resounded—utterly unexpected despite the brazen open carry. The gym was in use by hundreds of members. None with protection. Smoke couldn't believe the suits would risk collateral damage this haphazard. Bullets cut up the staircase and into the ceiling, ricocheted against steel girders, and angled back down to embed into the floor matting with dull intermittent thuds.

These guys definitely didn't want to talk.

A round of bullets shattered a massive picture window, and the panoramic view of the Pier 59 Golf Range was obliterated into shards of translucent hurricane-proof glass. The cracking explosion was cacophonous. Moreso, as the adjacent windows cracked with a reverberant screech.

Smoke side-stepped the wide-eyed gym clientele scuttling away from the destruction, dropping to the floor to avoid continued gunfire, and scrambling toward the pier's external fire escapes. These were New Yorkers in every sense. They knew what to do. Their actions were inherent. Methodical. Executive. Instinctively helping those who faltered. Taking control. Barking direction and urging those around them toward safety. They'd be okay. Or at least, Smoke hoped they would.

A bullet clanged against an elliptical by his shoulder and veered off on an unknown trajectory. The gym's fire alarms sounded, and a sprinkler began gushing water over the rows of machinery, spreading across the floor and down the steps to the café and reception areas below. Smoke slipped in the deluge, sprawling awkwardly across the linoleum, his broken finger cracking a second time, loud and painful. He cursed as he rolled beneath the ropes of a boxing ring and army crawled over the canvas toward the closest internal emergency escape.

Punching open the bright red door, adding another alarm to the mix, he caught his foot on the threshold and fell again with an angry, frustrated grunt. This was not going well.

The escape was a long tunnel stretching the length of the pier, lined with raw concrete, fire retardant foam, and flickering incandescent tubes. He pushed up from his knees, and ran, holding his injured hand tight in the damp heat of his armpit. He bit down hard on his lip to counter the throbbing pain of his finger. And the intense ache in his skull from having hit the pavement one too many times that morning. When bullet fire shattered an overhead light, he ducked, staggering sideways, and kept running. The suits were closing in.

The exit to 11th Avenue was still fifty feet ahead of him when he shouldered through a side door in the tunnel, slammed against an unexpected railing, and swung around it to climb a set of corrugated metal stairs. He rammed another door, one level up.

Then faltered in confusion.

In complete disorientation.

He was in a dimly lit office suite with heavy walnut furniture. Dark leather Chesterfields. Hundreds of leather-bound, legal tomes stacked high on shelves, floor to ceiling. A large picture window highlighted the Manhattan nightscape. High rises glimmered against the evening sky, the moon and stars sharp in the distance despite Smoke's certainty it was no later than 8:30 in the morning. His sight adjusted to the ambient light, and he slowly distinguished the dozens of dormant spotlights and fluorescents hanging from the industrial-style ceiling. Camera dolly tracks crossed the floor. Cables tangled and looped back and forth, a trip hazard underfoot.

In his mind, he heard the unmistakable double clang of a New York police procedural TV show—*dun-dun*—and realized where he was.

The studio set was unsettlingly silent, soundproofed against the city outside and the commotion back at the gym. He carefully felt his way through the dim light to the adjacent set piece—a morgue furnished with gray linoleum flooring, metal gurneys, and a wall of refrigerated cabinets. Four naked polyfoam cadavers topped the aluminum autopsy tables in the center of the room. They appeared as genuine as any of the dead bodies Smoke had encountered. Had been responsible for.

From behind him came the sound of footfalls, loud and clanking in the stairwell to the office set. He hesitated, then turned and ran straight for them.

The suits pulled themselves up short on the threshold of the office doorway, perplexed as Smoke had expected. Before their eyes could adjust to the dim, he swung a faux post-autopsy cadaver at full force toward them, hitting one suit square on, sending both man and fake carcass tumbling down the stairs. The nauseating crack of bone and fragmenting thud of skull against the corrugated metal tread did not come from the television prop.

The second suit lunged blindly into the dark, tripping, his brogues tangled in unseen cables. Smoke cracked his fist across the suit's face as he went down, knuckles bruising against jaw, cheekbone, and temple, flinching at the deafening report as the suit's weapon discharged. Smoke countered with a kick, hoping to loosen the gun from the suit's grip, but only clipped the barrel with the heel of his runner. Still, he followed through, torquing his body and throwing his substantial bulk into the suit's slighter frame. They crashed to the floor with a grunting thud. He took a blow to the eye before twisting the guy against him in a choke hold, the veins of his forearm and bicep swelling with the squeeze. The ripping pop of cartilage and sinew in the suit's throat was more than satisfying to Smoke as he tried to catch his breath, ignoring the loud and painful throb of blood coursing behind his eyeballs. He grappled for the gun with his free hand, the suit repeatedly smashing it and his broken finger against the steel wheels of a camera dolly.

"Who are you? Who sent you?" Smoke yelled through the pain as he gripped the suit's flailing hand, attempting to hold it still. Their clenched fists and the gun with them arced up and thudded against the suit's chest. "Tell me," Smoke shouted. He tightened his choke hold.

"*Vaffanculo!*" the suit said through gritted teeth. *Fuck you!* His breath stank of unfiltered coffee and tobacco. It was the unmistakable burned-rubber smell of *Gauloises* cigarettes that Smoke associated with the dank alleys and sex-fueled cellars of *Le Marais* in Paris. Anonymous midnight encounters amid Parisian Bohemians. Gender and sexual preference irrelevant in dark subterranean passages.

The blast, muzzle flash, and recoil of the gun reverberated for a second time. A bullet squelched through the suit's torso, the force throwing both of them backward to be further entangled in the cables, and Smoke was palpably aware the bullet's trajectory had stopped less than a spine's width from his own sternum.

He lay askew amongst the twisted knot of cords for several moments, gulping for air, willing the erratic thump of his heart back toward normal. Then he kicked the suit's legs off of his and kneed the bloody torso to the side to free himself and regain his footing. His head buzzed. He bent low and gripped the suit's face, turning it back and forth.

Did he know him?

The guy was blandly appealing, with a dirty blonde French crop, a sharp nose and jawline, and thin crimson lips. His plaque-edged teeth were dulled gray by cigarettes. Smoke patted down the jacket and pants. The gun blast had partially obliterated a European Passport in the breast pocket. Aloïs Laurent, twenty-three, a *Rue du Colisée* address in Paris, France. A slim plastic wallet held two *Carte Bancaires* credit cards and $6,000 in American bills. A fob pocket held an unbranded mini smartphone—credit card thin. He pocketed the lot, then with open hands patted down the suit's torso, arms, and legs. A second European Passport was inscribed with the name Aloysius Laurentius. This one with an address in Florence, Italy. The shirt pocket held an electronic door keycard for a suite at The Hotel in the Meatpacking District.

Lights flared on in the adjacent morgue studio set.

Smoke ran his hands along the lengths of the body once more to ensure nothing had been missed, then crept backward out of the office, discretely pulling the fire escape door closed behind him. Halfway down the stairs, he stepped over the twisted remains of the television corpse, which had obviously met a nasty end on the streets of New York City in a recent episode.

The second suit at the bottom of the stairs was not dead.

His neck was bent at an unforgiving angle, his body limp, his eyes blinking wildly with fear. Tears streaked his cheeks, his face an exact duplicate of the one at the top of the stairs. A twin.

"I'm sorry," Smoke said. "Your brother is dead."

The suit pressed his lips tight and squeezed his eyes shut as Smoke searched the pockets of his jacket and pants. Two more EU passports, varying names and residential countries. Mathéo Laurent of Paris. Matteo Laurentius of Florence. More credit cards, American bills, and a second mini smartphone. He pocketed them as muffled noises issued from the office set at the top of the stairs. The TV production crew had found Aloïs's body.

"Mathéo, tell me who sent you. Who sent you to kill me? *Dis-moi qui t'a envoyé.*"

"*Je te dirai si tu me tues.*" Mathéo's words came out with broken, jerky breaths. *I'll tell you if you kill me.*

Smoke blinked at his response, but then nodded.

"*Putains! Medici Firenze,*" Mathéo said with little breath. His languages and accents were slurred, slipping from

French to Italian, grammar lacking, but with an educated lilt. Blood coated his tongue and lips, and the bones in his neck crunched as he spoke.

"Medics, doctors from Florence?" Smoke asked, confused.

"*Non. Famiglia Medici*," Mathéo spat. "The family Medici. Fucking whores!"

Chapter Eighteen

On the top deck of the Staten Island Ferry, Smoke struggled to wind down, his mind racing, the bench hard and uncomfortable beneath the ache of his butt. He tried to focus on balancing a foam cup of bitter coffee at his knee while munching on a toasted everything bagel with cream cheese to at least satisfy his rumbling stomach. He glanced at his bare wrist, then up at the overhead sun, wondering what time it was. Not yet noon. Maybe 10:30. Clouds approached on a warm breeze from the west.

The Statue of Liberty was massive at such close quarters, demanding his attention. Her patinated gown flowed down to sandaled feet, and the broken shackle and chain. Her upstretched arm held firm to the torch, enlightening the world. The morning sun added a sheen, deepening shadows across the folds of copper sheathing, highlighting the raised symbols on the tablet held to her breast. Liberty had a relatable French connection, but he couldn't think of any such connection between him and the French twins.

The Medici Family. What could Mathéo possibly have meant by that? What connections could the twins have to an Italian family dynasty and bloodline that had died out centuries ago? And what did that have to do with him?

The boat crested a swell rolling through New York Harbor. The vessel tilted and Smoke held out his coffee as it sloshed from the cup.

He noticed a smear of blood along the side of his runners—most likely belonging to Aloïs. Smoke licked the pad of his thumb and bent down to wipe the shoe clean. Then he checked his hands, arms, T-shirt, and jeans. No more blood. He'd taped three of his fingers together, centering the broken one that was now hued a mottled, dark blue. The Ibuprofen helped, but not much. He awkwardly stood and attempted to stretch the ache from his arms, torso, and legs.

Mathéo had been hard to kill. Not physically, but for reasons Smoke had not encountered before. His blue-gray, tear-filled eyes had held his attention as he'd cradled the young man's neck. Even with a gentle touch, the bones cracked and crunched like cereal, offering no protection to the spinal cord that had compressed in the fall down the stairs from the studio.

"*Tu pourrais encore vivre*," Smoke had muttered. *You might still live.*

"*Non*," Mathéo had said, the single word emphatic.

Smoke had thumbed the blood from Mathéo's lips, then placed his palm against his clean-shaved jaw, swiftly jerking it up and sideways, irreparably severing the nerve tissue encased within the shattered vertebrae. Death was instant. The blue-gray eyes still held his gaze, but now without the slightest spark of life.

Now on the ferry deck, he pulled out the twins' mini-smartphones, removed their batteries, and then nudged the phones back into his pocket. Next were the four passports. He flipped through their pages as the boat climbed another swell. The young men shared addresses in Paris and Florence. The Parisian address was in an exclusive urban residential area. An entire building, it seemed. Smoke could only imagine its value. Despite Aloïs's lack of dental hygiene, the twins were clearly far from destitute. They'd landed yesterday at Teterboro Airport in New Jersey. A short town car drive into Manhattan via the GWB or the Lincoln tunnel.

"Private jet," Smoke muttered beneath the call of gulls soaring above the vessel.

He remained on Staten Island only long enough to buy a burner smartphone, a fresh, flaky *gah-nole*, and a real *caw-fee* before boarding the noon boat back to Manhattan.

Passing once more beneath the inspiration of Lady Liberty, he thumbed *Aloïs Laurent* into his burner's internet search engine. None of the links appeared relevant.

Mathéo Laurent.

The first viable link was to an Instagram account. Definitely him. Definitely a party boy. Sun-bleached blonde and tanned. Instagram happy. Popular with the girls. Surrounded by a lot of big-boy toys. Cars. Yachts. Jets. Smoke recognized the French and Italian Rivieras in his photos. Nice. Monte Carlo. Sanremo. Portofino. Cinque Terre. Some photos were likely on the Tyrrhenian or Aegean Seas, by the look of the rugged coastline beyond the furled spinnakers and bare-breasted women holding flutes of champagne. The profile's bio linked to a *FansOnly* account. He employed Mathéo's credit card to pay the €100 subscription fee. Blatant nudity for a price. For fun, when money and reputation were of no consideration or consequence.

Smoke raised an eyebrow. Mathéo had a lot more than just money to entice a close bond with the women in his life. He flicked past the photo gallery and clicked on a video. Mathéo with a woman of about the same age. Euro movie star looks.

Both possessing the unbridled beauty of youth. They played to the camera as they laughed and kissed and fucked in the opulent salon of a Provençal or Italian Villa. Not a care in the world. The camera panned, catching the reflection of its operator in an antique Baroque mirror. Aloïs. Naked. Youthful Mediterranean masculinity. Settling the camera, Aloïs joined his twin and the young woman on the divan, the bond between all three unaffectedly intimate.

Smoke's thoughts drifted inward, the Manhattan skyline unfocused ahead. These young men—these boys, really—had had everything. Why would they risk it all? Was it the daring and ego of the *untouchable*? Or was it the fear of something much worse?

Chapter Nineteen

Smoke strode into The Hotel reception and slammed the electronic keycard on the counter.

"Aloïs Laurent," he said. "*Ma carte*, it is, how you say, non-*fonctionne*. I will return *dans une demi-heure,* ah, in half of the hour." He strode back out onto the street before they could question him, glad Gabrielle had not been present to hear his butchering of a language they both spoke well. God, he hoped she was still alive. The thought of her bleeding out unconscious on the sidewalk left him cold. His flesh crawled, and he shuddered.

He took a chair at an outside café on 9th to bide his time before changing his mind. Within five minutes he was standing at the roof bar atop the Gansevoort Hotel, double fisting two martinis, leaning against the pool deck's glass balustrade. He savored the smooth, chilled Grey Goose. The sun was still high overhead, glinting off the double-tall windows of converted warehouses scattered across the Meatpacking District, and off the rolling waves of the Hudson River a few blocks to the west, as it reversed its flow with the incoming tide. Fourteen stories below his perch, the avenue was alive with locals and tourists: shopping, eating, drinking. He pushed back his curls and closed his eyes to feel the breeze on his cheeks. He wished he still had his aviators, probably long smashed by the wheels of cars traversing West Street.

"Magnificent," said a woman as she sidled up beside him and pretended to admire the view. She had that privileged nasal tone that should stay out in the Hamptons, or Sag Harbor, or wherever, on the farthest reaches of Long Island. Smoke didn't bite. He didn't want to peel the skimpy pink bikini from her spray-tanned flesh or chew on her dramatic, over-plumped lips. Maybe another time, but not today. Definitely not today. He didn't even want to know her name, which was probably Barbie, or Bethany, or Briana. Yeah, Briana, he decided.

She ran the point of an acrylic fingernail the length of the thick vein traversing the bulge of his bicep. She followed its course, apparent even at his shoulder beneath the well fitted cotton of Hugh Danver's T-shirt. He tossed back his head and drained the first martini, ignoring her advances.

"I'm staying here at the hotel," she said, dropping her hand to the generous curve of his pec without respect for any boundaries he might or might not have. Briana was undoubtedly a young woman who could have whatever her money, or her daddy's, or mommy's money could buy. Still, his nipples hardened with the touch, and he thought back to the *FansOnly* video: the Laurent twins with the beautiful young woman, all of them naked and aroused. "You like that, huh?" Briana said. "I see you do."

Smoke drank the second martini in a single draft, then threw her a tight but welcoming smile. "I'll have to take a raincheck, baby girl. But I'm certain you'll still have a wonderful time while you're here in New York." He threw her a wink and headed toward the elevator.

He walked the cobbled streets back to The Hotel and slammed his open hand against the reception desk a second time. "*Excuse-moi.*"

"Of course, Mister Laurent." The receptionist handed him a new keycard in a logo-embossed cardboard sleeve. Across the back was handwritten: *Mr. Laurent, Suite 1737.*

"*Merci beaucoup,*" he said.

The suite was on the seventeenth floor, and worth at least five thousand dollars a night with its impeccable black and gold décor, and expansive views north, west, and south. A bottle of *Moët* sat on ice, an unopened envelope leaning against the crystal bucket. He locked and chained the door behind him, then looked around. The walk-in wardrobe held two suitcases, each monogrammed with a twin's initials, their contents unpacked, freshly pressed and placed into silk-lined drawers or draped over cedar hangers. A combo-locked, ridged metal case stood between the suitcases. He didn't need to open it to know it held a disassembled high-powered rifle. A laptop lay on the bedside table. He hesitated at the window, contemplating the distant concrete barricade where Gabrielle had been dragged, and the stretch of West Street he'd slammed against face first.

Then he fell onto the bed and pulled the computer onto his lap. The sheets smelled of the twins. And *Gauloises* cigarettes.

"Damn it," he said.

He returned to the wardrobe, searching for a packet of cigarettes amongst the *Garçon Français* socks and underwear. He found a carton alongside a sterling silver *Cartier* lighter etched with the words *Palle! Palle! Palle!* He ripped the cellophane cover from a pack, tapped out a stubby white cigarette, lit it, and drew in a deep, erratic breath.

It had taken him years to drop the habit in his late twenties. He'd just have one. Just one.

The heavy nicotine muddled with the alcohol coursing through his arteries. It lightened the ache in his skull. In his bones and muscles. He toed off his runners and socks and dropped back across the black and gold damask eiderdown, sliding the laptop onto his thighs as he continued to puff.

There was no password protection on the device.

The untouchable ego of the rich, he thought for the second time.

The laptop was brand new, without email, or apps, or internet connection. There was nothing beyond its original factory settings except a single folder on the desktop labeled "NYC." He clicked it open.

Inside the folder were two Word docs and multiple jpegs. The first document was titled "Smoke," which he opened to find details of his life. Birth date. Birth mother. Each of his foster parents and their addresses. And their crimes. One full page was his *expunged* juvenile record, followed by details of his hard-earned degrees at Harvard and Georgetown Universities. The decoy residential address was in boldface. His €2 million yearly stipend and his bank account number in the Caymans were italicized and underlined.

His head lolled back and he stared at the ceiling, dragging deep on the cigarette and noting the location of a blinking smoke detector near the suite entrance. He blew away from it.

The document held no hint of the multi-legged redirects he'd established between various credit unions and banks across Europe and the midwestern United States to safeguard his accrued funds.

And, more crucially, it gave no reference to the only person he loved without question. The only person he spoke of to no one outside a very tight circle.

There was a map graphic with starred points tracing his approximate movements throughout Manhattan, clustering around Chelsea and his favorite training routes. Thankfully, it appeared accurate only to within three city blocks. He assumed they'd been tracking his cell.

The second document in the folder was titled "Gabrielle." He deleted it without reading, respectful of her privacy.

Next came close to 100 high resolution photos capturing recent moments of his and Gabrielle's. Both together and with others. Intimate and mundane. He noted the guy Gabrielle had kissed and slapped as a diversion at the Carlyle Hotel—the one who'd been wearing the Hermes suit—not wearing the Hermes suit. Yep, the tattoos were real after all. Some photos of Smoke documented first-degree felonies beyond any reasonable doubt. Others recorded his penchants for running, dancing, fucking, docking, and kissing.

He took another drag of the *Gauloises,* its effects shimmering to the lengths of his toes.

He was thoughtful as he finished the cigarette and lit another. Then he deleted each of the docs and photos, emptied the computer trash, and erased the files and folders from the hard drive. He'd handle the drive more thoroughly later. A hammer should do it. Perhaps followed by the flame of that nice little engraved lighter, and then the depths of the Hudson.

He flicked on the television, doubting he'd find any good news.

The set opened on an old episode of *Friends*. *The One with Five Steaks and an Eggplant.* He scrolled through the television guide to ABC.

Breaking News.

The NYPD had tied the Stuyvesant murders to another in Tudor City, and yet another on Wall Street.

Details at 6:30.

This was far from over.

He stubbed out the cigarette, peeled off his jeans and T-shirt, and crawled beneath the sheets.

Chapter Twenty

He awoke with a start. The dim reflection of early evening shrouded the suite on the seventeenth floor of The Hotel, the lights of Newport and Hoboken on the Jersey side of the river glistening in the distance. Searchlight beams swept across the panoramic nightscape.

Tossing off the bed covers, Smoke lit another cigarette and walked naked to the window to contemplate the view. He leaned against the glass, cool and comforting against his flesh. He let out a moan at the relief it provided. The throbbing ache in his head had dulled, and his broken finger was now little more than a pulsing numbness. One of his fingernails was torn and bloody, and he placed it momentarily into the moisture of his mouth before taking another deep drag off the cigarette.

Ice popped in the crystal bucket centered on the petite dining table at his side. He had no taste for the *Moët* but thumbed open the envelope leaning against the bucket to read its contents. The note inside was addressed to the twins. Crass verbiage bordered on disgusting. The signature scrawled across the bottom was *Rafaella di Toledo*.

Smoke narrowed his eyes, rereading the note. It was an invitation to a high-end fashion show on Little Island tonight. A summons from Rafaella... *di Toledo*. It had to be that hideous creature who'd hosted the Hell's Kitchen soirée he'd attended with Eleonora… Eleonora had called her Rafaella.

Continuing to puff on the *Gauloises*, he contemplated the arc of the searchlights emanating from Little Island on its concrete tulip stilettoes in the Hudson shallows. The unfiltered cigarette burned down to the tips of his tobacco-stained fingers before he tossed the remnants into the bucket of melting ice and again dressed in Hugh's clothes. He raised his arms and sniffed his pits. All good. He studied his reflection in the picture window. Should be fine. One of Manhattan's top fashion designers had advised him long ago, in a SoHo gutter while they snorted high-end Colombian dust off a Euro model's girthy nineteen centimeters, that New York *everyman* chic had nothing to do with runway fashion and everything to do with attitude and the body providing the contours. As long as the material was dark, preferably black, it was easier to backdoor it surreptitiously when events demanded. You might earn extra kudos and photos in the local gossip rags if you had a new movie or book coming out, perhaps a salacious relationship with a top one percenter; or over a million Instagram followers.

It had probably been the blow talking.

He guessed he was going to find out.

And perhaps despite going in blind, he might also garner some clue as to what this was all about. With the twins out of the way, he had no concerns beyond determining the truth.

When he arrived, he made his way through the crowd of gawking onlookers clamoring along the sidewalks and flashed the invitation. A beast of a bouncer motioned for him to proceed onto the black carpet crossing the southern bridge toward Little Island. This route was calm compared to the island's main entrance bridge, further north. A long line of limousines stretched along the greenway. They pulsed and hummed in the psychedelic flash of hundreds of cameras as someone of importance, money, beauty, or all three, stepped onto the carpet. The crowd took up the chant: *Rhianna! Rhianna! Rhianna!*

Yup. Worthy of the adulation earned, Smoke thought.

He passed through the gauntlet of metal detectors and a cursory pat-down at the edge of the island. The stiletto shaped piers rose dozens of feet out of the water, supporting grassed embankments, foliage, and mature groves of trees above them. The elegant, feminine curve of the concrete construction had always fascinated him and was a favorite part of his daily run. The main concourse at the manmade island's center was inviting. Meditating hills and botanical trails climbed multiple stories around its perimeter into the twilight. Tonight, the glitterati of New York's high fashion and social status held court. Smoke wished he'd worn a suit—at least a jacket. But furtive attention from those around him bolstered his confidence that he and his *everyman* couture were more than welcome as part of the eclectic scene of fashionistas.

"Veuve Clicquot, sir?" a server asked.

"San Pellegrino," Smoke said.

The server motioned to another, and Smoke soon held a flute of crisp sparkling water to his lips. He sidled through the crowd of the beautiful and the rich. And the absolutely stunning. His heart skipped a beat when he glimpsed his Broadway and movie star crush. He'd attended the opening night of Sondheim's *A Little Night Music*, in which her starring role as Desiree had been so evocative, and he'd had no other choice than to fall unequivocally in love with the unattainable. She was stunning in every sense. Beyond stunning in the flesh.

And then he spotted Rafaella and winced.

Hideous creature.

"Thank you for the invitation," he said as he approached.

A range of emotions attempted to play across her face. Surprise, and then the instinct to suppress it—her facial reactions held in check by copious injections of Botox and fillers. "My pleasure," she said with uncertainty, glancing past him before returning her attention to him. "You are alone? No Eleonora to hold your hand?"

"Tonight, it's you I want."

"Oh. That is unexpected." She ran a fingertip around the rim of her champagne flute. "I would've thought I was thirty years too young for your tastes. Still with my own natural collagen and teeth."

Smoke doubted that. He sucked in a deep breath. "Tell me about Aloïs and Mathéo. Or do you call them Aloysius and Matteo?"

"You've met the boys? Yes, of course you have. And you're still standing. How fascinating." She placed her empty flute on a tray. "They prefer the accented French variation despite their birth in Tuscany. I'm sure it's only a rebellious phase, but each to their own. What would you like to know?"

"Why did they come to New York?"

Her smirk was cruel. "Why does anyone come to New York? I'm certain a man of your means and proclivity already knows the answer to that question." She pressed her hand to his chest. "I'll admit, I can see what Eleonora, and most likely the boys, might see in you. But honestly, you're not my type. A bit too preppy." She leaned in closer and breathed in his scent. "*Gauloises!* Hmmm. You *are* well acquainted with the boys, aren't you? Don't let Eleonora catch you cheating. She can be a mean one."

Smoke sipped his water, attempting to reorganize his thoughts. "You don't know why they're here?"

Rafaella reached up and pulled his face down to her own.

"Do you think I'd tell you if I did? Why are *you* here?" she asked. The brush of her lips aside his as she spoke, her spittle sickly sweet from the champaign, had him pulling back in disgust and wiping the back of his hand across his mouth.

Anger shimmered over Rafaella's face. For a second time, she glanced past his shoulder, this time with a barely perceptible nod.

The brute approaching them was of slender build, but solid, with a not unattractive angular face that Smoke knew he needed to commit to memory. Late thirties. Thick, dark sweptback hair. Well manicured brows arching above a strong Roman nose. Heavily lashed lids over near-black eyes. Generous lips. The suit and shoes were Italian. Unbranded "stealth wealth" style. Bespoke and unduly expensive.

Now Smoke definitely felt underdressed. It angered him he hadn't been more prepared.

"*Signore* Moretti," Rafaella said. "I expect you're already acquainted with our friend here."

Moretti patted Smoke on the back, slid his open hands down either side of his torso, pits to hips, and then drew him into a tight, welcoming hug. He kissed both of Smoke's cheeks, and there was a subtle hint of *Acqua Di Parma* along the clean-shaved jaw.

"*Sì,* I am intimately acquainted with Tommaso and his appetites," he said. He held tight to Smoke, murmuring in his ear. "*Mio amico,* what an opportunity! Should your ultimate tragedy be here at this *grande* gala, or shall we continue to play, how you say, *il gatto e il topo*?"

"Cat and mouse," Rafaella translated.

Smoke knew exactly what Moretti had said and meant. The six-inch bulge of the weapon beneath the weave of his Italian suit was hard against him in the embrace.

And Smoke realized he'd just met himself. Or, at least, someone who did exactly what he did.

"Aloïs and Mathéo didn't need to die today," he said to Moretti. "Why did you send boys to do a man's job? Your job."

Rafaella glared, shocked. "They were making amends. They offered their services in recompense for exposing—" Her face flushed and she bit her lip. Then she turned from them and strode off into the crowd, taking another *Veuve* from a server's tray as she passed them.

"How about you and I slip away for a quiet *conversazione*, Tommaso," Moretti said in his unaffected romance accent, motioning toward the cityscape. "And if you like, we can discuss how you'd prefer this evening to end. That is how you do it, is it not?" He smiled. "How could I find your style anything but charming? *Bellissimo*."

The hairs on the back of Smoke's head stood up. "Let's just do it here. Give Little Island a killing to add to its Wiki page," Smoke growled. Disgusted with himself, he wondered how he had so smoothly and blindly walked into this situation. And how he was going to get out of it.

Alive!

Moretti kept his arm draped across Smoke's shoulders, his hold warm and tight as they made their way through the crowd and around a grove of immature red oaks to a service door beside the outdoor amphitheater. He pulled the door open and beckoned for Smoke to enter. Steep steps within led down to a run of slim, steel walkways straddling the artificial island's concrete stilettos, and the service door slammed shut behind them, loud and jarring, as they climbed downward. Recessed lighting accented the damp shadows with the Hudson flowing mere feet below them. It was cold and noisy as it swirled around the piers, echoing through the dramatic curve of arches, much louder than the gala above them. Smoke likened the space to a flooded Gothic crypt awaiting its first body.

His.

"Such a romantic grotto you've brought us to, *Signore* Moretti," he said over his shoulder as he walked along the grated walkway.

"*Per favore, chiamami* Simone," Moretti said, pulling a handgun from his jacket.

"Okay then, Simone. You'll probably need a muzzle suppressor down here."

Moretti reached inside his jacket.

In one moment Smoke turned and with the full strength of his quads, slammed his right foot up and between Moretti's thighs for full, jarring contact. The action met its mark, the impact shuddering through the Italian's body, his gun jettisoned out into the water.

With a pained gagging grunt, Moretti returned with a twisting fist punch that dropped Smoke flat onto his back, the air knocked from his lungs, his foothold slipping to dangle his legs down either side of the slim grate. The Italian stumbled on the follow-through, and Smoke swung his legs up to grip Moretti's, buckling him at the knees and bringing his bulky deadweight on top of himself. There was no room to throw a fist in the confines of the metal balustrades, with the horizontal wire cables pulled taut between its uprights. They gripped each other as best they could, muscles tensing as each attempted to gain the upper hand, to wrestle the other into an untenable position, to constrict movement and preferably stop the flow of air or blood. Moretti twisted and made purchase on Smoke's throat, fingers digging deep into the muscle behind the larynx. He pressed a thumbnail hard against the carotid artery, all but stopping the blood flow. Smoke quickly felt faint, the pressure in his face intensifying as he continued to struggle against the Italian's hold.

He was fading.

Fast.

He could feel and hear the myriad of tiny blood vessels across his cheeks and eyeballs popping and breaking as he struggled to breathe. To stay conscious. Somehow, he freed an arm. He reached around his opponent and grappled for a hold, but there was nothing soft about the Italian's body. Every inch was lithe, hard muscle. He stretched for Simone's face, repetitively thumping cheeks and lips, eventually forcing his fingers into his open mouth. He dug two in between gum and tongue, his knuckles grated between clenching teeth as he pressed his thumb hard up against the soft underbelly of Simone's jaw. He squeezed fingers and thumb toward each other through the flesh and yanked the mandible roughly sideways. It was the same brute force he used to do a clean and jerk lift of more than his body weight at the gym.

A sharp crack resonated as the jaw dislocated and tendons tore. Simone yelped and jolted sideways, slipping beneath the wire and falling awkwardly into the churning water below. Smoke rolled onto his side with the sudden release of constraint, coughing and wheezing, spitting bloody saliva and barely stopping short of throwing up. The ache in his head had returned to full force. He leaned over the edge of the walkway as he caught his breath, waiting to see whether he would vomit. He knew he'd feel better if he did. Simone's body bobbed to the surface of the river below, his face beneath the rolling swell.

"Shit."

Despite his history and his job, Smoke was unwilling for another death on his hands in such quick succession. Especially another that was not explicitly sanctioned before execution. He rolled off the gangway and plunged into the surge.

The Hudson was cold, oily, and gritty, intermittently echoing the noises of the city, and the gala above them. It embodied a stink beyond words as it repetitively slapped against his face, putrid and sickening as it coated the inside of his mouth whenever he gulped for breath. He clumsily turned over Moretti's body. Simone was alive but unconscious, with no need for CPR. And judging from the awkward bulge of his jaw, it'd be a while before he'd be able to tear a slice of pizza with his teeth.

Smoke kicked furiously in the surge. The gangway was several feet above them, beyond his reach. He pulled Simone into the crook of his arm and kicked away from the concrete pylons of Little Island. The river's current hastily swept them from the shadows to course amongst hundreds of ancient wooden piles. A petrified forest jutting out of the river. Decayed remnants of luxurious piers that had once welcomed the survivors of the Titanic and bid farewell to those aboard the fated Lusitania.

He struggled to hold both his weight and Simone's above the swell as the current jettisoned them from the rotted piers and out into the open water. He was not a swimmer. His energy waning fast. But he held tight to Simone, unwilling to let him drift and sink, even as waves from the Midtown Ferry cut across their course to send them under.

Smoke

A fluorescent brown darkness and a dull thumping drone surrounded them as Smoke frantically thrashed his legs and pushed upward. He broke the surface, an oily discharge coating his mouth and tongue as he took in a deep breath before the slap of another wave. The water abruptly whirled and eddied, throwing them out toward New Jersey, then back in toward the Manhattan shoreline to dump them unceremoniously on Gansevoort Beach, a thousand feet downstream from Little Island.

"*911*, what's your emergency?"

"Crazy guy. Right? Some kind of foreigner. From New Jersey or somewhere like that. Came runnin' out of the watah at Gansevoort Beach, threatenin' ta kill anyone who approached. Said he'd already murdered two guys at Chelsea Piers earlier today. Yuh with me? I gotta go. Right? He's—"

Smoke ended the call, tapped the battery out of Aloïs's smartphone and relaxed upon the lounge in Suite 1737. He took a drag on another *Gauloises*.

Chapter Twenty-One

The cell phone chimed on the seat beside her.

"Lucy O'Donnell."

"He's smart. Called in a disturbance on Gansevoort Beach with Aloïs Laurent's cellphone before killing the signal. The call bounced across every border in the Eurozone, then back to hit *911* here on the island. We nailed him on the EU reroute with voice recognition."

"Any other intercepts?" she asked.

"No, local systems can't compete. And only we have his speech signature."

"What was the disturbance?"

"Moretti. We collected him before the NYPD even had a chance to turn on their lights and sirens."

"What is Simone doing here?"

"Dunno. Didn't pressure him. He's worse off after the altercation. Might need a dentist. We dumped him at his hotel with a box of painkillers."

"Has NYPD figured out who or where our subject is?"

"No. Are we ready to…"

Lucy leaned back into the plush leather of the town car.

"Leave it for now." She ended the call.

Her cell rang again almost immediately.

"Lucy?"

She didn't hide her surprise. "Tommy, hi!"

"Is it too late for a quick drink? Maybe some dumplings or something?"

"Not at all. I need a couple hours' break from this case, anyway. It's doing my head in."

"Barracuda Bar in an hour?" Smoke asked.

"Sure. One of my favorite haunts. See you there."

* * *

Lucy was already at the bar nursing a Cosmopolitan when Smoke walked in, his attention instantly drawn to her backlit silhouette. She looked smart in DKNY jeans and a dark cropped jacket over a white tank. The Hotel had had a fast turnaround on laundering Hugh's pants and T-shirt, but Smoke's runners had not fared well in the Hudson. He'd had to squeeze his sockless size thirteens into a pair of Aloïs's Ferragamo loafers. They were tight, but the soft leather stretched enough to make them almost bearable.

He slid onto the barstool beside Lucy's. "Hi, again," he said.

"Hi." Her concern shone through the single word. "Are you okay? You look pretty rough, even in this lighting."

He smiled and held up his bandaged finger. "Just tripped the curb on West Street during my run today. Nothing a Cosmo or two won't remedy. How has your day been?"

She held his gaze as the on-point bartender slid a Cosmo in front of him. "You don't want to know," she finally said. "Besides, if you found out, I'd have to kill you."

He clinked his glass with hers—"Cheers to that,"—and took a sip. "I really enjoyed the other night. Though I wish I hadn't had to leave so early."

"Understandable," she said. "I appreciate someone who takes care of their responsibilities no matter the disruption."

He nodded, silent as he contemplated his next words.

"Hey, I know we don't really know each other, not yet anyway, but I was hoping I could ask a favor of you. I don't want to compromise your job, and I'll understand if you can't help."

Lucy watched him, waiting.

"A good friend of mine was hurt earlier today, and I don't know how to even start checking to see if she's okay. I thought, because of where you work with the police, maybe you might know. Her name is Gabrielle. Gabrielle Davis."

Lucy appeared thoughtful, turning her glass atop its coaster on the bar. "The spokesperson for the NYPD mentioned that name during the press briefing this evening. It should be on the networks by now if the media deemed it newsworthy. Something in relation to a drive-by near the Whitney." She glanced at his bandaged finger.

"Is she okay?" he asked.

Something in Lucy's countenance shifted, and it seemed she dropped any pretense. "She is. The medical team at Bellevue stabilized her before airlifting her to Walter Reed."

"The Army hospital in Maryland?"

Lucy nodded. "Perhaps she requires one of their specialists. Is your friend military?"

"Ah, no. Oh, I don't know. Maybe ex." Smoke shrugged, wishing he'd read the Word document on Gabrielle. He zoned out, his focus somewhere in the depths of his Cosmo. Then he shivered, letting out a deep sigh as if he'd been holding his breath since that morning's events. Relief flooded him, and he wiped brusquely at his face.

"Thank you," he said, shivering again as his body relaxed further. He wanted to kiss her but knew he shouldn't. Still, he leaned forward and touched his lips to her cheek for the briefest of moments in thanks, then pulled back. She appeared neither surprised nor offended.

She whetted her lips and had just opened her mouth to speak when a group of guys, boisterous and flamboyant, entered from the dancefloor at the back of the bar. They pushed through the lavish drapes of crimson velvet, the kaleidoscopic light of mirror balls and the reverberation of Donna Summer sultry about them. They clustered around the stools and leaned against the bar. Shirtless. Sweaty. Exhilarated.

"Six Chuck Norrises, Bubba," the Alpha bellowed. He flashed Smoke and Lucy a Cheshire grin in easy recognition. "Make that eight, babe," he said to the bartender.

"Hold on to your hat with this one," Smoke muttered.

The Alpha clinked shot glasses with each of the men in his pack before turning to Smoke and Lucy. He had a meaty chest and belly, an eight-pack almost completely concealed by a few too many Monte Cristos. Approachably sexy. They tapped glasses and downed the shots. The alcohol immediately numbed Smoke's tongue before the burn of hot sauce flared. He took a quick swig of his Cosmo to dilute the heat, but it only made it worse.

"It's been a while, stranger," the Alpha said, his voice deep and calm.

Smoke was about to answer when Lucy reached out and caressed the Alpha's cheek.

"Not tonight, Jimmy," she said. "I'll call you. Promise."

The bear of a man leaned into her touch with half-closed eyes, then lightly kissed the inside of her wrist. He threw Smoke a sly wink, then turned to herd his pack toward the dancefloor again.

"We've more in common than I thought," Smoke said.

"Perhaps. We are on an island, after all." Lucy swiveled on the barstool and set her hand tentatively on his. "I'm starving. How about you?"

He rolled his hand to grip hers. "Ravenous."

They held each other's gaze a moment too long. Lucy's thoughts were unreadable, but the eye contact was evoking emotions in Smoke that he hadn't felt since....

God, he needed a cigarette.

They stopped at a K-pop food truck on Death Avenue for takeout: dumplings, BBQ beef, and kimchi. Then they climbed the stairs up to the High Line—an old elevated train line repurposed into a pedestrian greenway that weaved amongst the high-rise condominiums of Chelsea. They strolled north along its boardwalk toward Hudson Yards, a few stories above the honking flow of street traffic. They sidestepped the old train rails and ambling couples, admiring the plantings of grasses and foliage that somehow made Manhattan feel more intimate than it ever was. The ambient luminosity of the city rose all around them—unashamedly brash, resonant, and loud. Even at this time of night.

They settled on a bench cloistered amongst shrubbery. It offered unobstructed views into the windows and private lives of millionaires whose homes clustered along either side of the parkway. High-salaried executives. Privileged socialites. Panoramic views of greenery taking precedence over privacy. Plate glass walls promising glimpses of *Rear Window-style* intrigue.

Smoke opened the takeout boxes on the bench between them as Lucy pointed her chopsticks toward the fourth level of a nearby condo. A semi-dressed couple kissed and slow danced through their kitchen, oblivious, or not, to their audience.

"I've always thought of the casualness of New Yorkers as comforting," she said. "That with our forced proximity, we recognize we're part of something much larger. That we don't need to hide our true selves, our idiosyncrasies, or differences. Put it out there for everyone to see. Maybe admire. Or just to ignore as an acceptable norm."

Smoke held up the box of dumplings toward her. "I agree." The news of Gabrielle had sunk in more deeply to soothe his nerves, to relax his thoughts. "It's probably the confidence from having made it here. Hell, just being here and surviving with everything that's continually thrown at us." He settled his attention on the couple in the window. The lights of their condo dimmed, but still the undulation of shadows told their story. "There's deservedly great pride in that, something that bolsters the brazen New Yorker attitude in all of us." He lowered his gaze. "And yet I think we all still keep some small part of ourselves hidden. Just for ourselves. Just in case." He glanced at her, uncharacteristically shy, happy she was there with him. By his side. "Do you draw your curtains, Lucy?"

She tilted her head. "No. Should I?"

Smoke noted the mischievous spark in her eyes. He grinned, relieved, then selected a strip of tenderloin and dropped it into his mouth.

"Never," he said, chewing. Then he slid off Aloïs's Ferragamo loafers and stretched his toes.

Chapter Twenty-Two

His mouth tasted sour from the previous evening's food and alcohol, and he regretted not brushing his teeth before dropping into the plush, cozy bed around a quarter past three. He'd been exhausted. Exhausted and elated.

Gabrielle was safe.

For now.

Smoke kept his eyes closed against the early morning glare as he kicked off the sheets and fingered his molars to extract a sliver of beefy Korean BBQ. He was oddly disoriented, not yet awake, unable to recall saying goodbye to Lucy or strolling the several blocks back to The Hotel. A dull pain pulsed in the depths of his skull, mirrored by the tender ache of morning wood rising from his groin. He wondered if he'd ever share a bed with Lucy, though he'd be content even if the friendship remained as it was—fresh, simple, and reassuring. He was dreaming and he knew it. If she ever found out who he was, that he was connected to the case she must surely be working, he may as well just hold out his wrists for her to slap on the cuffs. Still, he could dream. Still, he could hope everything might work out. Still…

He slid his hand down the shaft of his cock to pull back the subtle sheathing of his foreskin. He was hard, sticky, and hypersensitive. More than aware of the elevating beat of his heart. The crawl of flesh and rippling of nerves. The escalating, rhythmic catch of breath at the rear of his throat. And the intensifying tremors throughout his musculature that crested in unison with his easygoing effort. He finally gave in to the convulsive release of tension that had been building since he'd crawled from the secure warmth of Eleonora's bed.

For several moments he did not move, did not breathe, could not sense the beat of his heart in his chest. Then he sucked in a deep breath and held it within him before slowly exhaling, biting down on the side of his lip. The gentle thud of his heart became apparent once more as he relaxed into the familiarity of spent calm, the soothing easiness and warmth of splattered semen dripping down the sides of his abdomen and chest. His cheeks. Sluggishly drifting back toward sleep, through barely parted eyelids he glimpsed the twisted, crumpled bulk beside him on the bed.

Dead eyes staring. Accusing. Less than a breath from his own.

He scuttled sideways in alarm and fell awkwardly from the mattress to the floor. He landed on his butt and heeled himself backward, away from the bed toward the wall, yanking the top sheet with him. Elgan Glyndwr.

"Fuck! Fuck! Fuck!"

Smoke took several deep breaths to compose himself. A myriad of impossible explanations swirled in his head.

"How the fuck?"

Elgan still wore his suit and buffed Diors. And he was still very, very dead. Slumped on his side, with his face partially buried in the pillows, his pale baby blues had turned a milky white, staring at Smoke. Through him. Reproachful and wretched. The sharp jawline and cheekbones highlighted the sunken skin between them, the deepened wrinkles on either side of his mouth, his lips slack and bloodless. Blue.

There was a knock at the door.

The only door to Suite 1737. There were no adjoining suites. No windows that opened. The well appointed floors, walls, and ceiling were solid. Fireproof, soundproof, escape-proof.

There was a second rapid rap-tap-tap. "Room service," said someone who, Smoke surmised, was most likely not room service.

He crept toward the door, dragging the sheet with him, wiping at his chest and face. The distorting fisheye peephole revealed a young man in a starched black uniform and cap, a trolley at his side.

"You can leave it there," Smoke called through the door.

The young man turned to look down the hall.

"Sorry, sir. I'm not allowed to do that. Hotel health and safety codes. I won't be but a moment in the suite." Again, he glanced down the hall. Smoke caught his squint and a slight lift of his chin.

Smoke saw no other option than to let it play out. He pulled the duvet over Elgan's body, gathered the sheet around his own naked bulk, flicked the chain and latch, and pulled open the door. He tensed every muscle in his body, ready to evaluate and swing with whatever came next.

"Good morning, sir," the attendant said, averting his gaze as he pushed the trolley. No one followed him into the suite.

"I didn't realize my, um…" Smoke briefly took in the rumpled bed, "…ah, my husband had ordered breakfast." He rearranged the sheet around himself and went to get Aloïs's wallet, wary of the attendant's every movement as he set up the dining area with a white tablecloth, silverware, and cloche-covered food. The young man leaned an envelope against a petite vase holding a single orange blossom.

"No problem, sir."

Smoke slipped a hundred from the plastic wallet and pressed it into the attendant's hand. "Tell me, when *did* my husband order breakfast?" he asked.

The attendant looked from Smoke to the messy bed, then down to the carpet. "It may have been within the last twenty minutes, sir. The kitchen is undeniably proud of its fast turnaround for our guests. Especially with such a unique order. Thank you, sir. Have a nice day." He rolled the trolley out of the room.

Smoke dropped the sheet as he kicked the door closed. He pulled on Hugh's pants and shirt and grabbed the passports, wallets, his burner, and the twins' slim mini smartphones, sliding them into his jeans pocket. He reached for a hotel toothbrush and shoved that into a pocket as well. The Hudson had irreparably fucked his runners—he accepted that now—and he had blisters from the twin's loafers worn the previous evening. He leaned against the edge of the bed and pulled on Elgan's Diors. They were bespoke to Elgan's measurements, about a Euro size 49. Over twelve inches of hand-cobbled elegance. Almost a perfect fit.

Smoke hesitated, scanning the room, trying to think, knowing he didn't have the time. He needed to get the fuck out of there. But he also needed to know what he was missing. He lifted the two cloches. Both were a creamy Florentine dish of offal—chicken livers, hearts, and testicles, braised and adorned with the crest and wattle of a rooster.

Bile surged at the back of his throat, and then his eyes darted to the envelope resting against the vase. His name was scrawled in bold calligraphy. *Smoke*. He ripped open the envelope to find a full-color postcard from the Met: the Bronzino portrait where he'd first engaged Eleonora. He flipped the card over. There was a single word in the same rich scrawl as the envelope.

Medici.

"Fucking whores," Smoke recalled Mathéo saying before ending his life.

He pocketed the *Cartier* lighter, nudged the open pack of *Gauloises* under the tight fit of his sleeve, and left Suite 1737 to run down the corridor. Away from the bank of elevators. He pushed through the fire escape door with his shoulder but stopped short at the stair rail. The heavy footfalls of a dozen or more men running up the concrete shaft echoed and bounced up the seventeen stories of the stairwell. He leaned back into the hotel corridor, pulled the four passports from his pockets, and flung them as far as he could down the hall. They flew past the door of Suite 1737, toward the main guest elevators and the other fire escape. Stepping back into the stairwell, he carefully closed the door and crept up to the next level. He hoped his pursuers' destination was short of his location. It had to be. He knew it was. He stood in the shadows, motionless, as a SWAT Team mounted the landing and entered the seventeenth. They were kitted out in body armor, helmets, and eyewear, their torsos wrapped in assault webbing packed with ammunition and flash-bangs. He counted twenty submachine guns, carbines, and assault rifles as they rushed across the landing. Flash-bangs resounded from the hotel corridor, followed by the thump and roar and shout of the team as they entered the suite in full force. The smoke and stink of the grenades permeated the air.

Smoke wondered if he should climb down the stairs or up.

Up.

He took several deep breaths to compose himself before he pushed open the door on the nineteenth level and stepped out into the Penthouse Lounge Bar.

It was empty. Too early for a drink.

He was well aware of the clientele and prices of this luxury space once the sun fell below the horizon. He'd once dropped a cool grand on martinis for Gen X and millennial millionaires on the night "She who must not be named" exulted in high heels atop the bar, with a diamond-encrusted brassiere, corsetry, and a band new face. The group he'd eventually gone home with that evening had been similarly dressed. Similarly fabulous.

The bar extended onto an open-air roof deck, a score of hotel guests reclining on chairs and oversized ottomans scattered across the artificial turf. They were taking in the morning sun. Admiring the unobstructed million-dollar views encompassing all of southern Manhattan, the sky and harbor a deep blue above and below the Statue of Liberty.

Smoke pulled the fire alarm.

"Fire on the seventeenth! Fire on the seventeenth!" he shouted.

The panic amongst the guests was immediate, intensifying when the siren split the early morning silence. It was a loud clarifying *whoop whoop whoop*, accompanied by a cyclic, commanding, robotic voice ordering evacuation. Then the roof-mounted pressurization fans kicked in. Their drone swiftly grew into a high-pitched whir as they forced air into the fire escapes. Heavy fire doors slammed shut throughout the penthouse. The frantic mob crowded down the closest escape, Smoke amongst them.

Chapter Twenty-Three

He'd spent an hour pacing the grand halls, corridors, and tunnels of the Port Authority Bus Terminal. Doubling back. Retracing his steps. Ensuring no recurrent or familiar faces before he retrieved the leather satchel containing Elgan's laptop from a locker. Even then, he dawdled on a train platform below Times Square for another hour. Watching it fill and empty with commuters, again and again, noting any stragglers. Satisfied he wasn't being surveilled, he climbed the stairs to the surface of Manhattan and headed east toward the library. It was a place where he felt safe. A place with many people. Many exits. Many cameras.

But then, so had been Chelsea Piers Fitness.

He'd always considered Astor Hall, the main entrance lobby of the New York Public Library, as nothing short of spectacular. But he'd long thought its marbled grandeur to be little more than a prelude. One to whet the appetite for the treasures held within the building and, perhaps above all, within the breathtaking Rose Reading Room on the third floor.

He settled into the farthest corner of the room at one of its large oak tables.

Deep in thought, the unsettling images of Elgan's sagging corpse beside him on the bed pulled at Smoke's attention.

He needed to get it out of his head. He looked toward the sumptuous ceiling that spanned the length of two New York City blocks. Opulent plaster moldings framed a vast mural of fleeting clouds, the scene punctuated by dramatic tiered chandeliers. He allowed himself to fall amongst the clouds, his thoughts gradually relaxing with the ambient noises of literary relief. The ruffling of pages being turned. Wooden chairs scraping across the tiled floor. The soft, mesmerizing intake and exhalation of breath. The subtle hum of students, academics, and reverent tourists scattered throughout the room. The smell of books and knowledge. Finally, his mind cleared, though he could hardly hope the scene in suite 1737 wouldn't forever skim just beneath the surface of his thoughts. He needed to focus.

He pulled the laptop toward him and tapped the Enter key. Again, no password or biometric protection. The lack of security infuriated him.

The laptop flared on, displaying a desktop backdrop of three gold balls in a triangular configuration against a blue background.

"Palle! Palle! Palle!" Smoke muttered and he pulled the *Cartier* lighter from his pocket to confirm its inscription. "Balls! Balls! Balls!" he translated out loud. The symbol on the laptop's background had something to do with the Medici. He figured that much.

He clicked the email icon, but the device had no email account registered.

Next, he selected the document icon. It led to hundreds of sub-folders, Word docs, PDFs, and spreadsheets. Folders within folders within folders. Thousands of artifacts. He glanced up at the clouds, took in a deep breath, and clicked on the first file.

The sunlight beaming through the arched windows above slid slowly across the floor and tables. The rays climbed the opposite wall, until they shone right through the space, from window to opposite window, highlighting the chandeliers and muraled clouds to an impossible brilliance. He'd spent the better part of the day, into the very late afternoon, trolling through the laptop contents. The spreadsheets documented extreme wealth. Astronomical numbers in multiple currencies. Many of the Word docs profiled companies and forecast financials. One folder held copies of title deeds for buildings and land scattered across Manhattan. Across the Americas. Across Europe and Asia. Thousands of deeds. Dating back through the centuries. The two dozen he eyeballed were all stamped with variations of crests, shields, and logos, all with one thing in common: three dots, circles, or balls. One crest interpreted them as oranges, another as gold rings, and another as planets.

Smoke pulled at his lip in frustration. He didn't understand what he was looking at, or for, and it felt like he was getting nowhere. It seemed like stuff a hedge fund manager would keep on their laptop. He clicked into the computer's C drive and drilled past the usual folders of software and application data. There wasn't anything out of place. It all appeared pretty basic, at least to his rudimentary computer knowledge.

The abrupt screech of a chair at the far end of the room pulled his attention. He tensed, his back straightening, as a young woman strolled the length of the reading room, her gaze drifting from side to side but always hesitating when cast in his direction. She was fit. Athletic. An ease of movement. She wore nonrestrictive khakis and a jacket that could easily hide a Glock or knife. Several tables away, she casually reached behind her neck, and Smoke's muscles tightened, ready to spring from the hard wooden seat. He rose to his full commanding height, breathing deep and slow, filling his lungs and bloodstream with oxygen. His limbs were simmering with a spike of adrenaline, his focus sharpening, the pulse of blood through his veins grounding him, providing a beat to accompany any required movement.

But then she was close enough for him to read her face, and he relaxed. The hand at her neck flipped a long mane of hair across her shoulder. She smiled at him as she passed. When she stopped and turned, Smoke felt comfortable with her outside his immediate field of vision, no need to confront her as she took out her phone and snapped a picture of the room. Of the light streaming in through the windows. Of the motes of dust lifting from generations of knowledge. Of people seeking answers. He was just one of them.

He settled back into his chair and knuckled the Pictures icon on the touchscreen. The folder contained a single jpeg—a group photo of seventy or more people across multiple generations. Some shared obvious familial characteristics, but many didn't. All were gathered around a banquet table on a grand terracotta tiled terrace overlooking the ocean. The menacing slopes of Mount Vesuvius rose on the distant horizon, confirming the broad curve of coastline behind them was the Bay of Naples. Smoke pulled out his burner and snapped a picture of the photo.

There, standing near the right side of the group in the photo, was Eleonora di Toledo. He squinted and leaned closer to the screen. Yes, it was her. She was resting her hands on the shoulders of the two people sitting in front of her.

Daan and Angi Stuyvesant.

Smoke stroked the stubble on his jawline as he studied the three of them and their placement within the larger group.

He doubted Daan could be Eleonora's son. His complexion and features seemed unrelated, and the family name was clearly different. He thought back to his time with the young couple. The softness of their lips and touch. The pleasure of tongue against flesh. Of flesh between tongue and palate. Of flesh within flesh. The tender moment when…

He shook his head, realizing Angi could be Eleonora's daughter. Or niece. Surely, she was one or the other.

But Eleonora had proffered no awareness of their deaths. Their *murders*. He tried to recall her face as they studied the Bronzino at the Met. As they had talked. There was some emotion there he'd incorrectly read.

The crack in her voice, the glisten in her eyes, the slight tremor in her hand, curling toward a fist at the edge of his vision.

He felt the blood drain from his face, then he suddenly flushed with guilt.

"What the hell am I doing?" he muttered. "What have I been doing?"

He clicked on the web browser to search for Angi di Toledo, wondering if that could be her maiden name. The browser kicked him into the NYPL intranet to input his library card number and password.

The instant he made the connection beyond the library's firewall, Elgan's laptop emanated a high-pitched pop and died.

* * *

It was after 8 pm. The vestibule of the Plaza Residences felt unexpectedly daunting in its opulence, but also in light of what he knew—and didn't know about Eleonora. Smoke held his back a little too straight as he gripped a bottle of merlot by the neck. He attempted to rake his curls into place, but they were wild and greasy against his scalp. He was looking more than a little disheveled when he checked his reflection in the hotel's main lobby doors. His clothing was a little too stretched, a little too rumpled, a little too stained. And the shoes, as magnificent as they were, needed more than a fifty-buck shine. He'd severely scuffed them during his dramatic departure from The Hotel.

Uncomfortable, he nudged the end of his toothbrush further down into the depths of his jeans pocket.

He'd attracted the attention of security—an unassuming but solidly built guy who took position at the 59th Street door. He was nonthreatening but intent on Smoke's every movement.

"Sir?" The concierge beckoned for Smoke to approach as he hung up a call. "Ms. di Toledo is not currently taking visitors. Madam assured me you would understand."

The security guy stood a little taller and tilted his head.

Smoke wiped at his mouth and nodded.

He set the bottle of merlot on the concierge desk. "Could you please have this delivered to Ms. di Toledo with a message?" he asked.

"Of course, sir." The concierge slid an embossed envelope, a piece of letterhead, and a Montblanc across the desk, then took possession of the bottle of wine. He checked the label and raised an eyebrow. Neither vintner nor vintage seemed to impress.

Smoke scratched out a note and sealed the envelope, clenching his fists when he glimpsed his fingernails, still dirty and ragged from his dip in the Hudson. The security guy held open the door for him to leave. "Thanks," Smoke said through gritted teeth.

Outside, the last of the day's Manhattanhenge was blinding along 59th Street. The sun rapidly dropped toward the horizon, perfectly aligned with the city grid. Smoke stood with his back to it, then hunkered down on the curb beside the rusted tailpipe of a Buick Enclave. He lit a *Gauloises* and took a puff, but stubbed it out to chew on the bristles of his toothbrush instead.

He flicked through the burner phone, its battery hovering near eighty percent, and scrolled to the photo he'd copied from Elgan's laptop before dumping the dead machine back into a locker at the Port Authority Bus Terminal. He stretched the image with his fingertips, focusing on each face in the group, one at a time.

The photo was at least a year old, maybe two, with Giulia Rossi still alive beside her husband, Jameson De Vries. They were a handsome couple holding hands. Happy. In love. He passed the visage of Rafaella without hesitation, searching for Liz and Elgan. But finding neither appeared in the photograph. Only one twin was present and he didn't know whether it was Aloïs or Mathéo. Aloysius or Matteo. He scanned every face several times, zooming in and out, concentrating on those he'd killed. Wondering why they'd been killed. Wondering why he'd killed them.

What was it Rafaella had said about the twins?

He pressured a knuckle against the dent of his temple. They'd been making amends, she'd said. For exposing something. Exposing what?

He opened a maps app and zoomed out from his location in the Manhattan gutter. He brushed across the Atlantic and panned to the Italic Peninsula jutting into the Mediterranean. Making his way down the Italian coastline to the Bay of Naples, he thumbed a course along its dramatic southern cliffs. He kept referring back to the group photo, with elements of the terrace and structures at its edge. The tropical foliage. The grand vista of the bay and Mount Vesuvius in the distance. On the screen, he honed in on Sorrento and the Grand Hotel, recognizing the colors and tessellated tiles of the terrace. The clifftop balustrade.

He tapped on the hotel hyperlink, then the call icon.

"*Ciao. Buongiorno, Grand Hotel*, Sorrento."

"*Ciao. Buongiorno*. Apologies for contacting you so early in your morning. *Mi chiamo* Daan Stuyvesant, calling from New York City in the United States. I stayed at your hotel a year ago or so and was wondering if the same room would be available this October."

"*Un momento, Signore* Stuyvesant."

Smoke picked at the filthy bandage compressing his finger as he waited, running a fingernail under the others in a less than successful attempt to clean the grit from underneath. He lifted his hand to his nose. The grimy dressing smelled of horseradish and mayo from the deli sub he'd consumed for lunch, muddled with his own accumulating stench.

"*Si, Signore* Stuyvesant. The same suite with a bay view terrace accommodating yourself and *Signora* Stuyvesant last July will be available throughout October."

"*Grazie*. I'll call back to confirm dates." He ended the call and returned his attention to the photo. In particular, to Giulia Rossi who, days after this picture, would fall over 200 feet from the George Washington Bridge into the Hudson.

If he could work out why the targets needed termination, and who benefitted, perhaps he could determine who wanted *him* dead.

Who he worked for.

And more importantly, whether he was one of the good guys.

Or the bad.

Chapter Twenty-Four

He climbed the stairs to the fifth-floor walk-up in Hell's Kitchen. The building stoop was neat but deserted, the main door ajar without a doorman or any apparent security. The shag on the stair inside was worn, as he recalled, loose threads of fuchsia pile frayed at the edge of each step. Wallpaper, patterned with a spiral design from the seventies, was peeling from the wall. Both paper and carpet were damp, bolstering the underlying odor of mildew and rats' nests assaulting his nostrils. At the top landing, he pressed his ear to the door of the studio where he'd attended the soirée with Eleonora. There was no noise from within other than the slow, steady drip of a leaking faucet.

He knocked on the door and waited. He tried the doorknob. It was locked. For several moments he remained still, closing his eyes to listen to the building. Suddenly, his ears pricked. In the street outside, amongst the ever present hum of traffic, was the approach of sirens. Fire engines. He leaned over the landing rail to peer down to the lower levels and confirm the common areas were empty. Then he waited for the FDNY Engine's approach. Predictably, the wail of sirens compounded into a reverberating onslaught of stutter tone air horns, conveniently muffling the noise of him throwing his weight against the door. The latch splintered through the jamb and the entry flew open. He stepped quickly inside and slammed the door shut behind him. With his back against it, he waited for his sight to adjust to the low light, hesitant to enter the space until he was certain it was empty. It seemed it was. He reached out and blindly ran his hand across the wall and flicked on the light switch. The space was as small as he recollected. Maybe 300 square feet. It wasn't soundproofed against the incessant cacophony of the city. In particular, the wail of the fire engines pushing through the intersection half a block away. An open rear window provided the dull vista of a skewed soot-blackened wall. The dirty brickwork echoed the metal-on-metal of a nearby restaurant kitchen somewhere at the bottom of the alley. Likely the Thai place on the backside of the block, beckoning with aromatics of fish sauce, galangal, and bruised coriander. The aroma was far superior to the stench of the building's interior stairwell.

Smoke's first thought was Rafaella did not, could not, live here. It was simply a pied-à-terre for the subversive elements of an otherwise unknown life. He'd noted her couture during the soirée, and again at the event on Little Island. No one with that tailoring would take residence here. He considered the studio as a subterfuge. He checked the closet and kitchen cabinets to confirm his theory. All were empty. The refrigerator held remnants of a good time. A few bottles of rosé. A chunk of brie. The open shelving held glassware and a sampling of crockery, but that was all. He crossed the room in three easy steps to check the bedside tables. Lube, an open box of condoms, another of cigarette papers, and a mason jar of marijuana buds. He thumbed back the latch and sniffed the weed. It was high end. Californian. Granddaddy Purple Kush.

He nudged a couple of papers and buds into the half empty *Gauloises* packet at his sleeve, then checked the bathroom. It had no door. He stared point blank at his face in the mirrored cabinet above the toilet and, despite himself, chuckled. He looked like shit.

He opened the cabinet, hoping to find other drugs, something for his finger and every other bruise that ached the length of his body. Two pills remained in an unmarked bottle. They looked like they might be painkillers. He swallowed them dry with a mouthful of spit as he thumbed open a folded piece of paper from the top shelf. It was a utility bill, but with an address for Rafaella di Toledo further up the neighborhood on 50th Street between 9th and 10th. A luxury residential tower Smoke had often admired from a sidewalk table outside his favorite Hell's Kitchen gay bar.

* * *

The eighteen-story residential tower imbued pre-war elegance, dramatically gut-renovated into the twenty-first century. Quintessential art déco capped by a dramatic bronze crown, it far surpassed all other buildings in Hell's Kitchen for indulgent excess, with an entrance door revolving into an expansive, decadent lobby.

The doorman immediately caught Smoke's attention.

"Good evening, sir. May I assist you?"

"Yes, I'm expected at the di Toledo residence."

The doorman held a finger to his ear, listening to an earpiece. "Ah, could you be more specific, sir?"

"Rafaella," Smoke said, the name grating in his mouth.

The doorman smiled, quickly scanning Smoke from head to toe. Again, he pressed a finger to his ear. "Of course, sir. I've confirmed your invitation. Many of Ms. di Toledo's guests have already arrived. Please come with me." They bypassed the main bank of residential elevators, and the doorman held an electronic fob to a brass door emblazoned with an art déco starburst. He held out his open hand for Smoke to enter a private foyer.

"The elevator shall arrive momentarily, sir. Enjoy your evening."

Smoke stood alone in a polished ebony vestibule, surrounded by the honeyed perfume of three dozen black tulips in a Royal Copenhagen vase that would not have been out of place in a museum. The far wall was thick plate glass showcasing a Mercedes-Maybach angled beside a Bugatti La Voiture Noire, both pristine in their black marble vault. There were no buttons in the elevator cab. It simply arrived and lifted him to the penthouse level much faster than expected. The doors slid open to a double-height foyer topped by a brass deco skylight. Above the chevroned glass panels were the sunset colors of the evening sky, offset by the tower's brilliant brass crown. The impact of the structure was immediate. He felt privileged. Powerful. Despite his awareness that he was willingly stepping back into dangerous territory. He had everything to gain. Everything to lose. But he didn't see that he had any other choice.

The elevator door closed behind him, and again he was confronted by his broken reflection in the starburst of brass. Sweat stains had bloomed from his pits with the jog uptown through the evening crowds of Hell's Kitchen. He ran his fingers through his hair, but it did nothing to enhance the image.

The décor from the foyer to the condominium was seamless through wide open double doors. Floor, walls, and ceilings were immutable tones of white on white on white, enriched by varying textures of massive travertine tiles, silk-covered walls, and hand-polished plaster ceilings. The furnishings were modern. Minimalist. Comfortable. White. There were no visible luminaires. No crass chandeliers. No pendants or spotlights. But there was a glow. Exactly where it needed to be. Music sublimated the ambiance, unrecognizable but familiar as it transitioned between elements of the Baroque, Classic, and Romantic. Apart from the guests scattered throughout the room, two immense, frameless canvases provided the only relief of color. One was primarily viridian. The other Tuscan red. Both with great swathes of thick oil paint swept across them. The undulant ribbons of vivid color all but obscured what appeared to be Renaissance-styled paintings beneath. Purposely over-painted, hidden, obstructed from view by something new, indescribable but vital. Between these two canvases was a third, just as massive, but almost oblivious between its two garish bookends. White oil paint, the same tones as the room, allowed only thin slivers of a masked Renaissance scene to rake through. Smoke squinted to decipher the fragments.

Rafaella approached him across the travertine.

"It's good to see you with most of the *pretty* rubbed off. You might be worth fucking after all," she said. She gripped Smoke by the elbow and led him away from the reception room. He followed her without comment. Up the stairs to the mezzanine level, through a bedroom suite, and into a dressing chamber with views over the rooftops of Hell's Kitchen.

"Sit there," she said, pushing him backward.

He sat on the edge of the counter as directed, wondering how this was going to play out. He didn't have a plan, purely a gut feeling this was where he needed to be. The only thing he knew for certain was that he wasn't going to fuck this hideous creature.

"I appreciate a guy who looks and smells like a real man. More than rough around the edges." She smirked. "But you might've taken it a few steps too far."

"Afraid I'll offend your friends downstairs?"

"Nonsense." She held an ampule of eye drops above his face. "Look up," she said. "They are bored and as boring as all get out. But you… you're interesting. I see that now. And they'll see it too." She squeezed drops into each of his eyes. "Does that feel better?"

He blinked several times, nodded, and glanced into a magnifying mirror beside him. The shots of blood webbing across his eyeballs slowly vanished. Rafaella wet her hands in the vanity sink and ran her fingers through his hair, untangling and gathering back the curls.

"Do you mind if I handle this?" she asked, motioning randomly around his head.

"You mean my face?" he said.

She didn't wait for a response as she opened several drawers, looking for something. "We have similar complexions, and since everyone already thinks we're up here fucking, I'd like you to look slightly more composed before we go back down."

"So, you're telling me you've ruined my reputation before I've even met my new acquaintances?"

"Shut up and light me a cigarette." She lifted a blending brush to his cheeks while he tapped out two cigarettes from the *Gauloises* pack, placed both between his lips, and lit them. He held one out toward her.

"A proper gentleman would place it in my mouth," she said.

He placed it in her mouth, the turn of her lips not as repugnant as he recalled.

"Moretti did a real number on you, but the bruising and the broken capillaries across your cheeks should dissipate." The *Gauloises* hung precariously from her lip as she spoke.

"I'm assuming you haven't yet seen what Simone looks like."

She raised an eyebrow but continued to blend over the bridge of his nose and curve of cheeks before pulling back to survey her work. "He'll be here later this evening, so I guess I'll compare the two of you then." She licked the pad of her thumb and wiped it across the stubble beneath the line of his cheekbone, then leaned into him, his thighs on either side of her hips.

"You don't like me, do you?" she said, the corners of her mouth lifting.

"What gives you that idea?" he countered.

She narrowed her eyes, taking a deep drag off her cigarette and blowing the smoke out of the side of her mouth. He did the same but allowed the smoke to drift lazily from his nostrils and open mouth as he contemplated her stance between his legs. He wasn't going to fuck her.

She appeared thoughtful as she finished the cigarette and stubbed it out in the sink.

"Let's push this evening into their Eleven Madison Park brunch conversations for the next week or three." She removed the dangling cigarette from his mouth, took a final quick puff of it, and threw the butt into the sink with her own. "You taste nice," she said quietly, as if she hadn't meant to say it out loud.

The lipstick she selected was a velvet black-red. The same as the darkest slivers of Renaissance cutting through the dominant colors of the massive paintings downstairs. The same as the gloss of her mouth. She held her face close to his as she applied it to his lips, taking care at the defined edge of the cupid's bow.

"Were you born with a cleft lip?" she asked.

"No. A foster parent didn't like my face as much as you seem to."

It was then he noticed her right cheek, slightly more pronounced than the other, a shadow of a bruise not quite covered by concealer. He gently touched the back of his fingers to it, his action more tender than he would have thought possible under any circumstance.

She abruptly pulled back. "What are you doing?"

"I'm sorry," he said. "Who did that to you?"

"Who do you think?" she spat, her lips twisted into the hideous curve he'd first noted at the soirée when she'd confronted Eleonora.

He nodded his understanding, not requiring clarification that Eleonora was not all sweetness and light.

"Well, I'm glad you're more than just a pretty face."

"I apologize," he said. "I shouldn't be here. Especially dressed like this amongst your guests."

Rafaella slid her open hands along his thighs on either side of her. Then she gripped him by the hips and pulled herself hard against him. "I suspect this is exactly where you need to be. Just take care when you find what you're looking for."

She wiped the back of her hand over his mouth, smearing the lipstick across his lips and into the stubble.

"There. Perfect," she said.

Chapter Twenty-Five

There were two dozen guests, a handful recognizable from the Sorrento photo, and he realized he'd need to commit them all to memory. All were well groomed and dressed. Place any single one of them on the streets of Uptown Manhattan and they'd pass barely noticed. But not here. Not gathered in the same room. The appreciation of unbranded stealth wealth couture was both unavoidable and consequential. The ragged Bohemian jacket paired with uniquely tailored ripped jeans and hand-cobbled brogues. A slim single-breasted vicuña wool blazer and chamois slacks. Suits and skirts hand-cut and hand-stitched to precise and exquisite contours. Silk, cashmere, leather, and linen. Zero synthetic fabrics. It was everyday wear created and constructed by top—nameless—fashion houses for each particular person in the room. Never to grace another figure, or appear on runways or in catalogs. Smoke doubted that any one of the guests was wearing less than $10,000 of bespoke couture. An understatement as he reconsidered the footwear.

Beyond them, a massive marble dining table was set for a sit-down dinner.

He introduced himself as Tommy, reticent to divulge more, unaware of what the guests may or may not already know. Rafaella left him in the company of Augusto and Felice, a familiar-looking couple from Dumbo, though she didn't stray far, her gaze always tending in his direction.

"Please, call me Gus. Only Rafaella dares call me Augusto, something she's done since she was an insufferable five-year-old." He held out his hand, the nails trimmed and buffed to a shine, his skin soft as Smoke took it and pumped it twice.

Smoke motioned toward himself. "Apologies for my state. It's been a rough couple of days and I didn't expect Rafaella to have guests this evening."

"Oh, I'm sure." Gus glanced at Felice before returning his attention to Smoke. "I think we've met before. Maybe at a club down near Christopher Street, or here in Hell's Kitchen?"

"The Eagle?" Felice asked.

"That's certainly possible," Smoke said. "But we also chatted for several minutes at the Boathouse wedding reception last week. You were both a bottle or two of champagne ahead of me."

"Of course," Felice said. "You wore that tuxedo well."

"You wear *this* well," Gus added, reaching out to tap Smoke's shoulder.

Others joined them, with Smoke committing the mostly Italian sounding names to memory with each introduction.

It wasn't long before the name Jameson De Vries surfaced in the conversation. Not Italian. Smoke assumed Frisian. Dutch.

"I don't understand why they've done an about-face and designated it a murder," he heard someone say. "Jameson has been so despondent since Aunt Giulia died. And from the vague descriptions of the crime scene, it seems he chose his own demise—whether intentional or by accident."

A server offered a platter of fried arancini balls to the group amid the conversation. *Palle! Palle! Palle!* Smoke thought, selecting one and biting into it, content to listen to the conversation without disrupting its flow.

"Perhaps because it happened so soon after the Stuyvesants. Handsome Daan always was a cheeky bastard and definitely hot-headed, but I didn't see that one coming."

"Have the authorities provided any details on why they've kept that investigation open? And how it's linked to Jameson's death?"

"Apparently they identified the DNA of a single, unknown male at both scenes."

"What kind of DNA?"

Gus shrugged. "Angi and Daan were open, both with their relationship and the types they appreciated sharing it with." He took in Smoke's bulk beside him. "Perhaps it could've been a threesome gone wrong, but from what I've read, there were no defensive wounds. No sign of a struggle. From either Daan or Angi."

"Same with Jameson. He was going under pretty quick at the Boathouse bar earlier that evening. Perhaps the wedding was too much for him."

"But again, there's the DNA linking both scenes. Sure, Jameson was related to Angi and Daan by marriage. But he barely, if ever, ran in the same circles. I don't recall ever seeing them in conversation."

Smoke recalled the hours spent with Jameson at The Townhouse, then lounging on his sofa, then sprawled across the rug of the Tudor City penthouse. A gentleman in every way. The taste of whiskey and cigars on his lips. Their tender moments. Talking through the night, mostly about Giulia. A man desperate for company. Not unlike Elgan who seemed, in their short time together, to crave nothing more than the gentle touch of another human being.

"And who were the others supposedly killed by the same culprit?" Gus asked.

"Some Welsh guy, and a young woman from downtown."

Smoke washed down the arancini with a sip of water. "Elgan Glyndwr and Liz Bayer. Didn't you know them?" he said.

Gus shrugged, his face as blank as the others.

Over Gus's shoulder, Smoke saw Moretti standing on the far side of the room near the terrace doors. His attention was tight on Smoke, shaking his head and mouthing the word "No."

"At least that's what I heard on the news," Smoke said.

"They added two more to the body count this morning. Some fracas at Chelsea Piers, but they haven't released the names. Man, if the NYPD is right that this is all on one guy, he sure has been busy. It all seems pretty random to me."

Moretti motioned for Smoke to join him out on the terrace.

Smoke excused himself.

"*Che cazzo!*" Moretti said. "Are you trying to get yourself killed?" His voice was barely a whisper, the movement of his jaw almost undetectable. A swollen, garish purple bruise extended from his right temple down his face and beneath his collar. The underside of his jawline was puffy and black.

"Afraid I'll put you out of a job?" Smoke said.

Moretti sighed, then winced in pain. He closed his eyes, his features motionless as he slowly breathed through pursed lips.

"Tommaso. I wasn't assigned to kill you. I was assigned to protect you and Gabrielle. Unfortunately, the intel sourced by my handler was confusing and missing reliable facts. I had to board a flight to New York without any briefing of what I was heading into. By the time I landed at JFK, Gabrielle had already taken a bullet and you were nowhere to be found."

Smoke contemplated Moretti's words. And his face.

"Then why the charade in front of Rafaella?"

"The less aware she is, the better."

Smoke nodded, without fully grasping Moretti's meaning.

A server approached with a tray of wine glasses.

"Do you have anything harder?" Smoke asked.

"Yes sir, full bar."

"Good. Two Grey Goose martinis. Straight up. Twist."

Smoke flipped the cigarette pack from his sleeve and tapped out the weed and papers. Several *Gauloises* were left, but still he scrunched up the packet and threw it onto a nearby table. He licked a paper and rolled a joint.

"This will help," he said when the server returned with the martinis. Moretti sipped his, relief on his face as he carefully swallowed the chilled liquor. Moreso when Smoke lit and handed him the joint.

"I guess I should apologize about the jaw."

Moretti waved his hand. "You could have left me to drown in the river, but I'm told you dragged me ashore. I'll just be grateful for that."

They leaned against the travertine balustrade, passing the joint back and forth in silence, a breeze drifting off the Hudson. Both sides of the great river were littered with light, but it was the vast wattage of Times Square and Midtown that dominated their panorama.

"Who said I pulled you from the river?" Smoke sucked in a lungful of the pungency, then handed the joint back to Moretti, his head buzzing and the ache beginning to leave his body.

"You ask the wrong questions, Tommaso."

"What are the right ones?"

"The ones that'll help us to work out what the hell is going on without getting us both killed." Simone suppressed a chuckle before gently pressing his hand to his jaw. "I'll need your contact number and the address where you're staying while your condo is being surveilled."

"Unfortunately, I'm homeless," Smoke said. "Plenty of funds, but no ID to secure a hotel room. I was planning on spending the night in Bryant Park." He turned his back on the view and immediately locked on Rafaella at the far end of the living room. "Yeah, I think it safer to sleep in the park." It surprised him when he realized he was smiling, but he quickly attributed it to the weed. Rafaella smiled back, the fullness of her lips reminding him of Eleonora. And Angi.

"*Senza senso!*" Moretti said. "I'll book an adjoining suite at my hotel until we work out something better to suit."

Chapter Twenty-Six

He was finally clean, his blonde curls wet from the vitamin-enhanced shower at the New York Palace Hotel. Sitting on the edge of the bed in a pair of loose slacks, he rearranged a backpack containing several sets of new clothes and shoes. He balanced a Bloomingdale's gift box on his lap as he wrote a note for Hugh. He hoped the meager explanation would suffice until their promised brunch at Elmo's.

Moretti entered from the adjoining room without knocking. "Do you still have the boys' cell phones?" he asked.

Smoke leaned over the side of the bed and reached into the pocket of Hugh's crumpled jeans. He'd keep them. They were a good fit. "I don't have the charge cords, so they might be low on battery. I've only accessed one a few times, for a couple of minutes at the most."

Moretti sat beside him on the bed. He powered one on, switched it to airplane mode, and joined the hotel's Wi-Fi network. Smoke followed suit with the second phone.

"What are we looking for?"

"We'll know when we find it, *mio amico*."

Smoke clicked on the Instagram app and started surfing the pictures. "What's the deal with their multiple passports—in differing Italian and French names?"

"The boys are… were… *Toscani*, with their original home in *Firenze*. Upon emancipation and with the release of their trust funds, they established a base in Paris to distance themselves from the family. They wanted a fresh start, but without losing access to their hereditary wealth."

"So, homes in Paris and Florence."

"Undoubtedly, two of many in their portfolio."

Smoke pulled on a fresh shirt from the backpack, buttoning it up to mid-chest before slipping on a lightweight black bomber jacket. "Did you meet them?"

"I crossed paths with them only once. A masquerade ball at Villa La Rotonda near Vicenza, for last year's Venice Biennale. They seemed good natured enough, of course with a confidence bolstered by their financial circumstance."

"What were you doing there?"

Moretti narrowed his eyes. "What were *you* doing on the George Washington Bridge on July seventeenth last year?"

Smoke side-eyed him, then returned his attention to the phone.

He was a few years deep in the Instagram timeline. The photos abruptly switched from Mediterranean old-world chic to the dichotomy of Manhattan's chrome-plated grunge. One picture caught his attention, and he stopped scrolling. The twins were sitting on a sofa, their arms around a young woman between them. A window silhouetted them, showcasing a glimpsing view of the Brooklyn Bridge. He turned the screen toward Moretti.

"Who's that?" Moretti asked.

"Liz Bayer."

"One of your recent kills."

"Yes, one the NYPD has somehow linked back to me."

* * *

Wall Street.

Smoke and Moretti walked into a residential building in Lower Manhattan. Mass-produced modern Baroque pieces squatted throughout the common areas. High-density, high-gloss black plastic furniture emulating a false regal charm. Crystals dangled from plastic candelabras—decorative light fittings pervasive in both high-end galleries and low-end hardware stores with a price point to match. The difference in quality and value was obvious even to an untrained eye. This was a failed attempt at the trendy Dark Academia décor.

Liz's apartment was on the twentieth floor.

"This is a pretty pedestrian rental building," Moretti said. "Members of the Family might own it, but they certainly wouldn't rent or live here. You don't remain rich by throwing dead money into another landlord's bank account."

Smoke stopped, tentatively peering around the hallway corner toward apartment 20C. There was no police presence, but yellow crime scene tape crisscrossed the entrance to Liz's home. He leaned against the door, then shifted his weight to throw his bulk against it.

Moretti slapped his hand against Smoke's chest to stop him, reached into his pocket, and handed him a lock pick. "Tommaso, *per favore…*"

Smoke twisted the pick in the keyhole and clicked open the door. Morning sunlight drenched the apartment, a sliver of a Brooklyn Bridge view, all dramatic swooping cables and Gothic arches. Triple-glazed windows kept the sounds of the city at bay.

They stopped at the threshold.

Someone had slashed and overturned the sofa. Had ripped the kitchen cabinet doors from their frames and strewn their contents across the room. They'd pulled the refrigerator and oven from the wall and tipped them onto their sides. Holes had been sledgehammered into the plaster ceiling and walls. Through a shattered sliding glass wall, they could see the bedroom was also in disarray.

"The police wouldn't do this," Smoke said.

"No, they wouldn't. But I know who would," Moretti said. "If there was anything here to find, it is already gone."

Smoke wasn't so certain. He scanned the debris scattered throughout the apartment, recalling remnants of his moments with Liz.

"*I wondered if it was you,*" she'd said. "*There was something about your manner. A sureness. More confidence than anyone Julianne and I had selected before. Not excitable like an out-of-towner. Not anxious, like a businessman who'd missed their train home to their family in Westchester or Greenwich. Nor cocky or slimy, like, you know, a lot of guys are. Just a gentle easiness. A confident tenderness.*" She'd slid a pod of dark roast into the coffeemaker and turned on the sink faucet. "*They warned me when I first accepted the portfolios, but I thought nothing of it. I thought it was just a conspiracy theory beyond the usual nondisclosure agreement to ensure I'd never dare break their trust. A joke, really, to keep me on my toes. But then I saw the incomprehensible values of their trust funds—both commercial and individual. And ever since, I've been second guessing their initial warning, and everyone who comes into my life.*" She'd fallen silent.

"*What makes you think it's me, now?*" he'd said.

She'd pressed her lips into a tight smile. "*Thank you for a lovely evening.*" She'd reached for a coffee cup, hesitating as her reach passed a New York Yankees baseball cap hanging by the cup shelf. She'd glanced over her shoulder at him. "*There's nothing I can do, is there?*"

"*No,*" he'd said.

Smoke quickly perused the room for the Yankees cap and found it discarded on the floor beside the oven. He stepped tentatively over the broken crockery and glassware to retrieve it. The brim and seams were intact, with nothing unusual or bulky beneath the material. But the squatchee atop the cap was the wrong shade of blue. He dug his nails beneath the button and pulled, and the small circular flash drive popped into his palm.

He held it up. "Is this why I killed her?" he asked.

"You tell me, Tommaso," Moretti said, his brow creasing.

The two men held each other's gaze.

"I was doing my job. A job I thought was imperative. A job I trusted was valid and, I expect, still is."

"Good," Moretti said. He nodded and took the flash drive from him. "And something on this USB might explain the House's reason for your assignment. And why you are now a target."

Chapter Twenty-Seven

The death-stained carpet stretched across the high-gloss floorboards of Jameson's Tudor City penthouse. Where Jameson had satiated himself and exhaled his last breath, forensics had cut sections from the expensive weave that were no doubt now secure in a crime scene evidence locker somewhere downtown.

It was late morning, the sun still slightly below the meridian, refracting through the multi-storied Gothic windows facing the East River and Long Island.

Moretti unlatched and knuckled open the terrace door to diminish the rotten stink hovering in the room. "How much of this condo have you seen?" he asked.

"Only the entry foyer and this reception room. Plus, the east-side terrace."

Moretti glanced up at the ornate ceiling and around them at the furnishings and paintings. "*This* is how you know you're in one of their homes. Despite how well we're paid, you and I do not live like they do, Tommaso. Any one of these artworks,"—he motioned toward the walls—"would outpace a decade of our salaries combined."

"And by 'they' you mean the Medici line of descendants."

"Some indirect lines, but yes, following a gerrymandered course of familial blood and money. And their immediate matrimonial contracts." Moretti pulled the flash drive from his pocket. "De Vries should have one of their customized laptops. The authorities might not have seized it, if it was in a different room from the crime scene."

To one side of the great fireplace, a corridor led to a wing of bedrooms; to the opposite side, another led to a media room and then a den. The den was in keeping with the richness of the rest of the condominium. Hundreds of leather-bounds leaned against one another upon floor-to-ceiling shelves, well loved and read. At eye-level Smoke could see first editions from the nineteenth century interspersed with modern variations. An original trilogy of *Frankenstein* without author attribution. A first edition of Polidori's *Vampyre* incorrectly accredited to Lord Byron. Alongside these stood twenty-first-century companions, expanding on the time-honored themes. Several signed baseballs and a team-autographed Louisville Slugger took pride of place on a shelf at waist height. Signatures that were several decades old and which Smoke couldn't decipher.

A laptop slanted amongst the paraphernalia of a paper-littered desk. Smoke recognized it as the same unbranded design as Elgan's. As the twins'. Setting it on the chrome-trimmed walnut desk, he dropped into the wingback and flipped open the display.

Moretti stood at his side. "They designed the first line of security protocol so only those with familial DNA can—"

The desktop flared on, three bright gold balls in a triangular configuration against a blue background.

"*Palle, palle, palle,*" Moretti whispered. He turned from the screen to scrutinize Smoke instead.

Smoke blinked, turning over his hands to peer at his fingertips, his gaze sliding next to the sensor pads on the keyboard. "Simone?" he asked.

"Now that's… unexpected." Moretti looked thoughtful. Then he handed Smoke the flash drive. "First things first. Let's see what we've got."

Smoke drilled down into the drive, copious folders of Word docs, PowerPoints, PDFs, and spreadsheets, clicking a sampling of each open as he surfed deeper and deeper. "Seems to be the same data as on Elgan's laptop," he said after several minutes of searching.

"You have Elgan's device?"

Smoke nodded. "It fried when I connected it to the internet. The carcass is in a locker at the PABT."

"Understood. What are these?" Moretti pointed to the bottom of the screen.

Smoke clicked on the first of a half-dozen .msg files. It was an email thread between Liz and Elgan. He and Moretti read message after message in silence.

"They realized how valuable this data is, beyond the obvious wealth it details," Moretti said.

"To themselves, or to others?" Smoke asked.

Moretti's eyes widened. "To both. Any knowledge of it could impact…." Moretti stopped himself short.

Smoke leaned back into the chair. "But why? Surely Liz and Elgan would have been making six- or seven-figure salaries to survive here in New York. How much money does someone need?"

"If I recall correctly from one of those spreadsheets, Elgan was making about $96 million a year. I expect Liz Bayer would have been high sevens at a minimum. But for some, even that is not enough when they're aware of other's true worth." Moretti tapped his thumb against his lips. "Also, wealth might not be the only consequence of distributing this information."

"What do you mean?" Smoke asked.

"Open that last spreadsheet again, the one dated last year."

He clicked it open. It was a list of a few thousand names. Both personal and corporate entities beside a column of values. All in euros.

"Search for a name you know."

Matteo Laurentius.

Beside Matteo's name was the value of his accumulating trust fund. Smoke's mind boggled as he ran his finger across the touchscreen, counting the number of commas. "That can't possibly be true," he said.

"I have no doubt it is," Moretti said. "That stupid kid, now lying naked and dead in a morgue fridge somewhere, held personal wealth greater than some countries. All debt free."

Smoke searched for Aloysius, Rafaella, Eleonora. Augusto. The values were ridiculous. Obscene. Amounts he couldn't comprehend, let alone calculate. "These people make the 'richest man in the world' look like a pauper. They could wipe out a country's national debt with the click of a mouse."

"And yet they appear on no published lists," Moretti said.

Smoke flicked through the spreadsheet, incredulous, allowing it to sink in. "Distributing this list would place a target on the backs of all its beneficiaries."

"That may not be the primary concern," Moretti said. "Stock market values… hell, the Fortune 500 seem trivial compared to these figures. This knowledge could destabilize everything. Individuals, conglomerates, countries. People with billions down to people with pennies. Whether conspiracy or fact, the entire world could feel manipulated or weakened by the slightest awareness of such wealth in the hands of so few—especially a single family. Hell, people already go crazy thinking there are two or three rich white guys with a few hundred billion each. How would they feel knowing the much larger scope and value of the Medici?"

The three balls on the desktop blurred as Smoke's thoughts deepened. He understood. "Any threat of exposure would warrant immediate retirement to void that risk." He shifted his focus to Moretti. "We don't dare tell anyone that we know this."

Moretti nodded; the color drained from his face.

Liz and Elgan's email messages were still open at the side of the screen. Smoke highlighted the last sentence.

"They wanted a cut," he said.

"Jealousy. The root of all evil. And it's close friend, blackmail." Moretti cocked his head. "*Silenzio*," he whispered.

A loud horrendous crack struck through the rooms of the condominium. Undoubtedly the entrance door rammed; its locks and substantial mahogany core obliterated. This was immediately followed by the thudding footfall of a coordinated team entering and fanning out through the ante-rooms and into the reception lounge.

Chapter Twenty-Eight

Smoke ripped the squatchee from the laptop and shoved it into his pocket. "Do you have a weapon?"

"Not anymore…," Moretti said, raising an eyebrow. "S*tronzo*," he muttered. Asshole. Under the consequences of his earlier action amongst the shadows beneath Little Island, Smoke was inclined to own the salutation.

"Is it the cops?" he whispered.

Moretti shook his head, leaning close to mutter at his ear. "No. I'll tell you later. If we survive."

In the main reception room, a deep-timbered voice shouted full-throated orders in Italian, commanding even through the heavy oak doors of the sitting room and into the den. Militaristic in their precision and strength. They were cleaning up. Or so Smoke surmised by the noise of the search. It seemed a methodical examination with slight but unavoidable destruction as they combed through the contents of the condominium.

Smoke slid open the desk drawer to look for any kind of weapon. There was a letter opener about six inches long, its edge sharp, its end pointed. He tossed it to Moretti, then grabbed the signed baseball bat.

Moretti discarded the opener on the desk. "There'll be seven on the team," he whispered. "If they recognize either of us or if we take out even one of their squadron, it is tantamount to signing our death warrants. We can't hurt them, nor should we. But if they find us here, we are dead. Either today or very soon after."

Smoke looked at the immense wall of key-locked Gothic windows before sucking in a deep breath. "How are you with heights?" he asked.

"Not good."

"Me neither."

Smoke nudged his shoulder against the lead mullions and transoms of the closest window sash. The old panes and metal were delicate and malleable, the ornate leaves of rippled glass splintering and bulging under his weight. The corroded latch that hooked into the wall's hewn stone finally cracked and gave way, letting the sash swing open.

Both men froze with the sudden sharp sound of the lock breaking, listening for any sign of the team outside the den filing in, weapons drawn, but there was no response. Moretti squeezed out through the slim opening onto the even slimmer ledge. Smoke followed, exhaling as much air as he could to make the tight passage. Buttons caught and popped from his shirt as he stepped onto the ledge. A gargoyle leaned from the wall near the east side terrace, but there was no balustrade between them and the stone creature. No handhold. There was only a slight ridge of stonework rising barely as high as the tread of their boots. Nothing separated them from the 200-foot drop to the hedging and gravel below.

Smoke couldn't help it. He looked down. His vision telescoped, slamming into the bluegrass, and poppies, and granite paving which could be only as fragile and as hard as they appeared at such a distance. His sight blurred, and he swayed. Gritting his teeth, he squeezed his eyes shut and thumped a hand hard against Moretti's chest. They both fell back, their bulks pressed against the masonry.

"*Che cazzo!*" Moretti muttered.

They sucked in a deep breath.

Sweat dripped from Smoke's brow, sliding into his eyes, salty and stinging. He wiped roughly at his face and flicked the perspiration from his lids. Peering in though the open window, he grabbed the transom and swung his leg around Moretti, straddling him to crawl back inside.

"Keep shuffling that way," he said, motioning with his elbow. "I'm going to give them what they're looking for." He slid back into the den, his breaths deep and anxious, his chest tight between window and casement.

He heard someone in the sitting area directly outside the den. Scurrying to the desk, Smoke nudged the squatchee flash drive into the laptop USB port.

The den's door knob turned, rasping.

Smoke ducked behind the desk, squatting beside the chair, hoping it might offer him a few additional minutes of life.

The door jerked open, dusty yellow light punching in through the crack, silhouetting a man with the prominent bridge of an aquiline nose. With him came the permeating stink of Jameson's last moments.

"*Pirrelli! Vieni ad aiutarmi con questo*," another, unseen man bellowed from the main reception room, and the door opened no further.

Smoke darted to the window as quickly and as quietly as he could. He slid through it onto the thin ledge and scuttled sideways along it, his eyes closed to the fall. He slammed into the stucco brick of the return wall before he dared open his eyes. Then he gripped the ledge and swung himself down onto the terrace, one floor below. Moretti had already picked the lock into the sub-penthouse and waved for him to hurry.

Smoke

*   *   *

The cocktail patio in front of St Bart's great hall was a pleasant, tree-covered oasis in Midtown East, steeped in the fumes and honk of Park Avenue traffic, only a footpath away. Open air high-tops huddled amongst the shadows and rifts of sunlight, embraced between the ornate Romanesque and Byzantine detailing of St Bart's Church on one side, and the dramatic art deco of the Waldorf Astoria on the other. The beer was cold and hoppy.

"So who the hell were those guys?" Smoke asked.

"When independent clandestine tactics fail," Moretti muttered, motioning toward Smoke and then himself, "it is overridden by a second line of defense. That team is anything but subtle. They have full knowledge of every guarded and unguarded detail of our operations and our lives. Every nuance, every success, every failure, every appetite. They must, by charge, be ready to step in when needed. I'm unaware of their official name, but I've heard them called the *Ruspanti*. They are always ready, but rarely deployed. During the last incident that I'm aware of, they razed a small estate and every one of its inhabitants in Puglia—fourteen residents retired on a hot summer evening. Authorities blamed the deaths on a virulent strain of the coronavirus."

"Surely the authorities did a full investigation."

The wrinkles deepened near Moretti's eyes. "No, Tommaso. Those in charge are rarely the ones in public office, or with badges pinned to their breast."

Smoke let the idea of the *Ruspanti* sink in, trusting he would never again encounter them.

He sipped his beer, smacked his lips, and let his thoughts wander from the morning turmoil. It was lunchtime in the city, and the bar was crowded with Midtown suits. Clashing conversations swung from politics to publishing, to fraud and money laundering; to weekend plans at Rhinebeck or Woodstock up in the Hudson Valley, or even further north into the Berkshires for a *Tanglewood* symphony—John Williams conducting his finest.

Smoke chewed on a smash burger, while Moretti scraped the whipped ricotta and wildflower honey from a baguette to fork onto his tongue.

"What next?" Smoke asked. "Should we check Elgan's residence?"

Moretti reached for one of Smoke's fries, sucked off the salt, and flicked the soggy remnants onto his plate. He shook his head. "No need. We've evidenced both Liz Bayer and Elgan were valid targets. Whether their actions were based solely on greed or also to further some radical ideology is not our concern. Besides, they are dead, so could not be continuing to steer evidence and liability in your direction."

"What about Jameson?"

"Also dead. And as evidenced by this morning's cleaning, also a valid target. The *Ruspanti* wouldn't have been there otherwise."

Smoke took another thoughtful sip of beer as a nearby taxi crunched into the bumper of another car directly in front of the bar. The cheer of the people mingling around them was more than a match for the resulting cacophony of car horns thumped by angry fists. "Welcome to New York City," he said with a chuckle before turning to Moretti. "The *Ruspanti*... Do you think they dumped Elgan's body in my hotel room?"

Moretti did not respond, his attention still on the Park Avenue taxis, and their drivers sharing escalating words. An indistinguishable language peppered with expletives honed on the streets of Brooklyn. Increased volume emphasized the ever more descriptive recommendations made by each driver.

"Simone?"

Moretti lifted his hand to touch his bruised cheek. The swelling was less pronounced, the sharp line of his jaw returning, but Smoke could see he was still in pain. He'd pay another visit to Rafaella's soirée studio to grab more papers and weed.

"Elgan's body," Moretti said. "It could be part of their cleaning, a misdirection. But I can't see any reason for them to point the loaded gun toward you. Each of your kills has been textbook, with adequate approval, subterfuge, and distraction. There have been no loose ends as far as I can see, and yet you are most certainly the target. What is the outlier, Tommaso? What was the change that set these events in motion?" Moretti suddenly froze. Then he touched Smoke's knuckle and lowered his voice. "Best you excuse yourself to the restroom and not return."

Smoke didn't need to be told twice. He thumbed the remnants of the smash burger into his mouth as he rose from his stool, but it was too late. Seven men were stepping up into the patio garden from Park Avenue. Sleek Lanieri tailored suits, cashmere, the epitome of Milano high fashion, the blackest of black in the depth of their noir. They fanned out through the crowd and circled their table. Each was as tall or taller than Smoke but with a muscled litheness flattered by the defined cut of bespoke Italian atelier couture. The Mediterranean hue of cleanly shaved jawlines and gloss black hair trimmed high and tight made them look untouchable. The conversations on the terrace amongst the less refined New York Sports Club physiques and Madison Avenue suits dropped noticeably in volume.

The *Ruspanti.*

No one uttered a word as the seven men blocked any imagined opportunity for escape. Their leader pressed into the tight circle, his shoulder hard against Smoke's. He held several bottles of Peroni in his massive hands and passed them out to his men and Smoke and Moretti without a word. Then he tapped the neck of his bottle against each of theirs' before taking a deep draft. Smoke caught Moretti's eye, then followed suit. The Peroni was crisp and distinctive with a citrus aroma. Not as sweet as the beer he had been drinking.

"*Grazie, capitano,*" Moretti said.

"*Grazie,*" Smoke echoed, and the leader lifted his chin in acknowledgment. The slight movement exposed the webbed grooves of a pistol grip inside his slim jacket lapel and, inadvertently, nothing but smooth tanned flesh beneath his crisp, white dress shirt. Smoke had incorrectly assumed the impressive swell to be armored Kevlar.

They drank in silence, each of the *Ruspanti* intent on Smoke and Moretti who, in turn, were intent on them. To Smoke, none appeared accusative or hostile. Or friendly. There was no emotion at all. It was a hard, cold study. An effort to size up strengths and weaknesses, indifferences, dangers, and desires, all while revealing none of their own. Smoke was well familiar with men who were unwilling or unable to drop their guard, even when that was what they sought.

None of these men wore rings, matrimonial or otherwise. All were well manicured, hands smooth with visible strength and dexterity. Likewise, none held distinguishing facial features. All were generically attractive, undoubtedly masculine. But none possessed any physical quality that might distinguish them from any other Euro Italian with classic good looks. Moretti fell into the same category. Handsome, and pleasant to look at, but indistinguishable in a crowd. Smoke glanced at his own hand, comparable to the *Ruspanti* in size and musculature. The only difference was the tape immobilizing his broken finger and the wisps of fine blonde hair on his forearm.

"*Tutto bene*?" he asked. We good?

"*Si, fratello*," said the *capitano*, in the same rich timbre that had barked orders that morning in Jameson's penthouse. He signaled for the team to leave the terrace, but he remained at the high-top, spreading his open hands across Smoke's and Moretti's backs. He pulled them close, his brow furrowing into a knot above the broad curve of his nose. Then he reached into his pocket to pull out the squatchee. "You need to stay ten steps ahead of us. Not one." His accent was pure, his scent earthy and engaging, his breath citrusy from the beer. The underlying threat in his words was clear. "Until this matter is resolved, don't trust anyone. Not even each other."

Chapter Twenty-Nine

Smoke thought it best to exit the train one stop early. The steep incline from the Spuyten Duyvil Metro Station infused a pleasant burn from his calves up through his quads and glutes. He ran up to the road's peak, then north through the streets of West Bronx into Riverdale. It was still familiar and welcoming territory for Smoke, even with his recent memories tinged by regret. He peeled off his tank and tucked it behind the waistband of his shorts. The afternoon sun was hot against his skin, his pace easy along the flatter terrain. He'd built up a heavy sweat by the second pass of the Stuyvesants' home, noting the sleek Mercedes convertible parked on its gravel drive, almost hidden within the mottled shadows of the hedgerow. Despite his experience, he was nervous and excited by what the afternoon might bring.

He turned west, then south, taking the length of the green-canopied Riverdale Park in his stride. The forested trail was cool and pleasant, the Hudson River glinting through the trees. The distant whistle of a citybound train resonated from the tracks along the lower shoreline. Sequestered amongst the greenery edging his route, the homes around here undoubtedly commanded massive mortgages and property taxes, the homeowners requiring at least one, most likely two, Manhattan salaries to maintain the illusion. But now he knew that hadn't been the case with Angi and Daan. Never had been. And never would be.

Back on the street, there were few people or cars to impede or distract him from what lay ahead.

When he reached the Stuyvesants' refurbished 1960s bungalow a third time, he slowed to jog up the curved length of the gravel drive. He climbed the granite steps to the front verandah and knocked at the double door. There was no sign of bright yellow police tape here. Not in this neighborhood.

His chest rose and fell as he caught his breath, perspiration sheening him from head to toe, dripping down his bare torso and legs. He checked over his shoulder to confirm the front hedgerow shielded him from street view, then wiped his brow with his forearm and knocked again. He toed off his runners to stand barefoot on the welcome mat, then cupped his hands to his face and peered in through the sidelight.

The checkered marble foyer cut right through the home from the front door to the greenery of the rear yard. A lap pool stretched the vista farther across manicured grass into the diffused shadows of a chandeliered pavilion, decked out with current-season Ralph Lauren furnishings mixed with antiques undoubtedly garnered from weekend jaunts to Connecticut and Massachusetts. To London and Paris.

Rafaella slunk toward him through the foyer, her stride practiced and smooth. She possessed the same wry smile as Eleonora. The same as Angi. Her silhouette was ample and feminine, cloaked in a white caftan that was little more than gossamer against her naturally tanned Euro flesh. She let it drop to the tile as she welcomed him in, then closed the door behind him.

Smoke pushed his shorts to the floor and kicked them to the side in one fluid movement, Trojans scattering.

Everything about Rafaella was familiar. The taste of her mouth, the pressure of her lips and tongue, the curve of her buttocks in his grip. And the strength of her legs around his waist as he lifted her up against the front door. They shared an unhurried tenderness. Raw and provoking in its sensitivity. Their movement around and into each other was deliberate and gentle. Intoxicating. Heady and pungent as they kissed, and licked, and bit, and eventually fucked.

Slow and thoughtful.

He carried her through the foyer and down into the pool, his flesh still burning inside her, their motion against each other escalating, becoming more urgent with the slap of water against them. But then he paused and pulled his mouth from hers, intent on her eyes. Studying the dark flecks radiating across the hazel. Breathing deep of her breath, as he intentionally slowed their frenzy. He subtly shifted his angle within her, challenging the convolutions of tender flesh until he recognized the spark he was seeking. Every muscle ached and burned. But there was no need to hurry. His focus was solely on her, satisfying her needs, and giving her pleasure.

Rafaella closed her eyes and tilted her head back, her mouth slack, her lower lip plump in the gentle bite between his teeth. Still, his movement within her was excruciatingly slow and considered, attentively checked by an almost unbearable urgency that was becoming harder for him to restrain. Her grip on his shoulders loosened as she relaxed into the moment, as he lifted her up out of the pool and padded around its edge and into the pavilion. His quads and glutes trembled as he lowered her onto a daybed, their connection unbroken as he pressed his mouth once more to the wetness of hers.

Time drifted around them as they continued their intimate exploration. No need for words as they came to know each other. As they acknowledged there were no boundaries between them they wouldn't cross. Not now.

He was close, and he knew she was as well. Unbearably close. Still, he held back, measuring his pace within the rhythm of her escalating tension and squeeze, edging forward, savoring the taste of her mouth, becoming more and more enamored with the fleck of eye and freckle of nose.

Rafaella abruptly gasped and convulsed beneath him. In response, he thrust hard and deep. His considered plunge and pull of flesh within flesh compounded her tremor and his own. It was an intensifying pump. His balls loose and aching with the repetitive, hard slap against her. She suddenly released, wet and warm, and he came, hot and viscous, within her. Cresting waves shuddered through them. Both fulfilling and draining. Swelling until eventually subsiding into a shared, pleasurable jerk. A body-length shiver.

Smoke maintained the aching tense of muscles, holding the weight of his bulk above her. His heart thumped, blood coursing through him, his breathing heavy and dizzying, the unsheathed head of his cock unbearably sensitive inside her. Continuing to throb. And ache. Threads of saliva stretched between their lips as they breathed only the warm breath of each other, and he gently lowered his mouth to hers once more.

This last kiss was long and ardent as the trembling waned, as he softened, his flaccid flesh still thick and warm and sticky in their connection. His eyelids wavered between open and closed with the brush of lips and tongue, all of his senses absorbed by her. By the lines of her face. The softness of her skin and hair, her taste, her smell, her warmth. The excruciatingly tender noises of their bodies, with his tongue and cock still inside her.

"I know you killed the twins," she whispered. "Is this when you kill me? Or am I already dead?"

"Shhh," he said, touching a fingertip to her lips. He bit down on his tongue as he pulled himself from her and rolled onto his back at her side. He stripped off the condom, reaching to cup his balls and massage the tender ache. Then he turned toward her, speculating how this was going to end. How this definitely needed to end.

"You have a lovely home," he said, wondering why she'd chosen this location.

Rafaella was somber. "It is gorgeous, isn't it?" Then she laughed, an expression that made her truly beautiful. "You don't even know how gorgeous. You've only seen the foyer and pool! And hardly even that as it's been more than apparent where your attention has been since I opened the door."

She abruptly fell silent and her smile fell, too, replaced by the hard lines of anger or annoyance. A coldness took hold. "Unfortunately, this is not my property. It belonged to a forsaking bitch and her deadbeat cunt of a husband, who are both better off where they ended up."

Smoke was taken aback and sank inward at the venom of her words, his pain no longer pleasant, a sadness taking hold. He looked away from her to take in the sky.

Now he wouldn't mind killing her.

Hideous creature.

Fucking hideous creature.

Chapter Thirty

He held his runners by the laces, his tank tucked into his shorts to hang by his thigh, as he barefooted it across the Stuyvesants' front lawn. Without glancing over his shoulder, he knew he shouldn't have returned. Not to this house. And definitely not to her. The thought of her lying dead across the high-end furniture and multi-layered floor rugs somehow warmed his heart. Yet he knew he'd never kill her unless sanctioned by the House. He wondered if he still worked for the House. If the House even existed.

He hunkered down on the grassy verge to pull on his Nikes, barely distracted by the engine firing pulses of an approaching motorbike. An Italian Ducati Monster passed, then U-turned on Independence Avenue to pull up beside him at the curb as he double knotted his laces. It was the leader of the *Ruspanti*. Simone had called him the *capitano*.

"Did she tell you anything?"

"How did you know I was here?" Smoke asked.

The *capitano* smiled, a curve of lips and flash of teeth that was far from unpleasant. "Get on, *fratello*." He tapped the leather seat immediately behind him.

Smoke swung his leg over the bulk of the Monster and positioned himself tight behind the *capitano*. The rapid acceleration of the machine caught him off guard. He dug his fingers deep behind the waistband of the *capitano's* slacks. Then he reached his other hand, the one with the broken finger, around the *capitano's* torso to hold low and secure against his hard abdomen.

The engine was loud and the breeze cool as the Ducati circled up onto the Henry Hudson Parkway. They white-lined it between the gridlock of cars, south over the bridge above Spuyten Duyvil onto Manhattan Island. Then they curved down past the Met Cloisters and under the viaduct to the edge of the Hudson River. The machine came to a stop in the parking lot of a waterfront restaurant.

"Best you put this on," the *capitano* said, whipping the tank from Smoke's shorts and tossing it at his bare chest. Again, that easy, self-assured smile. The *capitano* chose an outside table at the rim of the promontory, away from the other clientele, where the churning noise of the river's current would shroud their conversation.

"Have you eaten today?" he asked.

"You tell me," Smoke said.

The *capitano* didn't even look at the menu. "Two veggie burgers, extra *patate fritte*, and a bottle of Chianti," he said to the server. He pulled off his windbreaker to a thin white cotton T-shirt with short-cut sleeves. No tattoos to pull the focus from the well-defined arms and smooth hairless chest. He stretched, tight dark curls enhancing his pits.

"You never told me your name," Smoke said.

The *capitano* seemed thoughtful as he peered downriver toward the George Washington Bridge. Even to Smoke, the panorama of the bridge's span between Manhattan and New Jersey was impressive from this vantage point. "In the company of my men or when I am directing you to action, which I most surely will when required, you will address me as Capitano Cioni. Otherwise, Andrea."

"And right here, right now?" Smoke asked. "What is this?"

"This is when you call me Andrea." He gripped Smoke's forearm, then let it go. The server returned with the bottle of Chianti and two glasses. "I will decant. *Grazie*," Andrea said. He poured the red and handed a glass to Smoke. "*Cin cin, fratello.*"

Smoke sipped the wine. "How did you know I was in Riverdale with Rafaella?" he asked.

Andrea smirked. "She's passionate, is she not? Moreso, as she has ripened into a woman of her own confidence. Much more assured than when we were teenagers."

Smoke closed his eyes tight, biting his tongue against speaking his own thoughts on Rafaella. He took in a deep breath and opened his eyes. "Please, Andrea. I need to understand."

Andrea held his gaze tight, then took Smoke's hand and lifted it to the back of his own neck. He pressed Smoke's forefinger against a vertebra, and between the thick ropey musculature where Smoke could feel an unusual nub of bone. Or something. The *capitano* pressed his finger atop Smoke's, rubbing it back and forth. The small nub within the *capitano's* flesh seemed to click, to float loose beneath the muscle.

"That's natural, right?" Smoke said, in genuine curiosity.

Andrea then reached for Smoke's neck, his fingers wrapping around the cleanly shaven skin below the jawline. Smoke knew that hand had been used to kill, and would be again. Though his hold was warm and gentle, the strength within it was more than apparent. The thought of Andrea's hand crushing or fracturing the cartilage of his larynx, or snapping his neck, was too easy to imagine. Too easy to understand. Perhaps welcome.

Andrea pulled Smoke toward him, and tapped his fingers against the vertebra at the back of Smoke's neck. The same small bone, the same loose movement when pressed from side to side.

He drew back, his face barely an inch from Smoke's, his attention flicking from eyes to lips and back again. "You have only a slight scar, ambiguous amongst the fine lines of the neck, right at the hairline. Right here." He again touched a finger against Smoke's skin, then leaned back into his chair and sipped his Chianti. "Per your file, you were eleven when the grooming began. Of course, given your birth, there was never really any alternative, and the abuse incurred to mold you into who you now are is unfortunate. But well documented. I believe you were seventeen when an altercation at Harvard landed you unconscious in the hospital. Again, not unintentional. The incident provided them the opportunity to secure the device. It is rudimentary at best, but works well at close range."

"The House?" Smoke asked.

"No. The chip is a modern legacy of *Famiglia Medici*, from long before they handed you over to the House. The House wouldn't even know about the device."

Smoke raised an eyebrow. "I don't recall being handed over to anyone."

"No, you wouldn't," Andrea said, again touching Smoke's arm, but this time leaving the connection unbroken.

The contact was not unnerving. Indeed, Smoke found it subtly reassuring, and yet it punctuated a conversation he wasn't understanding.

He recalled bypassing the security of Elgan's laptop, and then Jameson's, when his fingertips had touched the bio-sensor. He'd thought they hadn't been using a password. "Am I a Medici?" he asked.

Andrea laughed, his exuberance slowly devolving into a deep and lasting chuckle. Still with that smile, he slapped Smoke's shoulder.

"You and I are two of uncountable bastards, *fratello*. Not pure enough to mainline a direct injection of their funds, but with enough blood they keep us close and well-tended. Just in case."

Their burgers arrived, and they ate in silence. Smoke gazed across the water as his thoughts deepened. The sun reflected against the GWB's sweep of cables, and boats dotted the glistening water beneath. Andrea was closely watching him, reading his expression and body language even as Smoke kept his countenance as unreadable as he could.

He swiped several French fries through a puddle of ketchup and bent them into his mouth. "Why don't we just cut it out? The chip I mean," he said.

"There's more than one," Andrea said plainly. "And we both have thirty-four years of scars along our bodies to make any search with a knife more damaging than helpful. Besides, they are relics. Few are even aware of them. And most are inactive."

Smoke licked the salt and grease from his lips as he considered Andrea's revelations. The thought of him officially being a bastard made him smile—a feather in the cap of his blank family tree. Then he felt the blood drain from his face as he recalled that morning's activity. "Rafaella?" he said, letting the name hang between them.

Andrea tilted his head and stroked his chin. There was the hint of an afternoon shadow along his jaw as his lips spread into a smile. "Don't worry. You'd need to go back several generations to find even a remote link to her purebred branch of the family tree. What did she say?"

"It may have been subterfuge, but she didn't seem aware I'd been at the Stuyvesants' home before. And what she said about Angi and Daan was… ah… not complimentary. She seemed more than happy they'd been retired."

Andrea nodded, the wrinkles about his eyes creasing as he considered that. "I know Rafaella can be a bitch. As much as you or I can be, when circumstance warrants. However, be mindful. There are factors you don't know about. And you're not the only one unfairly treated in their journey."

"Are you expecting me to take your words at face value?" Smoke asked.

"*Fratello*," Andrea said, locking his gaze on Smoke's eyes. "You need to know you can trust me. That I'd only lie to you if I determined it was the best or only course of action."

"You said at St Bart's I shouldn't trust anyone," Smoke said.

"I did." Andrea drained his glass of Chianti and poured another, his lips and tongue a deep cinnabar crimson.

Chapter Thirty-One

They stood on the upper terrace of the outside café bar in Bryant Park, within the moon shadow of the New York Public Library.

"I have this for you," Smoke said. He reached behind his jacket lapel, then pushed into Moretti's jacket pocket a bag containing a few buds and papers from Rafaella's stash. "You shouldn't light it here, but we can walk the streets later."

"*Grazie*. These should be the last I'll need. The pain has subsided to bearable." Moretti lifted an espresso to his lips.

At the far end of the park, near 6th Avenue, a massive cinema screen fluoresced with images of Meg Ryan and Billy Crystal. *When Harry Met Sally*. The croon of Harry Connick Jr drifted from hidden speakers, the smooth vocals settling over the picnicking audience and eddying amongst the rows of majestic London plane trees delineating the parkland from the surrounding streets and skyscrapers. Despite Smoke's caution, the skunk-grass smell of pot imbued the air, melding with the ubiquitous odors that less than subtly defined Midtown Manhattan. The drift of burned meat from the vendor carts askew on the sidewalks. The exhaust fumes, and the hovering remnants of that day's sun-warmed horse shit and urine.

Ahh, the sweet smell of a New York summer evening.

"Was there still a police presence at your townhouse this morning?" Moretti asked.

"Mm-hmm." Smoke watched Meg Ryan, his thoughts still on his conversation with Andrea—an interaction he still didn't understand.

"I'd thought you'd be back to the hotel by noon."

Smoke leaned against the edge of the high-top and fingered the neck of his San Pellegrino. "I needed to run. Get my head clear."

"Uh-huh." Moretti slowly nodded. He pulled the bag from his jacket and rolled a joint under the overhang of the high-top table. "What did the *capitano* say about me?"

Smoke took a swig of water. "Nothing. He just reiterated that neither of us should trust anyone."

"Did he have any idea who was—is—willing to expose the executions of five people so closely related to the Family? Or who wanted you and Gabrielle dead, and presumably still does?"

Smoke shook his head. "Perhaps they'll only be satisfied if I'm in jail."

"No, Tommaso. It never works like that. And you know it. You in jail would only make it easier for them—whoever they are—to kill you and resolve whatever their issue is. You were a target for a reason. You *are* a target."

They fell into silence, both intent on the cinematic conversation echoing from the speakers scattered throughout the park.

"What is this story all about, anyway?" Moretti said, motioning toward the screen.

Smoke peeled the paper label from his bottle. "Friendship," he said, thinking of Eleonora. Of Lucy and Andrea. Of the people who had passed through his life and those who were currently in it. "Whether friendship is even possible between a man and a woman without sexual implication. Harry and Sally actually had it pretty easy, if you ask me. Their time period was much simpler. Perhaps repressed. They didn't need to deal with today's ambiguity of gender fluidity and the broader acceptable spectrum of sexual attraction." Frustrated, he began shredding the paper label into strips.

"You make it sound onerous," Moretti said.

"Don't you think so? Any tentative relationship is now unnecessarily burdensome and complex. Muddied by undefined and uncertain sensual intentions. Or desires. By what the other person might or might not actually be looking for." He flicked the shredded paper onto the table. "I think we need to tread carefully, to be wary in any interaction and how it might be interpreted or misinterpreted beyond mere friendship."

"Are you sure you don't need a martini?"

Smoke shook his head, deep in thought until Moretti gripped his shoulder and pulled him from his reverie.

"If it's any consolation, Tommaso, I consider you my friend, and I have no desire to fuck you. Or fuck you over."

"Thanks." Smoke chuckled. "I appreciate the clarification, buddy. But you recall I almost killed you, right?"

Moretti shrugged. "I'm ordering that martini."

The bartender iced the cocktail glass in front of them, poured and stirred the Grey Goose and vermouth in the shaker, shaved and twisted the slim rind of lemon.

Smoke was thankful at his first swallow. It was exactly what he needed as his mind flicked, minute by minute over his interactions that day. Despite Andrea's consoling words, he still thought of Rafaella as no less than a fucking hideous creature.

"You were at the Little Island gala with Rafaella," he said. "What was her understanding of you being there? Of *my* being there?"

"A few years ago," Moretti said, "I ran her security detail for several weeks, when she'd attracted unwanted attention in Italy. She was aware of my skill set and commitment to the family and had no questions when the unwanted attention disappeared. It was a valid and verified kill sanctioned by Palazzo Pitti—the Italian equivalent of the House."

"But why were you there that night?" Smoke asked.

"My handler and I didn't know the full scope of the situation here in New York. We had no time to coordinate the operation and were coming in almost blind. I'd seen the surveillance of your townhouse but had no intel where you were and had no other leads on how to make contact. Given the high profile of the event on Little Island, and Rafaella's attendance, I advised her of my presence in New York in case my help was required."

Smoke detected no lie indicators in Moretti's expression or demeanor. He wanted to trust him. Needed to. "Rafaella seemed to know of the twins' intention to kill me," he said.

Moretti reached for Smoke's martini and took a sip. "There had been escalating concern over the twins' flamboyance with their trust funds. Their oblivious spending habits had attracted attention throughout the *Riviera di Levante*."

"Around *Genova*?" Smoke queried.

"*Si*. Their acquisition of several palazzos along the coast on the same day had caught the media's eye. We still don't know how that blatant risk exposure relates to the hit on you and Gabrielle, other than it does. And we have no confirmation yet whether either Palazzo Pitti or the House officially sanctioned it. There is some, how you say, *confusione*. Some back and forth between the two."

Smoke pulled the martini from Moretti's lips and tipped it to his own, taking a hefty gulp. "Which brings us back to Rafaella."

"She was aware of the situation with the boys in Italy and also that they'd struck a deal requiring them to come to New York. To make restitution. But she'd no details of their actual task until you let it slip that you were their target and that they were dead. She made the connection. Your revelation of their deaths was certainly a shock, even to one as callous as Rafaella, who is well aware of sanctioned retirements."

Smoke tried to make sense of Moretti's words. It didn't make sense to him.

"Surely, if Gabrielle and myself had been sanctioned targets they would have sent someone like you or me, not a couple of party boys making amends. I—"

The massive cinema screen across the park suddenly flashed white. It looked as if it was ripping as the film stock shuddered across the fluorescent fabric. The soundtrack slowed, jerking to a dull reverberation before popping and halting altogether. Both the screen and speakers were dead. The uproar from the crowd was immediate, a deafening crescendo. The wail of approaching sirens compounded their upset. A piercing doppler echoed amongst the tall office buildings surrounding the parkland. White and blue police lights strobed through the trunks and canopies of trees and shrubbery, glanced off fountains and memorials, and reflected across the acres of steel and glass, granite, and marble, stretching up into the night sky. A fleet of police and SWAT vehicles coursed along the perimeter streets, screeching against the curbs to blockade all sides of the green space. Black, military-looking Humvees thudded over the sidewalks and bounced up the steps to the higher terrace levels. People yelled and scattered.

Two of the bulky vehicles swerved through the center of the park, flinging picnic blankets and clods of dirt and grass. Cracking and ripping up stone pavers. Lights and sirens blaring. They skidded to a halt in front of the café bar.

Directly in front of Smoke and Moretti.

Chapter Thirty-Two

Smoke could only guess at the number of weapons trained upon him, Moretti, and the clientele of the café bar. From behind the glare of high beams at least three-dozen submachine guns and assault rifles were held at close range. Plus an uncountable cache of NYPD sidearms aimed by New York's finest. Massive truck-mounted lights were reversed into position along 42nd, their brilliance lighting the park as bright as day. Smoke could make out more armed vantage points along the rooftops of the older low-rise structures of 41st Street. Snipers. The lit silhouette of the Empire State Building rose behind them to the south, its upper tiers pulsing a menacing red in the darkening sky.

The panic and dissonance amongst the crowd oscillated with the unexpected onslaught and confusion. Partially blinded by the Humvee overheads, Smoke craned his neck and shielded his eyes, noting the bulk of the crowd was being ushered from the main lawn out onto 6th Avenue. They probably already knew the ending of the movie, he thought.

Automobiles and trucks blared at the disruption of their flow up-town and cross-town. Commanding voices barked orders above the disorganized fray, bullhorns amplifying indistinct words as police helicopters dropped between the neighboring skyscrapers to hover mere feet above the tree line, their clamor brash and choppy. Two of them landed on the cleared lawn. Their searchlights highlighted the café bar and the marble bulk of the library behind it. There was no out for Smoke or Moretti. None.

"Hands above your heads!" The words came distorted through a bullhorn. "No movement without my direct order! If any of you have any type of weapon on your person, drop to the ground immediately!"

Two men at the far end of the bar dropped to their knees.

"Face down! On the ground!"

The two men sprawled prone across the pavers, arms and legs outstretched, visibly shaking.

Smoke side-glanced at Moretti, then down at the bag of weed he had kicked to the side.

"All men! Down on your knees! Women! File toward 42nd! Slowly! Slowly!" Dark figures on either side of the Humvees motioned wide with their arms, directing the women toward the street. Separating them from the remnants of testosterone kneeling or spreadeagled on the pavers.

"Do you have your EU identification?" Smoke muttered out the side of his mouth. Moretti nodded, only a slight incline of his head. "They may not know we're acquainted. Do you understand?" Again, Moretti nodded, turning his body away from Smoke toward the patron on his other side. He shuffled subtly closer to the other until they were shoulder to shoulder. The unknown patron trembled in terror.

Uniforms escorted the last of the women from the terrace.

Fifty or more men remained on their knees amongst the high-tops, the two with weapons prone upon the pavers, perhaps seven yards from Smoke and Moretti. Two black-clad tactical teams rounded the Humvees and ran up the stairs onto the terrace. They spread out, weapons drawn, their backs to the high-powered beams continuing to blind those scattered around the bar. They barked orders as they grouped and split up the men, manhandling those not in Smoke and Moretti's group away from the terrace.

They then split those remaining a second time. SWAT dragged the two prone men with weapons by their feet across the pavement, thudding them down the stone stairs and into the shadow of the military vehicles to be processed. They were not the authorities' primary concern.

More choppers now hovered above Times Square, a block to the west, searchlights sweeping and Smoke recognized the media emblems on their sides.

The flagstones were hard beneath his knees and shins, more bruises to add to those already coloring his flesh. He held his hands above his shoulders, one hand shading his eyes from the glare.

And that's when he spotted Lucy.

She stood beside the SWAT team, similarly clothed in black, her weapon drawn and pointed.

Not at him, but at Moretti.

She glanced at Smoke with neither alarm nor recognition before pushing back a stray lock of hair and placing a finger briefly against her lips.

He got it.

He hunched his shoulders, raised both his hands above his head, affecting a tremble to those observing, and tilting his face from the light.

SWAT pulled the remaining men from the ground, one by one, loud and boisterous, jerking them to the side to be shoved behind the line of authority.

Then they circled Moretti and the man on his other side, threw them down roughly onto their chests, and cuffed their wrists at their backs. After binding their ankles with zip ties, they methodically patted them down. Moretti took it in silence, his new companion not so much.

Smoke remained immobile, his face held low, until someone manhandled him to his feet and rushed him from the bar, across the terrace, and out onto 42nd Street. It wasn't until his boots hit the pavement of one of the most famous streets in the world that he realized it had been Lucy frog-marching him across the distance. Her grip was firm on his waistband and around his wrist. No doubt another bruise.

"Madison Square Park in four hours," she said before running back toward the Humvees and, maybe, to Moretti.

Smoke released his breath through pursed lips.

Perhaps he did have a friend he could trust.

Perhaps.

Chapter Thirty-Three

The sky split open. A drizzle at first, then a steady rain as thunder reverberated amongst the high rises, the weather announcing the evening's true intent. It took Smoke an hour to walk through the Tenderloin of Manhattan to Madison Square Park. Not because it was so far, but because of the confusion and street closures and re-directs around 42nd. The pedestrian overflow from the disrupted Bryant Park event staggered scattershot throughout the city with no mind to traffic or signals or direction. The upset had also spread to those not immediately affected. Rumor told of armed serial killers on the loose in Midtown; of a terrorist attack without a specified location. The cacophony of sirens barreling throughout the grid of streets and avenues only compounded those rumors.

And no one seemed to want to use the subway.

Not tonight.

The rainfall was heavy by the time he reached Madison and 26th. The slender angled silhouette of the Flatiron building loomed tall against the dark, roiling clouds. But it wasn't the weather that worried Smoke.

He flipped up the collar of his shirt and jacket as he entered the park and made himself comfortable on a bench. The seat was huddled amongst shrubbery, protected by an overhang of elm, dogwood, and oak. But even with the thick canopy, it wasn't long before he was soaking wet, his sockless dress shoes filled with water, his suit sticking to his skin. The weather and the rumble of his empty stomach suited his mood, which had been tanking since his body count had escalated. Since Gabrielle, since Rafaella, since Capitano Cioni, since *Harry met Sally*. It was an hour before the rain slowed to a comfortable drizzle, and he shared the bench with an unknown companion in the quiet and deepening shadows of an otherwise empty park.

He was a homeless guy, pallid and grungy with thatched unkempt hair, who might have been similar in age to Smoke. It was hard to tell. He wore multiple layers of thread-bare suits, held secure by a shabby, soiled parka. Grime embedded his bare hands and feet. His ripped nails were long and tarnished black. And even in the mist, he stank. The putrid stench that came with living on the streets without sanitation or care. Bile surged in the back of Smoke's throat and he swallowed hard to keep it down, then quickly stood to leave.

He made it only as far as the wrought-iron gates before he hesitated. With his own life devolving into its current state, he could see how one might easily continue down the dwindling spiral to end up with nothing. To end up on the streets. On that bench. Perhaps that was better than being dead. Perhaps. He scrutinized the homeless guy a moment more, then left the park. Twenty minutes later, he returned with boxes of barbequed chicken and slaw, a six-pack of water, and another of beer.

The guy's name was Nate and, contrasting his disheveled appearance, Smoke found him to be personable and intelligent. A gentle, beguiling man. They settled into a cautious conversation as they ate, the rain beating down upon the flagstones at their feet.

Nate had lost his career, his rental, his friends, his girl.

"It hurt to lose my analyst job, but it was the last one that destroyed me," he said, shucking the lids off two of the beers and handing one to Smoke. "Has it got any better out there, or is the world still fucked?"

"Still fucked," Smoke said.

"Hmmm." Nate fingered through the box for a wing, then skimmed it through the mash and gravy. "And you? You don't look like you should be out here with me. Not in that suit. And not in this weather."

Smoke slouched against the bench, pulling the skin from a chicken leg before discarding it in the box with a flick.

"There must be something good in your life. Something in this city that makes the fight worthwhile," Nate said. "Please, at least tell me that's true."

Smoke sucked on his beer, knowing the answer but reticent to say it out loud.

It was something he never shared. Not with friends, not with acquaintances, not with anonymous liaisons. Just in case. Something he hoped even the *capitano* was unaware of. It wasn't in that document that outlined every blemish and brazen pleasure of his life. And without it, they'd never know who he truly was. Who he truly loved.

He looked at Nate, who'd had the rug ripped out from beneath him—one of the 100,000 New Yorkers gutted and cast aside by this fucking city, onto its streets and into its tunnels. Smoke knew he'd never see him again. There was no link between them. No risk. And somehow, he knew that under his current circumstance, it would feel good to talk about the one person he loved without question.

"I have a son," Smoke said. "His name is Theo. A three-year-old chatterbox with baby blue eyes and an adorable, very kissable pot belly." He smiled his real smile to himself for the first time in many days.

"Why are you here, then?" Nate asked, stripping the meat from the wing with his teeth.

"He lives with his moms in Park Slope. Normally I sleep over once or twice a week. I get the top bunk. But recently everything's gone to hell. I haven't had the time to spend with him." He sank into his thoughts, wondering when, or if, it would be safe to see his son again.

"Sounds like Theo's pretty lucky. Two moms, plus you."

Smoke brushed the box of chicken aside. He settled into the comfort of the beer, gripping it with both hands. His eyelids were heavy as he imagined Theo sleeping securely in Brooklyn, on the other side of the East River.

"Were you ever married?" Nate asked.

Smoke was abruptly pulled back into the uncomfortable cold wetness of Madison Square Park. "You know the questions to ask, don't you, buddy?" he said. He tipped the bottle and took a deep draft. Nate had zeroed in on a part of his life he'd long suppressed, and had never wanted to confront or talk about. He studied his companion across the lip of the bottle. And suddenly he was glad he had someone to talk to. Someone who wouldn't look down on him, who'd most likely even understand. Who'd been there. Who wouldn't judge him when he dared to spill his guts.

"It was true love," Smoke said. "The very idea of her took my breath away. Sucked it from my lungs. We were inseparable, our moments together tender as we shared our dreams, our hopes, our fears, our love. Some weekends we'd just lie naked and cuddle amongst boxes of takeaway and casks of cheap wine. Laughing, giggling, or crying, but happy." He fell silent for a moment, memories sweeping. "It was our second summer. July twenty-ninth. An evening I'd meticulously planned. A late supper in the garden of Tavern on the Green followed by a stroll through the pastures of Central Park, the towers of the city gleaming around us. A hired photographer surreptitiously capturing the moments. I'd booked a horse-drawn carriage through Midtown to propose at the top of the Empire State. But I couldn't wait. I'd never been so excited. I dropped to my knee at the crest of the Bow Bridge in the middle of the park and asked her to marry me."

Nate lowered his bottle of beer without taking a slug.

Smoke drew in a loud and profound breath and threw his attention into the sky, past the slim omnipotent bulk of the Flatiron building, blinking rapidly and glad it was raining.

"She—"

His face was wet, his breaths deep and shuddering.

"She—"

Nate reached for Smoke's arm but hesitated and pulled back without making contact.

Smoke clapped his hand across his mouth, then fully pressed his face into his hands, palms and fingers hard against his flesh to hold the emotions in check. But it was too late. They were overtaking him. He'd no choice other than to let them run their course. Something he'd long needed and which he now had no agency to stop.

He sobbed, loud and long and visceral, his body shuddering. His skull ached with the onslaught of raw emotion, every pain and uncertainty of the last days surging to the forefront. He let the waves crash through him until, he didn't know how much later, the grief subsided, solidifying into a pulsing ache directly behind his eyeballs. He slumped hunchbacked on the edge of the bench, quietly shivering, and wiped roughly at his eyes and nose.

"Sorry," Smoke said, the word catching in his throat.

Nate nodded, seeming to understand.

Beyond an interminable silence left between them, Nate responded in a gentle voice, the words hardly audible: "Tom… Tommy… You need to tell me the rest. You need to say it out loud."

Smoke slowly drew in another deep breath, his gaze unfocussed, the increasing rain beating down around them. He swallowed with difficulty, attempting to settle himself. "She gave no answer to my proposal," he muttered. "She didn't even say no. She just walked away and refused to see or speak to me ever again. I still don't know why." He was wasted and numb. A feeling in the depths of his heart he'd been holding too close for too many years.

A town car pulled to the curb and honked.

"Oh, fuck," Smoke muttered, knuckling his eyes. "Fuck!" He stood up, pulling at his saturated suit where it clung. "Hey, um… Oh fuck it. Thank you, man. I appreciate it. I really do. It was something I needed to… Well, you know." He gripped Nate's hand with both of his.

"I know." Nate's eyes were full of concern. "Thanks for the chicken and beer. If you need me, you know where to find me."

Smoke ran through the rain, sloshing across the puddles toward the town car and reaching for the door handle. He opened it, then slammed it closed again and ran back to the bench. "Nate, would you like to be inside, or do you prefer it out here?"

Nate's mouth lifted at the corners. A toothy, handsome smile. "I'm very brave, but I'm not an idiot. I'd not say no to shelter."

"Good." Smoke squinted against the downpour. "I have a… a friend with an unused studio up in Hell's Kitchen. I'll let her know you'll be staying there indefinitely. For as long as you need to get back on your feet. As long as you want." He dug into his pocket for Aloïs's plastic wallet and extracted the remaining cash. "Take this. You'll need it to fill up the fridge and to fix the lock on the front door."

Chapter Thirty-Four

His suit squelched as he slid across the rear seat of the town car. He thumbed the rain from his eyes. Lucy was also soaked, her hair clinging to her scalp. She'd removed the Kevlar vest but still wore black, a Glock holstered at her waist.

"Who was that?" she asked.

They sank into the plush leather as the car sped north along Madison Avenue back uptown.

"Just a homeless guy needing an attentive ear. Incoherent ramblings of someone who doesn't know who they are. And hasn't for a very long time." He pressed his eyes shut in an attempt to fully shake the upset and relief of Madison Square Park from his mind.

She turned from him and brushed condensation from the side window. Everything beyond was dark and rain-slicked. As Smoke pulled at the wet and twisted discomfort of his pants, he saw her focus was on him in the reflection. He also noted the rapid beat of her heart vibrating the wet chemise at her chest. Was she nervous? Was she afraid of him?

"What was that at Bryant Park?" he asked.

Still, she didn't directly look at him. "Don't worry about Moretti. He can handle himself," she said. "His diplomatic immunity is intact, and the NYPD will determine he wasn't in the US during most of the deaths." She wavered. "They might wonder about the timing of the Laurents, though. At most, they can hold him a few more hours without interrogation while they confirm his itinerary. And perhaps DNA. Though it's unlikely they'd get approval for that."

Smoke cocked his head. "Who *are* you? You said you were NYPD when we first met."

"My dad and granddad were. I never said I was."

Smoke pushed his hair back from his eyes, holding her gaze, awaiting an answer.

"Gabrielle is one of my direct reports."

Smoke darted his attention to the driver on the other side of the glass partition, then back to Lucy.

"You're a part of the House," he said.

She nodded.

He restructured his thoughts. "Why were you at that wedding at the Boathouse?"

"It's complicated. You were being considered for... I needed to determine how you'd react to distraction under pressure. I was—"

"So, our time together, our conversations, were part of your job." The muscles of his face slackened. He was exhausted.

"Tommy. No. Everything I said was true. I—"

Smoke shook his head. "Please stop. People keep saying words. Just fucking words. I don't need to hear any more." He rubbed brusquely at his face, then fell back into the seat, his blurred attention on the stream of traffic and lights ahead in the downpour. He shuddered and wished he were still sitting out on the bench in the rain with Nate. "Do you at least know why Gabrielle and I were targeted? Why everything went to hell?"

"Not yet. Though our analysts have confirmed Eleonora di Toledo used her contacts in the mayor's office to request an inquest into the deaths of her niece and nephew-in-law."

"Their names were Angi and Daan."

"Yes. That's what sparked the renewed investigation. But it doesn't account for the local authorities linking the other cases. And so quickly."

"The news reports stated DNA in common."

"Semen," she said. "Yours."

"Are you sure? That can't be true."

Smoke's mind wandered over the last several days. He'd used protection with Daan and Angi, the rubbers discarded at Grand Central Terminal when he'd returned to Manhattan. The condoms rolled on by Liz and Julianne were probably still stuck to the floor under a seat on the 4, where they'd been flung. He didn't ejaculate with Jameson during their time together or with Elgan on the train. Then the scene in suite 1737 of The Hotel tumbled and buoyed to the surface, finding Elgan's corpse in the bed beside him after he'd jerked off. His throat constricted with horror and disgust. His semen on the sheets and pillows of the bed, and most likely Elgan. And that room tied him to Aloïs and Mathéo.

"Still, I don't see how it's possible for every case," Smoke said.

"Although you were at each of those scenes, we both understand how simple it is to collect samples of ejaculate from any man we wish to target. Men are men. And you are the target," Lucy said. "We've no proof yet, but we suspect Eleonora as the source of the samples that might have then been planted. How many times were you intimate with her?"

Smoke closed his eyes. "Three, ah, four times. All at her condo at The Plaza." Eleonora had always disposed of the condoms.

"All before the other incidents?"

"After the Stuyvesant retirements, before the others."

Lucy bit her lower lip. "We have untraceable samples being flown in from overseas. Bratislava. We'll swap them out with the coroner's evidence and ensure cross-contamination with the DNA of the two male interns in the medical examiner's office."

Smoke pressed his hand against his jaw, attempting to crack the stiffness in his neck, the muscles seizing from the cold.

"What about the *Ruspanti*? They appear to be taking affirmative action."

Lucy turned toward him. "They have no jurisdiction within these borders. And, unlike Simone, no diplomatic immunity. They are a last line of defense, a cleanup crew, but if they come to the attention of the authorities in a compromising position, they are on their own. Neither House nor Palazzo will recognize them."

Smoke understood.

The town car swerved onto 51st, then south on Fifth.

"Despite what is about to occur, until we understand this situation, your stable datum is you cannot trust them. Not Capitano Cioni. Not any of his men. Take care with your every word and their every movement when you are in their presence."

"Give me one reason I should believe you over them."

"Two of the *Ruspanti* crossed the border into the US *before* anything required cleaning. Before you retired the Stuyvesants. I haven't determined yet whether they were subsequently tasked with scrubbing the aftermath of your assignments, or completing what the Laurents failed."

The car pulled to the curb in front of Rockefeller Plaza.

When the door opened, Capitano Cioni slid in beside Smoke.

Chapter Thirty-Five

The *capitano* was dry apart from a few drops of rain clinging to the cut of his buzz, his body radiating heat as he pressed in against Smoke's much cooler, wet skin. Smoke avoided eye contact, not wanting to give him anything. Not yet. Not after what Lucy had said. He needed to organize his thoughts.

They sped to the west side in silence, then south along 11th, beneath the towering enormity of Hudson Yards, into Chelsea. The town car pulled into the vehicle elevator of a multi-story condo. A handsome residential building with a stainless steel façade blooming from a terracotta base. They and the car ascended in silence, lights in the shaft flashing as they passed individual floors, and then arrived on the twelfth. Chrome doors yawned wide to welcome them into a double ensuite sky garage. A blue-black BMW with its top down was already parked.

Lucy stepped out of the car, waved her palm before a door sensor, and motioned for them to enter her home. The space was impressive. Industrial in décor, black steel and glass, curtainless. A floating wire-mesh staircase curved up to the second floor, backdropped by unobstructed views across Hudson River Park and the river itself toward the New Jersey skyline.

"I'm unable to offer a change of clothes," she said to Smoke. "But there are towels in the downstairs bathroom and a good Tennessee whiskey in the bar." She made pointed eye contact with him, presumably to enforce their earlier conversation, and then jogged up the stairs.

Smoke left the *capitano* at the bar, intent on the bathroom. Locking the door behind him—something he rarely did—he stripped, and showered away the cold numbness from sitting in the rain, then dried himself off. The external floor-to-ceiling plate glass wall appeared to offer no prospect of privacy or modesty.

"Do you draw your curtains, Lucy?"

"No. Should I?"

It made him slightly less sad, less angry about his confidence in her, that she'd been telling the truth during their conversation on the High Line. He would have to be content with that for now.

Squinting through his naked reflection, dark bruising still apparent down his side, from hip to toes, he couldn't tell what lay beyond the window. It appeared only black.

He dabbed his jacket and slacks with a towel to dry them as best he could, then pulled them back on, buttoning the jacket at his waist. A hairdryer civilized his curls but had a mediocre impact against the damp linen suit. He left his shirt hanging in the shower and plodded barefoot out to the living room. His thoughts were on the promised whiskey, and determining the purpose of this meeting. And which of the two of them he might dare trust.

An oversized chessboard sat upon a marble coffee table, the pieces fabricated of black and silver metal. The pawns were brownstones, the larger pieces embodied the more dramatic of Manhattan's celebrated buildings and skyscrapers. The Empire State, 30 Rock, Chrysler, Flatiron, Grand Central.

"White rook to B4," Lucy said as she descended the stairs, freshly showered and dressed in a gray and blue jumpsuit with her hair pulled back.

Smoke nudged the piece accordingly.

"Black knight to C6," Cioni countered, without looking up from his whiskey. "Checkmate by either side within the next four moves."

Smoke ignored him, leaving the knight in place, and accepted a glass of liquor—neat—from Lucy.

"It might be best if we sit outside on the loggia," he said. "I'm still kind of damp."

They sank into the low rattan lounges, the rain again falling heavy beyond the metal balustrade, the early morning dark and humid. Lucy kept the balcony lights off, and Smoke noted the ambient glow from inside was adequate for them to read the *capitano*, but not for the *capitano* to read either him or Lucy.

"When did you and your team enter the US?" Lucy asked without preamble.

The *capitano* smiled tightly, his legs open in a presumptive manspread, his hand splayed across the top of a thigh. He pressed his forefinger into the deep groove that defined the musculature of his quads. "I don't answer to you. Or anyone. Everything my men and I do is executed solely on my cognizance in the best interest of fulfilling our charge."

"Ditto," Lucy said. She calmly sipped her whiskey. "You all arrived on separate flights at different ports."

He nodded. "Standard protocol. A procedure the House also employs."

"You didn't all arrive in the country on the same day."

Capitano Cioni's countenance did not falter, but Smoke noticed he increased the pressure of his finger against his leg. *He didn't know*, Smoke thought.

"Two of your men, Pirrelli and Giordano, arrived by hired car two weeks ago. Before any of this started. They entered the country via the Champlain Port of Entry from Canada into upper New York State. You can corroborate via your channels."

He maintained his composure, though Smoke surmised a little too well.

"My men are beyond reproach," Cioni said.

"As are mine," Lucy said. "And yet we have this situation."

Smoke rested his foot upon his opposite knee and gripped his ankle. He winced as he tentatively touched the painful bruising along his Achilles tendon down to the underside of his foot, wondering if that injury was from West Street. Then he recalled slamming into the guardrail of the walkway beneath Little Island in the tussle with Moretti. "Do either of you know what tipped off Simone's handler regarding the situation here? That Gabrielle and myself needed protection," he asked.

Lucy raised her glass to her lips without comment.

"Gianetta, his handler, does not share her sources with anyone. Especially the conversations she's had with her direct reports," Cioni said. "Or with me," he added firmly, his attention tight on Smoke. "Doing so has proven unfortunate for all concerned."

"Okay. What made you deploy your team?" Smoke asked.

The *capitano* reached forward and grasped the bridge of Smoke's foot, pressing the pad of his thumb into the soft underbelly of the sole. "Massage here, *fratello*. It'll increase circulation and reduce the pain. It should also stop the heel from seizing. Though it might be best you cut back on your running for a while." His hand was warm, the grip solid but not unwelcome. When he let go, Smoke applied pressure to the spot designated. Cioni watched the rhythmic motion of Smoke's hand and foot.

"I'm entrusted to monitor all peripheral activity of the House and Palazzo. A watchdog of sorts. To ensure nothing endangers the status quo, the necessary discretion around the family's circumstances. If I determine something is untoward or requires immediate solution, beyond the established protocols of sanctioned retirements, then it is my decision and mine alone."

"Was I something that needed an immediate solution?" Smoke asked. "Was Gabrielle?" He stood and leaned against the balustrade, his back to the rain beyond.

Cioni drained his whiskey and held up his empty.

"The bottle is inside," Lucy said.

The *capitano* retrieved the whiskey bottle and refreshed all their glasses. "Certain duties are straightforward, and then there are those requiring nuance. *Fratello*, the tasks you and Simone are given require no decision beyond the how, where, and when of immediate or delayed retirement, and you both are superlative at what you do. Select elders in *Firenze* make the initial hard decision of any required retirement, a duty they do not take lightly, but even they might not be aware of some impeding factors. Despite our initial purpose, the *Ruspanti* has grown to secure that trust of eradicating any unforeseen loose ends. An overview, if you will." He leaned against the balustrade beside Smoke. "The direction for the Laurent twins to retire yourself and Gabrielle was unfathomable. It appeared to originate from the Palazzo, but it had no precedence, no logic beyond wiping out an effective arm of our defenses. And when I queried the elders, there was only uncertainty."

"Why didn't you just convey your concern to the House?" Lucy asked.

"Because I had no confidence in either House or Palazzo, based on the assignment to kill—" He glanced at Smoke. "It made no sense. I didn't know who I could trust. Who was compromised." The tight knot above his brow softened.

"Could Eleonora be the instigator of this?" Smoke asked.

"Eleonora…" Cioni was thoughtful of the implication. "As a senior family member here in the US, she's certainly aware of the due diligence required for authorization of retirement. But she is siloed from the elders in *Firenze* who make the final decision." He lifted his gaze to Smoke's eyes. "She'd never order your retirement, *fratello*. She's known of you since you were—" he glanced sidelong at Lucy "—since the House recruited you."

Smoke pinched the bridge of his nose, confused. "She knew who I was before they tasked me with her retirement?"

Cioni pulled back, his eyes wide. "*Che cazzo?*" He looked from Smoke to Lucy and back to Smoke. "Retirement? Eleonora? That most certainly did not parse through the counsel of the Palazzo." He fixed his attention on Lucy. "How did you receive that order?"

"It came through the standard channel. There is only one channel. We'd no reason to question it." All color dropped from her face.

"Angi and Daan were reason enough," Smoke said. "The House told Gabrielle they were an accident and it wouldn't happen again." He narrowed his eyes at Lucy. "*You* are the House. *You* assured Gabrielle."

"And yet it did happen again." Capitano Cioni said. "Someone has compromised the auth line." He lifted his glass from the table and threw back the remnants of whiskey. "Lucy, can you reconfirm the line into the House for those three retirements? Angi and Daan and Eleonora. I'll validate the Palazzo side. Check the encryption protocols and transmission for any indicators of intervention or redirects."

"What about Pirrelli and Giordano?" Lucy asked, striding inside.

Cioni nodded. "I'll investigate their arriving before the Stuyvesants' retirements and advise you of my findings." He ran toward the duplex entry foyer.

"Capitano!" Smoke called after him. "I'm coming with you."

Chapter Thirty-Six

Smoke pulled on his shoes in the back of the town car beside the *capitano*.

"Where are we going?" he asked.

"To the Plaza."

Smoke automatically checked his wrist for the watch he'd left on his bedside table so many days before. Only a sliver of cold sun bounced through the street grid from the easterly horizon. He stifled a yawn.

"It can hardly be 5:30," he said.

"It's not. But Eleonora will receive us."

The *capitano* twisted in the back seat. Without reserve, he smoothed down the blonde curls of hair on Smoke's chest. Then he pulled the jacket lapels closed and thumbed the top buttons through their loops. "Your ancestry is northern Italian, not southern." He spread his hands across the ample chest to even out the creased linen. "I'll take you to my tailor in *Milano* when we've resolved this matter. Whoever you are using does no justice to the *mascolinità* of your torso."

"Why do you keep touching me?" Smoke asked.

Andrea shook his head. "*Sei così Americano.* Because you are my *fratello*, my brother, and I am Italian. Isn't that enough?"

Smoke considered that. "Yes," he said. "Yes, it is."

* * *

"Well." Eleonora pulled open the doors of her condo and welcomed them into the vestibule. "Two of my favorite men. And together. How delightful. Gentlemen, shall we retire to the main salon, or is this to be more of a boudoir conversation?" She tightened the sash of her dressing gown as she turned and walked across the hardwood parquet. A decadent crimson lace trailed behind her toned calves, made firm by the four-inch heels of her bedroom Manolo Blahniks.

Smoke could still taste the earthy flavor of the smooth, blood-red leather on his tongue. "Perhaps we should start in the salon," he suggested. "We've taken liberty to order coffee."

"Pastries too, I hope," she said. "You both know the ones I like."

Smoke scanned Andrea. Yeah. He could see that. And he should have guessed as soon as the concierge heralded them toward the elevator after sharing only their first names on the phone call up to Eleonora's condo.

They settled into the salon, tall windows showcasing the awakening morning view of Central Park.

"I trust you'll excuse my appearance," Eleonora said.

Smoke considered her perfect.

Both men took a seat on the settee. A server followed in their wake and poured *caffè* then placed a platter of *cornetto alla crema* on the burr walnut coffee table. They were silent until he exited the salon and pulled the door closed behind him.

Smoke didn't hesitate. "When did you know I'd been tasked with killing you?" he asked.

Eleonora selected a pastry and set it on an elegantly patterned Florentine plate. "Before you did, my darling."

Cioni visibly relaxed.

"And that didn't worry you?"

"Should it have?" She stirred her *caffè*, the teaspoon leaving a swirling trail through the crema as she lifted her cup. "Tommy. There is a reason I chose you for the task."

Smoke's breathing slowed, his attention tight on Eleonora.

"I've known what you're capable of since you were seventeen. And I'll freely admit you entranced me as the naivety and inexperience of your youth diminished with maturity. You became a man. More certain of how to handle yourself and those we placed in your path." She pursed her lips and gently blew across the crema before taking a sip. "You wouldn't have killed me."

"How can you be so certain?"

The *capitano* stretched and rested his arm along the back of the embroidered settee. He touched his finger just once to the scar at the back of Smoke's neck. Smoke nodded, understanding, recalling the document and photos detailing the most intimate moments of his life in Manhattan. As well as the sanctioned retirements.

Seventeen.

He thought back, way back, to the trees along Palisades Avenue in Riverdale. Down on his hands and knees, scooping away the soil. Placing Taylor in the hollow and pushing back the dirt to cover cheeks and lips still rouged from intimacy.

Months later, Hayden.

Years later, Morgan.

Was Eleonora aware of *those* kills? They had seemed random meetings, a small part of his maturation, filled with youthful promise, affection, and understanding. Discovery.

They had wanted to be killed and he had wanted to kill them, to experience the ultimate together. To satisfy a forbidden desire. But now he wondered if Taylor, and Hayden, and Morgan had been placed in his path on purpose. If he'd been placed in theirs. To direct his passions. To determine his limits. By either the House or the Palazzo. The Medici.

"There was always a tenderness about you," Eleonora said. "Both personally and professionally. I found it beguiling. No action was ever taken in malice, or without just cause. Or without request or acceptance by those you—" She turned thoughtful. Quiet. "—by those you touched. In every instance, you took the time needed by yourself and those in your charge to receive the desired consequence. To accept and appreciate resolution by either their own hand... or yours."

The room fell into silence except for the quiet echoing tick of a gilt bronze clock on the mantel, and the diminishing patter of rain against the windows.

"The order for your retirement didn't originate from the Palazzo," Cioni said.

Eleonora said, "No. It didn't."

Smoke leaned back into the settee, settling the nape of his neck against the warmth of Andrea's hand. "*You* ordered it, didn't you," he said quietly.

"The directive for Angi and Daan's retirement was a shocking error, its origin still to be determined by the Palazzo," Eleonora said. "And yet, knowing exactly how you operate, I knew they would have accepted it as warranted. That there must have been enough reason in their own minds to consent. To welcome it." She quieted, staring into the depths of her coffee. "Because of that, all I can say is I needed to meet you in person. Wanted to know who you really were, beyond the dossiers and photographs. To experience being with you. And to confirm my assumptions were not unjust."

Smoke wondered if he ever actually had a choice in his life. Or had his evolution been solely in the hands of the Medici since he was seventeen? Taylor, and Hayden, and Morgan's requests had seemed organic. A desire that was both surprising and liberating but natural in their search for intimate connection. And Angi and Daan. Angi had relaxed into the onyx tub, her last kiss with Daan enviable and passionate, an intimate exploration that was more than just physical. A hunger satiated when she held her husband's hand, welcoming the blade as he drew it across her throat.

Smoke was numb. Lost for words. He didn't know how he felt about his life, about his interactions with every person he'd encountered since becoming aware of himself and his passions. He pressed his knuckles to the bridge of his nose. "If you knew it was a sanctioned retirement, erroneous or not, why did you request the mayor's office review the case?"

"I didn't."

Smoke tried to recall exactly what Lucy had said. *"Our analysts have confirmed Eleonora di Toledo used her contacts in the mayor's office to request an inquest into the deaths of her niece and nephew-in-law."*

"Rafaella made that appeal," Eleonora said.

"Rafaella? She certainly didn't seem to care for them, the last I talked to her," Smoke said.

Eleonora skimmed a fingertip across the pastry cream and placed it between her lips. "She has her own way of handling upset. And of showing affection. Best to note her actions rather than her words. She loved them like a brother and sister and was devastated by their deaths. Did you not wonder why she joined with you at their home instead of one of her own?"

A blush heated Smoke's neck and face.

"Has the Palazzo made any discovery regarding the error of Angi and Daan's retirement?" Cioni asked.

Eleonora shook her head. "I've not yet received a straight answer from *Firenze*. They are still attempting to sort through their mess of communications. The usual chaotic Italian bureaucracy."

Smoke bit into a *cornetto*, biding his time though he wasn't hungry. "The three retirements that superseded yours' in priority…" He hesitated, his attention flicking from Eleonora to Cioni and back. He was just going to say it. "I'm aware Liz Bayer and Elgan Glyndwr were organizing themselves to blackmail the family, to go public with their knowledge of the Medici wealth if extorted funds were not forthcoming." He bit his lip, searching their faces for any reaction. There was none, and that bolstered his confidence to continue. "But why was a retirement order issued on Jameson De Vries?"

"It might be best for you both to accompany me to his life celebration this afternoon." Eleonora stood and held out her hand to Cioni. "His nephews are hosting in Dumbo, as Jameson's home is not in good order after recent activity." She raised an eyebrow as Cioni kissed her wrist, but her face softened when she turned to Smoke, a thoughtful smile on her lips. "The authorities wouldn't have any reason to pursue you in Brooklyn, would they, my darling?"

Chapter Thirty-Seven

"Andrea, *fratello*, when did you first sleep with Eleonora?"

Andrea's face creased in reminiscence. "I assure you, we didn't sleep. It was her fiftieth birthday weekend. An intimate affair at Hotel Danieli in Venice. I was nineteen and a more than willing lover."

"Do you think she's beautiful?"

"I do."

"So do I." Smoke hesitated, then placed his hand on Andrea's shoulder as they walked. There was a camaraderie he'd not felt before. A brotherhood he'd never expected. It was strange to him.

They hurried across 51st to beat the light. The asphalt was still slick from the rain but the clouds had dispersed, replaced by a bright blue sky, the honk of taxis redolent in the crisp air of the New York early morning as it sped up towards another brash New York day.

* * *

The Dumbo penthouse commanded from several stories above the tideline of the East River. Rising higher still before it, the towering Brooklyn and Manhattan Bridges framed the condo's dramatic panorama of Downtown

Manhattan. Multimillion-dollar views. Hundreds of millions. The city shimmered, underscored by its incessant rumble and the whistle of watercraft skimming across the waves.

Augusto and Felice hosted the gathering on their enormous rooftop terrace, the perfume of Neapolitan pizza wafting from the wood-burning oven straddled between the home's inside and outside kitchens. An entourage of servers held cocktail trays low as they mingled amongst the guests.

"It was an open casket," Gus said. "I'd say he looked quite happy, given the circumstances."

Smoke loosened the knot of his tie. He was wearing a suit, blacker than black, borrowed from one of Cioni's men, the cut a slimline Italian. A perfect fit, eyeballed and selected by the *capitano*.

"I hadn't expected to see you again," Felice said to him, holding out his hand to shake Smoke's. "And with a different di Toledo on your arm. You're aware I'm also a di Toledo?"

"Only by marriage," Gus said pointedly, pulling his husband to his side. "But, yes, Tommy, you're more than welcome to stay for a more intimate apéritif once our guests have gone."

Eleonora stood at the far edge of the terrace, beneath the shade of a potted magnolia, a robust discussion in English and Italian consuming several guests around her. Cioni hovered close at hand, the brim of a fedora pulled low against the top of his shades.

Rafaella approached and nudged her hip against Smoke's. "Good to see you inside something Italian again so soon." She palmed the solid curve of his butt cheek and slid her hand down into the deep tuck of precisely tailored cashmere. She knew his body as well as he knew hers. His flesh shivered and crawled and flushed despite his mistrust, despite Andrea's and Eleonora's words in her defense, despite his refusal to be aroused by her touch. Her presence. She brushed her lips against his ear. "Next time, I fuck you," she said, the words less than a whisper. Definitely inaudible to those around them. Definitely something, despite his reservations, he knew he'd consider. And already knew his answer.

Fuck. Why was he so fond of strong, decisive women?

"My condolences to you all," he said, shifting away from her toward their hosts. "Do the authorities still suspect it was anything other than an unfortunate accident?"

Gus shrugged.

"You said he was sad," Smoke said. "That he had been for a long time."

"We were all upset by Aunt Giulia's death. But it devastated Jameson. The wedding was the first time we'd seen him since the funeral last year."

Smoke nudged his shades higher up the bridge of his nose. He noticed the discussion beneath the magnolia in the corner was escalating into a heated argument.

"Whose wedding was it, anyway?" he asked.

Gus wrinkled his brow with the question, clearly confused at why Smoke didn't know. "You were at the wedding and didn't know whose it was?"

"You were at the wedding?" Rafaella asked. "Sorry I missed it, and an opportunity to know you sooner. But I had my distraction and upset to deal with. Two people I cherished had just died." Her face suddenly paled, and she locked her attention on Smoke. "You were at the wedding," she said again softly, thoughtfully. "Of course, you were."

He reached out and gently grasped her hand, fully aware of the reason behind its tremble, that she knew why he'd been at the wedding.

"It was Jameson's son Luca's wedding," Gus said, eyeing Smoke and Rafaella's interaction. "They'd considered delaying it because of Angi and Daan's deaths." He dropped his gaze and sucked in his lower lip. "But the family, and Jameson, were adamant they continue. We all needed the blowout. A bit of joy."

"I—" Smoke grasped for his bottle of San Pellegrino. "Jameson died on his son's wedding night?"

Gus nodded, glancing over at the brewing argument.

Smoke followed his line of sight, recognizing two in the crowd as the bride and groom from the Boathouse reception. Luca was not as tall as his father but still possessed a robust bearing and form. His features were dark, his eyes puffy with emotion, his jaw unshaven.

I killed Jameson on his son's wedding night. Smoke's heart felt hollow.

He glanced back at Rafaella. "Are you okay?" he mouthed.

She nodded vaguely, still deep in contemplation.

"Luca's bride, Hannah," Gus said, nudging Felice. "What's Hannah's last name? She didn't take De Vries."

"O'Donnell," Felice said as a server offered them slices of perfectly charred pizza laden with prosciutto and arugula.

Smoke's attention snapped between the pallid tone of Rafaella's face and Hannah's last name. And Lucy's.

Hannah bore the same coloring as Lucy, the same delicate frame, the same eyes. Was she also House?

"It's complicated," Lucy had said when he'd asked why she was at the wedding. He swallowed a mouthful of water, his thoughts tumbling.

A slap resounded from across the terrace. The sharp clap of an open hand against a cheek. Painful to the ears. Smoke immediately tensed, and strode toward the fray. Eleonora held her hand tight to her breast. Luca glared at her, resolute, rubbing his cheek and jaw, his other hand clenched in a fist at his side. Cioni had stepped in between them, but that only seemed to incense Jameson's son.

Smoke was at a full sprint toward them as Luca swung his fist in unapologetic, misdirected retaliation at Cioni. He slammed into Luca, the impact compressing Jameson's son between his and Cioni's larger bulks, the wind expunged from all their lungs in a deep and painful grunt. They held Luca tight in a secure embrace, even as he crumpled between them, dulled into a quiet sadness. Smoke felt pressure rising behind his eyes, as he confronted the pain he'd caused the man in his arms. But he kept his attention tight to Cioni across the curl of Luca's hair, willing himself to remain emotionless, despite what he had done.

"Later, *fratello*," Cioni mouthed. "Later."

Smoke sensed his brother knew his thoughts. His regret.

Hannah was soon at their side, leaning between them to whisper to her husband. They loosened their hold, letting go when Luca found his feet and silently embraced his wife.

Stepping back, Smoke pressed his lips tight, breathing heavily through his nostrils. He looked around for Rafaella. But she was no longer with Gus and Felice, no longer on the terrace.

Eleonora had retreated to the balustrade, visibly shaking. Smoke lifted two glasses of red from a waiter's tray and joined her.

"Would you like to talk about it?" he asked quietly, needing the distraction from his own thoughts and suppressed emotions.

She accepted a glass and nodded, turning from the other guests.

They looked out upon New York and the two bridges, their entire view. For several moments, there was only silence between them. "The city is different when you're on the outside looking in," Smoke said, resting his elbows on the balustrade. "I don't think tourists or transient business people can ever truly get it. Unless you've lived and worked in its guts, survived in its guts, you can only imagine what it might be like to experience." He lifted his face to the warm breeze coursing up the river from New York Harbor. It was salty on his lips.

"He didn't mean what he said. We've all lost someone we love."

Smoke cuddled her against him. "I'm sorry, Eleonora."

She grasped his fingers and pressed them to her lips. "Darling boy. No need to apologize."

"May I ask what he said?"

"He said he was glad Angi and Daan were dead. So that I might experience what he and Jameson went through with Giulia's death last year."

"Oh, I see."

A police siren reverberated along the street below, a blue and white patrol car bumping from the cobbles up onto the foreshore walkway. It came to a standstill in front of the parkland's antique carousel and two cops exited, their lapel radios squawking. Capitano Cioni gripped Smoke's elbow and gave him a nod. It was time to leave.

Smoke pondered Eleonora's words and the scene on the terrace as they descended to the basement parking. They were less than halfway down when he turned to Cioni. "Was Jameson part of the Palazzo counsel in *Firenze*? Could he have originated the retirements of Angi and Daan, of Gabrielle and me before his own?"

Chapter Thirty-Eight

Smoke sat with Cioni and Moretti amid the Gilded Age opulence of the New York Palace Hotel courtyard, antithesis to the majestic marble folly of St Patrick's Cathedral across the avenue.

"The family seems unaware of Aloïs' and Mathéo's deaths," Smoke said. "But Rafaella certainly realized I'm directly involved with Jameson's retirement. And probably the Stuyvesants'."

"Rafaella knows about the twins," Moretti said. "She's smart enough to keep quiet and let it play out. And she'll do nothing to implicate you further than you already are." The bruising on his neck had reduced to a dull shadow, the skin again tight along the edge of his jaw.

"Two of my men have already escorted their bodies back to *Firenze*," Cioni said. "The Palazzo will announce to the family when they see fit."

The remark caught Smoke and Moretti off guard. "How will they explain the twins' manner of death?" Moretti asked.

Cioni sipped his espresso before answering. "It won't be the truth. The truth is less than palatable. Less than ordinary. They'll choose something aligned to the decadence of their lifestyle. Perhaps a drug overdose on one of their yachts in

Portofino. The Palazzo will likely also ensure the *medico legale* investigation and official statement suggests their bankruptcy, that they lived beyond their means, with no evidence to the true value of…" He glanced at Moretti and raised an eyebrow. "… Their trust funds."

Smoke leaned back in his chair, lifting its front legs from the flagstones, and balancing a piccolo of dark roast at his knee.

"Does that mean I'm no longer wanted for their deaths?"

"No," Cioni said. "You're still very much the sole target of the local police investigation for all seven deaths. Lucy is monitoring her channels and can confirm. There are also recommendations for the case to be escalated to the federal level due to the Laurents' involvement." He hesitated. "That automatically brings the death penalty into the conversation. If caught, a conviction could incur decades of appeals just to keep you alive in prison. The situation is noisy and proving hard to contain."

Smoke rotated the piccolo in his hand. "Lucy said the House would swap out the seminal evidence with corrupted specimens from overseas."

Cioni tilted his head from side to side, as if weighing the options. "It's doubtful they'd recheck until requested during an active trial. Again, that could take months or years. Justice is exceedingly slow in this country. Especially if they already have someone behind bars who *might* have done it."

"Shit," Smoke muttered beneath his breath. He drained the last of his coffee. "I honestly don't believe I left cum at any of the kill sites, other than during that fiasco at The Hotel. But even so, how could they tie it to my identity when, per the House, I'm not in any official public DNA system?"

"That's a question for Lucy," Cioni said.

"What do you mean?"

"You need to ask Lucy. She should advise you."

"Andrea. I don't trust her. I need to hear it from you."

Cioni held his gaze for several moments before turning to Moretti. "Leave us, *per favore*." Simone left without questioning the *capitano's* request.

"The House and Palazzo Pitti continually sweep all criminal DNA databases, CODIS, et cetera, for profiles matching any of our operatives. The sweep corrupts the files in real time before they are available to judicial investigations."

"But?" Smoke asked.

Cioni nudged his chair closer to Smoke and lowered his volume to barely a whisper.

"A junior analyst at the NYPD, who the House should probably hire—or kill—put in a special request to the Department of Defense DNA registry. To determine whether any of the samples in evidence were on that database. Her profiling of the killer, *you*, suggested professional military with high-level negotiating skills to ensure death without attempts at retaliation."

"What is that registry?"

Cioni wiped at his mouth, leaving his hand loosely at his lips.

"It's a US federal database containing DNA sequences for all military personnel. Its primary purpose is to identify the remains of those killed in action. The US government would like to avoid burying soldiers as unknown in their ultimate place of rest."

"Why would my profile be in there?"

Cioni hesitated again, wetting his lips. "Because you are a US military asset, *fratello*. Or were, perhaps, only for a short time during the paper shuffle that placed you under the organizational structure of the House. It was an unfortunate shortcoming in the documentation cleanup protocol by that entity."

Smoke shook his head. "What do you mean? I'm not military. I have no military training."

"Tommy," Cioni said, using Smoke's name for the first time. "Look at yourself. Your physical regimen and its result. Your scholarships to Harvard and Georgetown and the skills you perfected. You've garnered the same work ethic, dedication, and instincts you would've if you'd attended West Point or *L'Accademia Militare di Modena*, but without the reliance on working as part of a team. The Palazzo, and by default, the House, needed you to be self reliant. Autonomous in carrying out your duties. You're an invaluable asset and individual to them in every sense."

Smoke considered this, working through his thoughts, his life, moving events around to make them make sense. He couldn't make it make sense. "But I work for the House. Surely that's a direct reference to the family. The Medici."

Cioni shook his head. "They are now more a corporate entity than a family. One based on shared affluence and, yes, documented purity of DNA. They were, and are still, instrumental in honing, placing, and compensating you for carrying out their requirements. For keeping their members in check. For neutralizing any threat of revealing their obscene wealth which could destabilize the economic world outside their bubble.

"But you should also know that others at a high level recognize the necessity of maintaining that stability, that secrecy. In the United States, Homeland Security oversees and coordinates any required action. Specifically, a department of the Secret Service under the auspices of the House. The White House."

Smoke dropped his chair back onto all four legs, incredulous, letting the information sink in, anxiously rotating the empty piccolo on his knee.

Cioni grabbed his hand to hold the glass still. "There is a lot of focus on this situation. From the top down. Not just because of the possible breach of the auth line, but because of who you work for. And despite any uncertainty you might have with Lucy—that I might have with Lucy and the House in general—she is more likely one of the few we can trust. She's saved your butt more times than you can ever possibly know."

"The White House," Smoke echoed. "So, I *am* one of the good guys."

"Of course you are, *fratello*. But good guys can still end up in jail. Can still end up dead."

Chapter Thirty-Nine

The buzzing vibration of his phone awakened Smoke from a fragmented, nightmarish slumber. He was still in the borrowed suit, sprawled across the top of his bed in the New York Palace Hotel. He lifted his face from the pillow to peek out through the open curtains. It was barely nighttime, the spires of St Patrick's Cathedral silhouetted against the lights of Fifth Avenue immediately behind it, and the pulsing, lurid glow of Times Square to the west.

He fumbled to pick up the phone.

"What the hell is going on?" came Rafaella's voice.

He yawned and rubbed at his eyes. "What do you mean?"

"It's one thing to promise away my property to a homeless guy, but now you have to clean up."

"Hey, you said it was okay." He raked his fingers through his hair, trying to catch up.

"He's dead, Tommy. Your little project is dead."

"*What*?" Smoke was wide awake now, scrambling off the bed.

"The authorities are unaware. Thank God. And based on the details my assistant gave me, it certainly wasn't natural. Not with that amount of blood. You need to handle it." She hung up.

It was a twenty-minute walk to the Hell's Kitchen studio apartment. Smoke made it in ten. He ran up the stairs. The familiar splayed wallpaper, the assaulting colors, and odors. The door to the studio was closed, the shattered jamb and lock unfixed. He hesitated at the threshold, then pressed his knuckles to the door and slowly nudged it open. He didn't need another body added to his count. Nervous bile washed the back of his throat. He could smell the sweet metallic stink of wet blood.

He flicked the light switch. The bulb immediately sparked, popped, and died. But the dull ambient glow from the far window was enough to make his heart sink as he stepped inside.

Nate lay stretched naked across the couch, his hair cropped of the matted street dreads, and his skin scrubbed almost raw to remove the Manhattan grime. It looked as if he'd been forcibly stripped, the remnants of clean, new clothes shredded and strewn across the floor. Electrical cords bound his wrists and ankles, still attached to a new toaster and iron. Smoke, horrified, couldn't look away. Mottled bruising and raw abrasions blemished Nate's handsome, clean face and torso. His groin, hands, and feet were black with coagulated blood, and the couch was stained dark beneath him.

"Who the hell would even think of doing this?" Smoke said, distracted by the bent and bloody knife and spoon on the coffee table.

They'd stripped several of Nate's toes of their flesh and nails, the bones crushed and snapped. Likewise, they'd broken four of Nate's fingers and a thumb, the skin flayed, degloved down to the knuckles, the bones within exposed. His lacerated foreskin appeared to be an afterthought, beyond the more rigorous torture at the extremity of his limbs.

Nate convulsed, sucking in a loud rattling breath, and twisting with an agonizing guttural grunting. He pushed up from the couch, and Smoke caught him before he could fall to the floor, holding him close. Shocked, Smoke fumbled to untangle the cords from Nate's hands and feet, his anguish and guilt overwhelming as Nate spasmed in his arms. He pulled out his cell and thumbed in *911*. The operator asked if there was blood. Yes, there was blood. A lot of blood. The police would accompany the ambulance. But he couldn't leave.

"Tom. I'm sorry," Nate moaned.

"Who did this?"

Nate shook his head. He didn't know. "I'm so sorry."

"You've nothing to be sorry for."

"They wanted to know where you were but I didn't know." Nate held up his hand before his face in disbelief, his cheeks ashen, paling further still.

Despite his momentary lucidness, Smoke sensed Nate's body was shutting down. And fast. He could only wonder at its ability to exclude the pain of such horrific physical trauma. He tenderly grasped the damaged hand and pulled it to his chest as the sound of sirens approached, echoing.

"So sorry…" Nate murmured. "They made me tell them,"

Smoke felt his own heart skipping its regular beat, perhaps attempting to stop outright in his chest. He could barely bring himself to speak. "What did you say?" he asked gently, already knowing the answer.

Sirens reverberated from the street out in front, the noise resonating through the walls of the building as the medics and authorities kicked open the front door five stories down. Then came the heavy footfall as they climbed the stairs.

Nate shuddered in Smoke's embrace, tears streaking the bloody smears across his cheeks. "I'm so sorry, Tom. I told them about Theo. That he lived somewhere in Park Slope with his moms." His eyelids wavered, his eyes rolling back beneath them. The medics and authorities were now halfway up the five-story walk-up, the squark of radios approaching.

Anger welled in Smoke's gut. Not at Nate, but at himself, and at whoever had done this to his friend, and now knew about the existence of his son. He had to go. He had to go now. Holding Nate's face gently in his hands, their foreheads touching, his voice was merely a hoarse rasp. "Stay with me, Nate. Stay with me." Smoke looked from the studio door to the window, his frightened frustration mounting. "Please forgive me, but I've got to go," he said. "The medics will be here any second. Can you hear them on the stairs? Are you okay to be here for just a moment on your own? Just one moment. I promise…"

Nate nodded. "I am very brave."

"That you are, my beautiful friend." Smoke pressed his lips to Nate's wet cheek, tasting the salt of blood and tears, then scrambled across the furniture to the window.

Chapter Forty

The window sash slammed open with the force of his shoulder, and he climbed out past it to swing down onto an exposed sewerage pipe below. The torn insulation covering it was slippery under his brogues and he skidded, his balance thrown, and fell several feet before hooking an arm behind more plumbing on the way down. He winced at the rip of muscle in his shoulder, but the force was not enough to dislocate his arm, not enough to make him care about it. He held himself there precariously to catch his breath, willing the pain to subside. The shout of the medics echoed from the studio above into the tight confines of the alleyway.

Then came the high-pitched squeal of a defibrillator.

"Clear!" a medic called.

"Oh, fuck," Smoke muttered to himself, squeezing his eyes shut. "Come on, buddy. Come on."

Again, the defibrillator screamed.

"Clear!"

The beat of Smoke's heart was loud in his head as it thudded against his temples.

"Pulse! Good to go. On my count. One, two, three…"

Smoke lowered himself down the pipework to the next level, where he could secure a handhold on a window frame and jutting brickwork. He half-climbed, half-fell the remaining stories toward the bottom of the alley, finally tumbling onto a heaping mound of trash that defined the space from edge to edge. Cans. Bottles. Boxes. Food scraps. Rats stood on their hind legs, watching him from atop the rotting topography. They were defiant, daring him to approach. Smoke carefully crawled across the soggy, loose trash, skirting the rodents, until he found his footing on the far side of the heap. By the back door of a kitchen stood a chef, the black-and-white houndstooth pattern of his pants more a black-and-greasy-gray. He dragged on a cigarette held between pudgy nicotine-stained fingers as he glanced up at the open window, then at Smoke, before jerking his head toward the kitchen door for Smoke to go through.

Smoke tapped his Bluetooth earbud and hit the speed dial on his phone, at a dead run before he was even halfway through the filthy kitchen. He blurred past stunned patrons amid their pad thai and massaman curry to burst out the restaurant's front door onto 45th Street. Amongst the traffic. Vehicles honked and spewed fumes. He tried to flag down a taxi, whistling and waving. But in a city with ten thousand yellow cabs, there wasn't a single one empty on this block. Not one. The phone kept ringing in his ear.

"Come on, Pick up, pick up."

He turned on his heel and sprinted east, sticking to the blacktop, his hand raised to attract a cab, picking up his pace as he approached Broadway. Car horns continued blaring in his wake.

The phone went to voicemail.

"You've reached Dannii, Jenny, and Theo. You've got this."

"Get out of the brownstone. Get out now. Do what we said last summer. Please Dannii. Please, please, please."

Smoke tapped his earbud. "Fuck!" he yelled at the top of his lungs, exasperation mounting as he curved onto Broadway into the guts of Times Square, straight into traffic. Cars, buses, trucks, occupied cabs, and people jammed the *Crossroads of the World*. All at a standstill. Mesmerized by the vast wattage rising multiple stories all around them. Witches, and lions, and flying carpets. Brilliant and brash. The heartbeat of Manhattan. There was no way he was going to catch a cab here. No matter how many there were.

He slammed his fist against the hood of a limousine as he crossed in front of it, taking no heed of the driver's eloquent vernacular or the people he shouldered to get through the crowd. Two cops on horseback surveyed his trek through the milieu of tourists and scraggy cartoon characters but did nothing beyond lifting their radios to their mouths.

The gun-barrel view down Broadway stretched diagonally through the bowels of Manhattan toward Downtown. He dodged the traffic on 42nd as he crossed it without bothering to look. He waved when a cab heading toward him flashed its lights. But the vehicle swerved around him without stopping. He couldn't depend on them. He increased his speed, running along Broadway's bike lane, slamming his feet against the tar as he crossed street after street—41st, 40th, and 39th—in quick succession. Red lights, green lights, he didn't care. He kept running without slowing. He knew he *could* run to Park Slope in Brooklyn, but also that he'd never get there in time. His mind spun. Emotions bubbled. Then he tapped his Bluetooth earbud three times.

The call went through immediately.

"I need your help," he yelled above the honking traffic. A sharp twinge of pain struck from his heel up his leg into his hip. "They found out about Theo. They found out about my son."

There was a contemplative silence on the line as Smoke jumped the curb and slammed into the side of a Jeep Grand Cherokee that had lurched to a stop in front of him. He sidled around it and kept running.

"Where are you now, *fratello*?"

"On foot, heading south on Broadway, coming up on Macy's.

"Where do you need to go?"

"Park Slope."

"*Cazzo!* Keep this channel open. I'm on my way."

Smoke focused on the lights of the Macy's marquee a few blocks ahead, pushing aside the agonizing pain of his heel, concentrating on the form of his motion, the pump of his arms and legs, the steady breath in and out, in and out, aware of the traffic coursing alongside him, the lights of Macy's pulling him forward.

The traffic light ahead was about to change. Red. He didn't care.

He sprinted across 35th, a fender glancing his thigh before he hit Herald Square in front of the world-famous department store, almost twisting his ankle with the change in the pavement. Tourists and shoppers scattered out of his way before he swerved sideways to run amongst the moving traffic of 6th Avenue, squeezing between bus and truck to get back onto the diagonal of Broadway.

A cop car flashed its lights and pumped its siren once as Smoke passed before it, but otherwise ignored him.

"Where are you?" he yelled.

"Just pulling out of the garage. You?"

"I'll hit Madison Square Park in a few minutes. If you come straight down Fifth Avenue, we should collide. If you're fast enough. Otherwise, I'll be south of the park continuing along Broadway."

Smoke winced with the intensifying discomfort from his heel. He shifted his gait, landing on his forefoot instead of his heel with each stride. It wasn't as efficient, but at least it kept him moving.

"Four more blocks and I'm there, *fratello*. Be ready to take over. This Monster lives up to its name, but you'll be able to handle it."

Cioni swerved the Ducati onto the plaza at the Flatiron Building. Smoke, running the center line of Broadway, crossed 25th Street at the same instant and slid onto the Monster's leather saddle in front of the *capitano*. He immediately gunned the accelerator.

"Thank you," Smoke yelled over his shoulder, his voice broken and hoarse with lack of breath, the words amplified through the open Bluetooth channel.

"You should have confided in me."

Smoke didn't answer.

They white-lined through the traffic on Broadway, Smoke's attention firmly on Theo, wondering about Nate's torturers and how fast they might determine his son's location. He ignored the brakes as they crossed street after street, the Monster gaining momentum, its engine loud and reverberating within the canyons of Broadway.

Instead of following the street traffic around Union Square, he punched the machine up onto the pavers and coursed head-on through the greenery and merchant stalls scattered through the park, before swerving onto 4th toward the Bowery. It was a one-way avenue for several blocks. The wrong way.

That's when the sirens started. Blue and white NYPD cruisers appeared from multiple directions, thumping across the curbs, and screeching from side streets. Cars burned rubber and swerved into the gutters to stay clear of the pursuit.

"Bridge or tunnel?" Cioni yelled over the Bluetooth.

"Bridge."

"Which one?"

"Manhattan—it's the most direct."

He sped faster, the Monster's vibration adrenaline-pumping, its growl deafening.

Cioni glanced over his shoulder at the police vehicles. There were now six, sirens whooping and stuttering. Two more veered across the intersection at Houston, stopping all traffic from crossing their course. "Do you have a backup route their vehicles can't follow?"

Smoke fought off the growling ache in his skull. His hands and fingers were numb from clenching the grips. "There's only one."

"Good! Take it!"

Instead of turning onto the ramparts of the Manhattan Bridge, Smoke swung the Ducati south, directly past New York Police Headquarters, beneath the colossal archway of the Municipal Building, and up onto the pedestrian concourse of the Brooklyn Bridge. The machine rattled across the boards of the walkway several yards above the gridlocked roadway. Cioni's grip tightened around Smoke's waist, the two men fitted to each other, his body hard against Smoke's back. The machine's front wheel threatened to lift as the back wheel thrust them forward and Smoke guessed they were doing 150 miles per hour, faster than the speedometer—in kilometers—could register. Tourists and locals pressing against the walkway's balustrade were a frightened blur and the bridge cables were a vibrating hum as they covered the stretch from Gothic arch to Gothic arch in seconds. He pulled back on the throttle only when the path narrowed and rapidly curved down into the cobbled streets of Dumbo.

"Lights off, slow down, stick to the back streets, if you can," Cioni said.

Smoke reluctantly tempered their speed, his heart racing. He needed to be at the brownstone already but was also frighteningly aware he wouldn't make it if intercepted by the police. He double-tapped his earbud and rang Dannii a second time. Still no answer. He tapped back to Cioni.

"Andrea, they aren't answering. They always answer me."

Chapter Forty-One

The lights were blazing on all three levels of the Park Slope brownstone. Smoke switched off the Monster's engine upon approach and rolled the machine down the laneway behind the building and into the underground garage. Two cars were parked, which made him hopeful but wary. He rang Dannii's phone again. Still there was no answer.

Cioni pulled out his Walther PPK and handed it to him.

"What about you?" Smoke asked.

The *capitano* stretched his hands out before him and cracked his knuckles. Smoke got the idea.

They reached the first floor and already they were too late. The living room furniture was askew but intact, other than the shattered glass coffee table. But there was no blood. Not like the studio in Hell's Kitchen. Jenny and Dannii lay unconscious amongst the debris and disheveled sofa cushions, with no immediate signs of physical trauma or torture. Smoke stooped to check for pulse and breath, scanning the room and stair treads leading up to the first landing.

Cioni lifted a vial from amongst the remains of the coffee table. "Rohypnol," he whispered, tossing it to Smoke. He noted the multiple syringe stab wounds along Dannii's biceps, and Jenny's. The floorboards above them creaked.

"Is there more than one staircase?" Cioni asked.

Smoke shook his head. "Not inside. There's an old fire escape out the back. We'd hear if anyone lowered it."

They climbed the stairs. The second and third floors were clear. No sign of Theo. No sign of anyone.

Smoke was doing everything he could to hold it together, but still his breathing had become labored, his sight blurred. He settled himself, concentrating.

"It's you they want, *fratello*. Your son is just a means to an end."

"You think they won't hurt him?"

"They could've killed the two downstairs, but didn't."

"They mutilated Nate. He almost died. He still might."

"Nate?" Cioni asked, his brow knotted.

Smoke ran back down the stairs, favoring his left foot. "I need to call an ambulance."

"No. Call Lucy. She has secure resources to handle this."

Smoke made the call, hunkering down onto the floor and pulling Dannii into his lap.

Cioni squatted beside him and checked on Jenny, his fingertips at her neck to ensure her pulse remained strong. He pulled a lounge cushion beneath her head.

"Is that Theo's mother?" he said, motioning to Dannii.

"They both are."

Cioni nodded. "You should have confided in me. I should have been aware of Theo before it came to this."

"How do you know that wouldn't have brought this on sooner? You said to trust no one, and I did exactly that—"

"You did trust someone. Tell me about Nate."

Smoke rubbed at his face. "He's a stranger. A homeless man I met in the park, and he's the only one I've ever told about Theo. I needed someone I could talk to. Someone without ulterior motives, someone I didn't need to second guess, or withhold the most important aspect of my life from.”

“You could have talked to me.”

“I know that now, but I didn’t then. Nate was who I needed exactly when our paths crossed.”

“You said someone hurt him.”

“Mutilated him.” The blood drained from Smoke’s face as he thought of Nate crumpled across Rafaella’s sofa. “Whoever did it didn’t seem to care he is also a human being.”

“Tell me exactly what they did to him. Be specific.”

“Nothing short of torture. They degloved several of his toes and fingers. And made a crude attempt at a back alley circumcision.”

Cioni stiffened at Smoke’s words.

“Apart from valid religious covenant, a cut that simply proves dominance over another when they have no power to object. No power to preserve the integrity of their own body,” Cioni said, his disgust and anger clear on his face.

Several black SUVs and vans pulled up outside the brownstone.

“You know who did it,” Smoke said.

Chapter Forty-Two

"Is there anything else we don't know? *Anyone* else we need to cover?" Lucy's voice was calm, but her fingertips were red with her tense grip on an electronic tablet.

Cioni hunkered down in the back of the van, texting on his cell.

"No," Smoke said. "You know everything now."

"The damage to your friend in Hell's Kitchen was one of Pirrelli's trademarks before the Palazzo recruited him," Cioni said, joining them.

"The degloving?" Lucy asked.

"Yes. That and the genital mutilation."

Lucy flicked through the screens on her tablet. "The surgeon's primary concern is Nate's fingers. The damaged toes are a complete write-off, and the foreskin injury has been deemed cosmetic. He'll need multiple surgeries but should come through. Physically, at least." She read on in silence. "His work history is impressive, actually."

"Is Pirrelli responding to your texts?" Smoke asked Cioni, agitated, tapping his fingers against the seat.

"No. Nor Giordano."

The van plunged into the tunnel beneath the East River, with its echoing reverberation from hundreds of vehicles, its ambient stink of gasoline fumes.

Smoke ran his fingers through his hair and down the back of his neck. Pressing the scar on his nape.

"What about—" he started, but Cioni shook his head.

"What about what?" Lucy asked, looking up from the tablet.

"What about the rest of the *Ruspanti*?" Smoke adlibbed.

"Innocenti and Sangallo are secure in *Firenze*," Cioni said. "They won't be returning. Conti and Amidei are cleaning up at Elgan Glyndwr's residence in Montclair. There was far more compromising information stored there than originally thought."

The van rose out of the tunnel to skim along the western edge of the Financial District, One World Trade dominating the view through the side window.

"You should advise your field office there'll be a gas leak and explosion at Glyndwr's New Jersey address in the coming hours," Cioni said. "We'll contain the blast and there should be minimal peripheral damage beyond the property line."

"Do you suspect collusion in your team beyond Pirrelli and Giordano?" Lucy asked.

"No," Cioni said. "Though I'll personally interrogate and debrief each of my men individually. Those two are the newest members, with just under five years' tenure. The others I've known since we were children. Brothers in every sense of the word, except parentage. Until this evening, I would've trusted all my men with my life. Now—" He was thoughtful. "I still trust the original core team."

"What reason did Pirrelli and Giordano give you for their early arrival in the US?" Lucy asked.

Cioni held her gaze. "They were on their own time and claimed vacation. I had no reason to doubt them. They've always been open about their relationship and passion for travel. But I agree the 'coincidence' is far from reassuring. Especially after tonight's events."

"Where would they have taken Theo?" Smoke asked.

Cioni's face softened. "I don't know, Tommy."

Smoke stretched, pressed a hand against the van's ceiling, the other against the side of his head, cracking the bones in his neck. "Am I able to return to my condo?" he asked.

"Which one?" Lucy asked pointedly.

"Jane Street."

"Only for a quick in-and-out. Why?"

"I need my watch and my weapons."

Chapter Forty-Three

Smoke climbed back into the van at the curb of Jane Street. The cut of the borrowed Italian suit was closefitting, but adequate to hide the additional bulges below each breast and in the small of his back that supplemented his natural musculature.

"Anything?" he asked, sliding in next to Lucy.

"We've looped in Moretti. He's checking with his handler for any intel or chatter hitting their Euro contacts." Lucy scanned her tablet. "The House and Palazzo Pitti data analysts have proven your theory correct. Jameson did instigate the retirement of Angi and Daan. We suspect it was a misplaced retaliation against Eleonora. He blamed her for Giulia's death, despite copious evidence of his wife's betrayal of the family."

Smoke furrowed his brow.

"Giulia was about to funnel $700 million into child welfare and cancer research with no attempt at obfuscation. A good cause, yes, but she meant to expose her wealth and the wealth of the Family for her own personal benefit. She was aware her actions would endanger the Family's existing— *anonymous*—support for those same causes. Decades of support in far greater monetary value than her token amount. Many tens of billions in support."

"What did she want?"

Lucy pressed her lips together. "Giulia deemed tickets to the Metropolitan Museum Gala as more important than the family's anonymous donations."

"Tickets to the Gala," Smoke echoed.

"There is more to it that I'm not sanctioned to tell you. But believe me, the details are heinous and involve trafficking more than just Gala tickets. Let me just say she has never had the interests of children at heart in any of her dealings."

Given the high-level details, any qualms Smoke might have had about his involvement in her retirement dissolved.

"And," Smoke pressed, "in his position, Jameson would've been aware of myself and Gabrielle assisting his wife on the GWB. Can we also assume he incited the twins and their attempt at redemption? Targeting Gabrielle and me in the street?"

Lucy nodded. "We're still documenting the electronic trail, but it's now clear he heavily influenced that decision to approval. The analysts also believe he may have hired Pirrelli and Giordano as back-up, in case the twins failed their assignment."

"Any evidence of that?" Cioni asked.

"Funds from one of Jameson's investments are currently sitting in a Caymans escrow account, awaiting disbursement upon task completion."

"How does that link to any of my men?"

"He titled the account *Gian Gastone - Fumo la pensione*."

Cioni looked out through the windshield, the knot at his brow twisting.

"*Fumo la pensione…*" Smoke said. "That's a direct reference to my retirement, but who is Gian Gastone? How does he tie to Pirrelli and Giordano?"

Cioni slammed his fist against the door of the van. "Gian Gastone de' Medici," he said, "was Tuscany's last grand duke and *purebred* Medici. The architect of the *Ruspanti* back in the 1700s for his personal service. A vile individual in every way, with a penchant for young blonde men." He glanced at Smoke. "He paid hundreds of them in coins— *ruspi*—for their virility, something he was sorely lacking. The demise of his seed line went unmourned when he finally succumbed in 1737."

Smoke flinched at the number. Suite 1737 at The Hotel.

"It's beyond our resources to determine the next leg of this money transfer, but it seems a clear link." Lucy dropped her device onto the bench seat beside her and blew her hair out of her eyes. "There's €2 billion sitting there awaiting confirmation of task completion. It's excessive, but I guess everyone has a price."

"Yes, but not everyone's price is money," Smoke said.

"Theo is our priority, Tommy," Cioni said, touching Smoke's knee with his own. "We've released your cell phone number on all channels. If Pirrelli and Giordano are monitoring, they'll soon make contact."

"By default, the NYPD has also received it," Lucy said.

"Unfortunate," Smoke said. "How long before they might get authorization to triangulate my location?"

"They could have approval within the hour, but it's still a complicated process. The House will work to delay it as much as we can."

The van was headed uptown to be centrally located on the island, ready to go in any direction.

"How are Dannii and Jenny?" Smoke asked.

"Conscious and upset, as you can imagine. Once our medics give the all clear, we'll move them to a safe house. Most likely at the US Naval Observatory in D.C. to get them right out of the way. How much are they aware of your activities?"

"They aren't. All they know is I deal with corporate assholes who might retaliate. They figured that was expected in the business districts of this city."

Smoke's cell vibrated. He squinted at the number, then wiped the sweat from his palm and hit the speaker icon.

"Simone, what've you got?" he asked.

"Pirrelli and Giordano left a message at the hotel reception," Moretti said. "They're at The Campbell Apartment."

"We're on our way." Smoke ended the call.

Lucy leaned forward to direct the driver. "Grand Central Terminal. Drop us on Vanderbilt at 42nd."

Smoke's thoughts were running, second guessing their plan. He checked his watch. "That bar will be crowded with late night suits." His thoughts flashed to Liz and Julianne.

"They need you dead to collect," Lucy said. "A crowded bar is not an optimal location for a hit and run. Nor for a three-year-old."

Smoke pressed his clenched fists to his mouth, thinking how this could play out. "Can the House take control of all cameras throughout Grand Central Terminal? Not just to monitor and direct us, but also to stop recording? The NYPD already has too much evidence on me. We don't need to hand them audiovisuals of me killing two more."

Chapter Forty-Four

Moretti slid into the back seat of the van as it idled on Vanderbilt. He brushed the first drops of evening rain from his jacket, the damp buzz of the city reverberating in the confines of plush leather before he closed the heavy bulletproof door behind him.

Cioni was conferring with Lucy as Moretti settled in. "*Bene,*" the *capitano* said before letting out a deep breath and addressing them all. "It's just the four of us. No physical backup. If we fuck it up, then we wear it. I'll open a group conversation on my cell. Lucy will liaise with the House and advise on any remote support they might afford us, as well as convey real-time data on the activity of local authorities." He locked eyes with her and nodded. "Moretti, follow Lucy's lead into the main concourse. Ensure the service elevator to the bar is clear. Smoke and I will meet you both in the bar's foyer."

Moretti and Lucy exited the van. The *capitano* turned his back to the soundproof glass separating them from the driver to face Smoke. "There are few who wouldn't be enticed by the bounty on your head," he said. "And Lucy's assumption does not limit that temptation to Pirrelli and Giordano. If you see any of my men here, know it is not by my order. Also, be aware that per Palazzo nomenclature, the term *Ruspanti,* derogatory or not, applies to all involved in carrying out retirement directives. That includes yourself and Lucy, Moretti, and his handler. *Capito*?"

Smoke nodded.

Cioni clapped a hand onto Smoke's shoulder, then slid it up to the soft, close-cropped bristle at the back of his scalp. His face relaxed into a thoughtful smile.

"I look forward to meeting my brother's son."

* * *

The four of them double-tapped the Bluetooth channel open on their earbuds, sound-checked, and then climbed the stairs into The Campbell Apartment. The bar was pure Florentine palazzo grandeur. The gold-toned shimmer of brass sconces highlighted dark paneled walls, and iridescent frosted panes of leaded glass windows rose dozens of feet to an elaborate hand-painted ceiling. A winged lion embossed the stone chimney and fireplace beyond the long bar staffed by Versace-vested bartenders and stacked with shelves of high-end wines and liquors.

There were at least fifty suits crowded into the space. Standing room only. Even more up on the mezzanine level. The buzz of conversation and laughter was loud, hovering above the scent of perfumes and anxious sweat from long hours in Midtown offices. The intoxicating stink of pheromones, mixed with bourbon and brandied cherries, subtly bolstered the atmosphere.

Smoke pressed through the crowd, the glint of eye, the friendly flash of teeth, the lick of lip, the bite of cherry or olive a temptation by bargoers wanting more than to catch the next train home to their cat. Or their roommate. Or their family. Or no one at all. He doubted they'd be wearing those flirtatious smiles if they knew a *chance* brush of a knuckle against the hard bulge in his pants was actually against the length of a Glock 19.

He spied one of the *Ruspanti* at the far end of the bar.

"Which one is that?" he asked, loud enough for the earbud to pick up, catching Cioni's attention through the crowd and motioning with his chin.

"Pirrelli."

"Is he the alpha of the two?"

"No. He's not."

Smoke scanned the crowd and up toward the mezzanine.

"I don't see Giordano. Anyone?"

The other three responded in the negative.

He maneuvered through the crowd until he was against Pirrelli. Eye to eye. The *Ruspanti's* breath suggested at least one Manhattan had crossed his thin lips. He leaned in close to Smoke and sniffed, his forehead and cheeks sheened with oil, the tight pores of his nose plugged with tiny blackheads.

"You smell like trash, mister *Americano*," Pirrelli said, accentuating the word *trash* with a practiced Manhattan drawl.

Smoke slid his hand down into his pants pocket and pressed in hard against Pirrelli. "And I understand you have a thing for foreskins. I'm quite happy to blow a hole through this suit to separate you from yours. Though I'd probably destroy more than just the skin."

Pirrelli smirked. He looked past Smoke, then returned his attention to him. "Do that and your *bambino* mamas will definitely see your son again. One chunk at a time. Hand delivered over the next several years on the anniversary of his papa's death. *Nota bene*, that doesn't mean he'll be dead when we select and wrap the little gifts each year."

Smoke shook with barely contained anger. His finger was on the trigger, tensed and wanting nothing more than to squeeze it all the way. The heat of Cioni and Moretti nudged in close behind him.

"*Fratello*," Cioni said quietly, touching his knuckles to the small of Smoke's back. Despite the noise of the bar, the *capitano's* single word resonated loud and clear through the earbud.

Smoke released his pressure on the trigger but kept his grip on the weapon, pressing the muzzle firmly into the *Ruspanti*'s gut.

"What now?" Cioni said to Pirrelli.

The *Ruspanti* winked at his *capitano*, leaned against the bar, and lifted a hand to the bartender. "I'm going to stand right here and enjoy another Manhattan." He bent his arm to read the G-Shock Military watch on his wrist. "It's fortuitous there are four of you. I believe Grand Central Madison has four platforms. You'll want to have them all covered within the next, oh, five minutes."

Smoke was reticent to leave the bar without putting a bullet through Pirrelli's head, but knowing he'd do just that before the evening was over. He pushed backward, away from the *Ruspanti*'s oily sneer, between the bulks of Cioni and Moretti and into the crowd toward the door. He took no mind of social graces as he shouldered and elbowed people out of the way. Held no concern for their shocked looks, for the vodka and vermouth with twists of lemon sloshing from shallow cocktail glasses.

The other three barreled along in his wake.

"Lucy!" Cioni's voice echoed across the Bluetooth. "Is Grand Central Madison on the same security system as Grand Central Terminal?"

Smoke slammed through the entrance door of the bar out onto Vanderbilt Avenue, turning on his damaged heel to swing back in through the main doors into the terminal. The others close behind.

"Checking with the House," Lucy said, static breaking up her words.

The four of them crossed the upper mezzanine and descended the marble stairs to the main concourse with the same urgent cadence, the starred turquoise barrel vault curving twelve stories above them. Smoke hadn't been to Grand Central Madison, and didn't know its layout, or exactly where it was. All he knew was *down*. At least seventeen stories down, maybe more, below the more familiar Grand Central Terminal.

He hit a step on his damaged heel. His ankle gave out, and he went sprawling down the last few marble steps and across the floor. But just as quickly he was yanked back onto his feet by Cioni and Lucy, and pulled forward alongside them. The pain at his heel was less than tolerable, the pad bruised, cracked and raw, hardly cushioning the bone as he slammed his feet against the floor with each stride, taking another turn to leap down the next flights of stairs toward the terminal's dining concourse.

"Madison has its own independent systems, with video streaming to a monitoring station in Brooklyn," Lucy said. "My guys are working to access and deactivate. Hopefully, takeover."

The lights flickered as they ran down the single flight of escalators beneath the signage for the Long Island Railroad and Madison Concourse. They skidded from the marble onto terrazzo flooring.

"Take a hard right north," Lucy said in their ears.

Smoke rounded the corner between bulky columns to see the concourse of Grand Central Madison for the first time. It stretched at least a quarter mile ahead to 48th Street. Six Manhattan blocks, maybe more—further than his eyes could focus.

"Shit," he said.

Cioni and Moretti echoed his observation in Italian.

Hundreds of commuters idled, sauntered, or rushed throughout the concourse. Most lingered at the farthest end.

Points of colored tile and light punctuated the vast length of cool gray tones. Subtle hues of green, blue, purple, and cyan. Each point presumably designated exits to the grid of streets above ground and the banks of escalators descending hundreds of feet further down into the solid bedrock of Manhattan schist.

Smoke noted the distance to the first light, and increased his speed, favoring his heel, pushing through the pain, aware of the blood squelching beneath his sole and between his toes within the leather of his shoes. He bit the inside of his cheek against the throbbing discomfort.

The lights along the concourse abruptly extinguished, leaving them in pitch dark. Then the drone of air conditioning halted and the cool flow of air stopped. Smoke kept running, the others in his wake, not caring if he knocked a stray commuter to the ground, guided by the small pin-pricks of red light from the security cameras spread along the dead straight route.

Then they too blinked out.

Chapter Forty-Five

"We'll hit the first access point in twenty more strides," Smoke yelled into the darkness without slowing, closing his eyes to concentrate on the movement of his body and the direction, his hands outstretched before him. He slammed into commuters, unseen in the dark, barreling them out of his way, out of the course of those running just as blind in his wake. "Lucy, have you been here before? Do you know the layout?"

"The first bank of escalators will be on the right. They're steep, going down another nine or ten stories, at least 180 feet long. It's a couple of minutes ride."

"We won't be standing still for it," he yelled, his own voice resonating in his earbud.

Half the length of a football field, at a dead run downhill in total darkness.

"*Che cazzo!*"

Moretti said it, but Smoke knew they all thought it.

"The House is working on restoring the lights," Lucy said.

Smoke slowed through the inky blackness, his arms out to his sides, grabbing hold of Moretti, then Lucy, then Cioni in quick order. They veered to the right in a tight cluster.

"There should be four or five escalators per bank," Lucy said. "Only two or three in each bank will be descending."

Smoke skimmed his hand along the wall. He couldn't hear the mechanical noise he'd expected.

"Here. They're off," he yelled, feeling for the first set of rubber handrails, then grabbing the next, and blindly jettisoning himself down the steep set of treads. The steps rattled and clanged beneath his footfalls. He could hear the measured breathing of the others echoing around him in the escalator shaft, plus resonating across the earbud, but he wasn't certain who was who in the darkness. His damaged foot was now numb and raw, beyond any threshold of pain, but holding true with the effortless motion honed during marathons in New York, Boston, London, and Rome. Fortified further by a brutal marathon last year up Pike's Peak in Colorado. But that had been uphill. This was down—which he'd definitely not trained for. His quads twitched and burned. And screamed.

"What happens at the bottom?" Moretti yelled, in between loud breaths. His words bounced against the curve of the ceiling above them.

"There's a mezzanine in the first cavern, perpendicular to this descent," Lucy said, sounding uncertain. "There'll be stairs or maybe more escalators to the island platforms and dual tracks above and below it. The mezzanine level will also access a second cavern directly beyond the first. It should be straight ahead. And it will have the same island platform configuration. Above and below."

Cioni called it: "O'Donnell first up. Moretti first down. Smoke second up. Cioni second down."

The lights abruptly ratcheted on, and the escalators surged with a grating mechanical shudder. They were all thrown forward with the change in momentum, shoulders and knees taking the brunt of the impact as they awkwardly tumbled down the steep decline, colliding with the sharp edge of the corrugated metal treads. Smoke twice caught the underside of his chin as he toppled, the treads cutting deep into his stubbled flesh, scoring the bone at the underside of his jaw down to the marrow. He ended his fall at an awkward slant, his legs angled above him before he rolled to regain his footing and continue the run down. The others were also back on their feet, Lucy sliding across the metal balustrade onto the steps behind him as her original escalator now chugged upward.

He struck the mezzanine, pushing forward through the first cavern into the second, and quickly hobbled up the steps to the platform between tracks 203 and 204. Pressing his hand to his throat did little to stop the flow of blood from the gash, the front of his shirt and jacket saturated a dark glossy crimson. He was light-headed, his vision a blur.

Smoke didn't know what he expected on the platform, but he knew instantly he'd made a mistake.

Giordano stood a few yards from the top of the stairs, recognizable from their meeting on the cocktail patio of St Bart's. And it was his suit he had borrowed and was now wearing. Smoke had barely loosed the Glock from his pocket when the first bullet slammed into his chest with a cracking, wet thump.

A second instantly followed.

He was knocked backward with the force, his arms limp and twisted as he slammed onto the terrazzo, the air forced from his lungs with a grunt, his skull smashing against the stone with an unsettling hollow crack.

The *Ruspanti* approached and stood over him, his Walther PPK the only thing Smoke could see through his bloody blur. Giordano squeezed the trigger a third time; the bullet thudding into the bloody, ripped swell of Smoke's breast.

Chapter Forty-Six

Cioni plodded up the stairs, his arms wide, his hands open, his weapon dangling from his pinky by the trigger guard. The lights of the platform flickered, the few visible commuters urgently scattering toward the far end of the platform, away from the commotion. Their frantic footfalls echoed along the cavern.

"*È stato facile, fratello*," Cioni said to Giordano. "Much easier than we expected." He chuckled. "*Americanos*." He flipped the pistol and pushed it into the holster beneath his jacket. Nudging Smoke's hip with the tip of his boot, he pulled out his phone and snapped photos. "O'Donnell is dead," he said without emotion as he thumbed a text and pressed the "send" icon. "But we should get out of here before the House turns the security cameras back on, or the station master realizes they've lost control of their systems."

"What about Simone?" Giordano asked, checking the clip, then casually wiping his weapon with a microfiber cloth and securing it behind his lapel.

Cioni shrugged. "One less to share the money with." He eyed Giordano. "Have you given my last texts any more thought, Dante?" He reached up and caressed Giordano's cleanly shaven cheek with the palm of his hand. The

Ruspanti closed his eyes and shivered as he leaned into the gentle touch.

"I have, Andrea." He opened his eyes, his attention hovering upon the *capitano's* mouth, and smiled.

"And Pirrelli?" the *capitano* asked.

"Let me handle him. I'll fulfill that *pensionamento* when we return to *Firenze*. It's the least I owe him for the pleasure of our years together."

Cioni nodded and reached for Giordano's hand, pulling it to his abdomen. He glanced at Smoke's body, then scanned the length of the platform. "Where is the *bambino*? Young Theo."

Giordano rolled his eyes. "*Fanculo. Che importa?*"

Cioni stopped. Hesitated. "Where is he? Dante, I need to know now."

"*Perché?*"

Cioni expelled a frustrated breath through his nostrils.

"Oh, fuck it," he said, dropping all pretense.

He crushed Giordano's hand in his, swung it around and thrust it high behind the *Ruspanti's* back, snapping ulna and radius with the torquing movement, the broken shards of splintered bone tearing through the forearm and cashmere sleeve. "Where the fuck is the child?" he yelled.

Giordano's eyes were wide in horror and disbelief. "He's with Pirrelli. At the summit of One Vanderbilt—"

His words ended with a deep, guttural shriek.

The blast from Giordano's pistol resounded.

And the bullet instantly shattered Cioni's femur near the hip, and his leg went slack beneath him, blood pumping from the artery at his inner thigh. The *capitano* grabbed Giordano by the neck as he stumbled, digging his fingers deep into the sinews, strong fingernails cutting into the skin. He lifted him up and javelined him headfirst down onto the platform. The *Ruspanti* crumpled across the yellow line, his face imprinted by the raised bumps of tactile paving, his leg and shattered arm dangling over the edge, his weapon skittering across the platform.

Cioni went down with a squelching thud.

He pulled his belt from its loops and yanked it high and tight around his thigh. Then tore the length of his pants leg up to his groin to further tourniquet the limb, before army crawling across the platform toward Smoke. Blood smeared bright and wet and viscous in his wake.

He propped himself up as best he could and ripped open Smoke's jacket and shirt to confirm the damage. Three bullets had dug deep into the webbing of the Kevlar vest. Each deformed by the impact with the ceramic plate. He fingered around it and the blood-saturated padding, trying to discern any penetration. There was none. He pressed his ear to the exposed flesh, Smoke's breast warm and sticky with blood against his cheek. The broken sternum, ribs, and cartilage crunched beneath the weight of Cioni's head, but he detected the slow cadence of a heartbeat. It was barely beating beneath the strain.

"Tommy!" he yelled, leaning over him to check his breathing. "Tommy!" He urged Smoke's mouth open before pinching the nostrils closed. Then he pressed his mouth to his brother's, forcing his breath deep into his lungs. Smoke's chest rose and fell with an audible crunching of bone. Cioni held his fingers to the taut muscles of his neck, ensuring the pulse continued before blowing in another chestful of air. Smoke abruptly convulsed and flung his eyelids open wide.

* * *

He gagged and coughed, the burn and crack of his sternum and ribs agonizing as he attempted to take in a breath on his own. The pain crested with each rattling hack.

What was going on?

What happened?

Cioni hovered above him, his face creased in concern. But then he smiled, his eyebrows arching high. He pinched Smoke's cheeks and kissed him on the lips.

"*Bastardo!* Don't do that again!" He kissed Smoke a second time, then fell down onto his back beside him.

Smoke scratched at the straps of the Kevlar; his fingers clumsy and slow.

"Leave it," Cioni said, grasping Smoke's hand to stop his fumbling. "The vest is holding you secure. Don't touch it until you get some heavy-duty painkillers."

Smoke propped himself up onto his elbows. "Gaah! Fucking hell!" he grunted with little breath as the splintering pain seized him. He glanced toward Giordano, quivering at the edge of the platform, barely alive, eyes staring vacant, and then at Cioni, taking in the mess of his leg. Blood was pooling around them—too much blood.

The platform tunnel echoed with the deep screeching hum of an oncoming engine.

"Where's Theo?" he yelled above the growing noise.

"One Vanderbilt. At the summit with Pirrelli."

Smoke tapped his Bluetooth earbud as he awkwardly pulled off his blood-soaked jacket and dress shirt, clenching his teeth against the pain of movement, the breathtaking grind of broken ribs and ripped cartilage.

"Lucy," he said. "Status?"

He wound his bloody cotton dress shirt loosely around Cioni's bare upper thigh. "This is gonna hurt," he said, not waiting for a response before he pressed his thumb deep into the puckering exit wound, compressing the artery, then wrenching the shirt as tight as he could, tugging it with his teeth.

The *capitano* attempted to sit up.

"Stay down," Smoke yelled, pushing his hand flat against Cioni's chest.

"The NYPD has triangulated your cell," Lucy chimed in. "They're amassing around the perimeter of Grand Central Terminal."

"Simone," Smoke said. "I need you here with me and the *capitano* in the second cavern. Upper platform. *Pronto*."

"I think it's messing with their locators that we're so far underground," Lucy said. "They can't exactly pinpoint you within a several block radius around the terminals. Not yet."

The lights flicked off, then staccatoed back on along the length of the platform. The screech of the train brakes was piercing as the Long Island Railway engine slowed its approach.

"Nearly there," Simone said, his voice distorted through the Bluetooth.

"You're gonna have to carry the *capitano's* dead weight on your own, Simone. His leg is completely fucked. Lucy, how do we get him out of here?"

"Stand by…" Lucy said.

"The search perimeter has also just expanded to the top of One Vanderbilt. That's where Theo is," Smoke said.

"Understood. Stand by…" Lucy said.

Moretti ran up onto the platform, at the same instant the oncoming train hit Giordano's splayed body. He wasn't dead. Not yet. Though he probably wished he was. His head rolled as the train wheels tugged his body down through the slim gap between engine and platform, his face a revelation of horror as his skull bowled along, then cracked with a vacuous crunch to be lugged down beneath the train toward the rails and concrete ties.

Moretti didn't miss a beat, looping his arms under the *capitano's* pits.

"There's a shuttle leaving from the platform directly beneath you in forty seconds," Lucy said. "I'll organize for the House to meet you at the Jamaica train station with medical transport."

Smoke helped Moretti lift the *capitano*. "You got him?" he asked, ensuring he did, before scooping up Giordano's weapon and running for the stairs down to the mezzanine. "Lucy, I need direction. How do I get to One Vanderbilt from here?"

"Stand by."

He glanced over his shoulder as he ran from the second cavern into the first. Moretti and Cioni, his leg dragging clumsily behind, were taking the turn toward the lower platform and shuttle to leave the scene.

"Lucy!" Smoke said.

"Don't take the escalators. There's a corridor off to the side. An elevator will get you up to the main concourse. One Vanderbilt has its own underground entrance foyer at the southern end."

"Got it." He was in the corridor, his thoughts with Theo somewhere above him, not slowed even by the numbness of his foot and calf, or the pain of having to breathe, slow and shallow. The elevator doors open ahead of him.

"We're going to kill the power and lights again as soon as we can," Lucy said. "NYPD and SWAT are swarming Grand Central. Another squad is ready to deploy at the northern end of the Madison concourse. I'll be joining their ranks in the confusion."

The elevator rose quickly through the schist.

"Tommy, you need to dump your cell," she said. "They'll be able to pinpoint your exact location as soon as you hit the concourse. Let me know the instant you are out of the elevator, but then get rid of it."

"Understood. I'm gonna need a medic and a cleanup crew with a body bag at the top of One Vanderbilt in the next few minutes."

The elevator door shunted open.

"Here!" he yelled, before rock-skipping his cell across the terrazzo tiles. It shattered as it bounced, flipping when it hit the lip of the escalator to jettison down the slanted shaft back toward the platform caverns deep beneath the surface.

He ran.

The lights went out once more, throwing him into total darkness.

And he was on his own.

Chapter Forty-Seven

Theo.

The doors into One Vanderbilt's underground foyer were locked, scaffolding pushed against the glass and walls, and all throughout the space. A mini dumpster inside held remnants of light fixtures, broken ceiling tiles, and wiring. Boom lifts supported wooden crates of replacement lighting awaiting installation.

Smoke fumbled in his pocket for Moretti's lock pick.

Clicking the tumblers into place, he sidled in and latched the door behind him.

Not a moment too soon.

Green lasers swept through the darkness outside the secured foyer doors. SWAT had arrived on the Grand Central Madison Concourse.

The smell of the room was odd to him. Much like that of a new book with page edges gilded in metal foil. Not yet opened. Not yet read. By anybody. And definitely not him.

He faltered through the maze of metalwork and plastic drop sheets. Ducked under suspended metal planks. Skirted spools of electrical and ethernet cabling. Ambient light from Grand Central Terminal, or perhaps the Avenue above, somehow filtered into the space, lighting his path with an unsettling, shadowed ruddiness. Now and then the drop sheets flared an insipid green as the SWAT lasers swung through the darkness in his direction. He tripped and ripped through the last hanging plastic sheet onto the floor. Accent lighting clicked on around him, and he found himself in a long, black corridor, footlights skimming low along the lower edge of the walls, urging him forward. The elevator at the end of the passage was dark and mirrored, slimline lights strobing from ceiling to floor as the doors slid shut and he shot upward toward the summit of the skyscraper.

And Theo.

Glimpses of himself flashed in reflection with each flicker of light. Blood and sweat and stink, both his and Andrea's, saturated his suit pants. His torso was bloody and bare except for the tight confinement of the discolored Kevlar vest, the bullets still embedded. The vest's straps were uncomfortably tight against his damaged rib cage. They cut into his skin where they looped beneath his pits through the matted curls of blonde hair, now stained a dark black crimson. He tilted his chin in the wavering light, attempting to assess the bleeding gash on the underside, before scraping his fingernails across the dried blood encrusting his pectoral. He immediately regretted it. The twinge of pain was harsh and unforgiving. Sadistically brutal.

The elevator hit the ninety-first floor within seconds, his bulk feeling lighter with the momentum of the slowdown. When the doors slid open, he tensed and gripped his Glock with both hands out in front of him, ready to shoot. His backup gun and Giordano's pistol remained securely tucked into the waistband at his back, their warm, unyielding barrels reassuring against the hard muscles of his ass. The only part of his body that didn't ache.

He stepped out into the corridor.

It was dim, his sight slow to adjust, but at the end of the passage was the suggestion of massive picture windows, city lights, and the flash of lightning. The crystal of his Patek Philippe watch had shattered, its hands twisted, presumably when he'd hit the platform. He had no idea what time it was. Maybe midnight. Maybe one or two. How long had he been unconscious?

He stopped, aware of the tap of his dress shoes against the floor. Crouching down, still holding the gun before him, continuing to scan the darkness ahead and behind, he pulled his laces loose and slid out of the brogues. It was good to be barefooted, to stretch his toes, syrupy blood making them slick. He padded on without sound, without breath, casting his attention through the dark, searching for any movement or subtle change within the shadows.

Searching for Theo.

He came to the end of the corridor but remained in shadow.

He was slow to comprehend the scene before him.

The Empire State Building fluoresced red and purple, the pinprick of Manhattan lights all around it. Not one Empire State Building. Not two. But thousands of them reflected back and forth, up and down, toward infinity in every direction. The night's ferocious weather made the unexpected view even more unnerving. Gusting wind threw clouds across the sky and amongst the skyscrapers. Lighting flashed and bruised their depths.

Pirrelli appeared in the middle of all this, looking for all the world like he was suspended in midair. He was cradling Theo's small limp body, the two of them replicated uncountable times in every direction, tinted a sickly magenta by the Empire State's pulsing light.

Theo.

Smoke's heart ached and his throat felt dry as his son's name caught at the back of his mouth, unspoken. He tensed and stepped out onto the glass floor, his bloody feet slippery, splaying his toes to hold a steady grip. The garish multitude of the room's parallel and oblique glass and mirrored surfaces instantly reproduced and retroflexed his image. A quiet physical strength within the turmoil.

"You're more resilient than we gave you credit for," Pirrelli said. His voice echoed beneath the dull clashing drum of weather outside against the huge panes of glass.

"You don't seem surprised." Smoke was wary of anyone else who might be in the shadows of the mirror installation.

Unreflected.

He slid another bloody step forward, refusing to look down at the mirrored abyss beneath his bare feet, even knowing it was an illusion. One that insinuated a drop at least as far as Vanderbilt Avenue ninety stories below. Instead, he glanced up, but baulked at the image of his broken and bloody body suspended within an infinity of mirrored nothing. He concentrated on his son. *Theo*. Still in his pajamas and quilted robe. Tiny Ugg boots secure on his feet. His thumb held firmly in his mouth. And his small chest rising and falling with a steady breath.

"Give me my son," Smoke said, his voice balanced, without menace. Measured. The intonation of a father who knew exactly what to do. Knew exactly what was at stake. "My bullet won't miss, no matter how fast you think you are. No matter how clever you think you might be." His words came across with depth and empathy as he held his aim true to Pirrelli's forehead, reaching out his other hand toward Theo.

Beads of sweat collected in the furrows of the *Ruspanti's* brow and stained the pits of his jacket.

Smoke took another careful step farther out into the center of the illusion.

"How did you know we were up here?" Pirrelli asked.

"Guess."

"Dante wouldn't have told you."

Smoke assumed he meant Giordano. "He didn't tell *me*." He took more tentative steps, halting only when the *Ruspanti's* nervous heavy breaths ruffled the blood-matted curls across the top of his chest. "He told Capitano Cioni."

"The *capitano*?" Pirrelli blinked, confused. "But he…"

Smoke maintained eye contact as he pulled his son into the crook of his arm. "What did you give him?"

"Rohypnol. A small dose. Enough to make him pliant. Where is Dante? He and the *capitano* can explain all of this to you."

Smoke recognized the uncertainty crossing Pirrelli's face, and he knew without a doubt what he was thinking. He'd fallen into his own similar confusions in the past. His own blind love. And trust.

"You hurt a friend of mine," Smoke said. "Inflicted damage that no man should ever suffer."

"It served our purpose."

Smoke struck the heel of his Glock across Pirrelli's temple. The *Ruspanti* blanched but held his footing.

"And my son. What would you have done to him?"

Pirrelli shrugged. "Does it matter?"

Smoke struck him again, the blow splitting his brow and cheekbone open, splashing blood down to his jawline.

"Is that the best you can do?" Pirrelli asked. "You'd be dead by now if I had the gun."

Smoke kept his breath slow and shallow, protecting and loving the boy nestled in the crook of his arm. Focused on keeping the ache from wracking his body. On steering the conversation in a carefully orchestrated direction based on instinct and experience. Too much experience.

"But you do have a gun. The bulge at your abdomen is more than obvious. Or, if you like, you can use this one." Smoke reached around to his back, pulled Giordano's Walther PPK from his waistband, and tossed it to Pirrelli.

Pirrelli stared at it in confusion. "How do you have Dante's weapon?"

"Dante didn't need it anymore."

"What do you mean?"

"He's dead. Cioni killed him."

"The *capitano*? But…."

Smoke noted the crack of voice. He let the horror sink in. Kept his own features emotionless as he recognized the face of someone who'd lost the one they loved more than anything else in their life. The crumple was slow but certain, wrinkles deepening about the eyes, the sluggish well of tears, the dilation of irises. An unchecked tremble of lip and chin.

"But…"

"You have a gun," Smoke suggested.

"I don't understand."

"I have no qualms about killing you, but only if I need to. Only if you give me reason to."

Despite the *Ruspanti's* actions, despite what he'd done to Nate, what he did and perhaps intended to do to Theo, there was no official sanction for his retirement. Smoke might be an executioner when an action was warranted. He could live with that. But he was not judge and jury. He refused to let his fury lead his actions. No matter how easy it would be to squeeze the trigger. "Do you want me to kill you? Do you need me to kill you?"

Pirrelli slowly shook his head.

Smoke repositioned Theo in his grip. "What is your given name?" he asked.

Pirrelli glanced up beneath heavy, wet lids. "Alessandro."

"Alessandro," Smoke echoed. "You have your gun in your pocket. And you've got Dante's gun in your hand, still warm and marked with his fingerprints. From when he attempted to kill me."

Pirrelli turned the weapon in his hands and took a step back, indecision and sentiment clouding his features. Smoke stepped with him.

"We both have a choice right now, Alessandro. I've made my decision, but I need you to make yours."

Pirrelli had backed into the expanse of glass showcasing Manhattan. From the Empire State Building right across to the Verrazzano Bridge stretching over the narrows to Staten Island. He slid slowly down it and sank onto the mirrored floor.

Smoke hunkered down with him, knowing he'd made the impact he needed. He placed his Glock on the floor beside his bloody foot. "Alessandro. It's all right. You're making the right decision. You wouldn't make it if it weren't correct." Smoke didn't pity the man slumped before him. He knew him too well for that.

Alessandro abruptly thrust the barrel of his partner's weapon deep into his own mouth, chipping teeth, punching it hard against the back of his throat.

He gagged as he sobbed. And shook.

And squeezed the trigger.

"Stop!" Smoke commanded. He smacked the back of his hand against Pirrelli's chest and grabbed the top of the pistol in one fluid movement, blocking the hammer so it could not strike the firing pin. "That's not the answer. That's never the answer. Never." Smoke's heart was pounding in his chest, the crunch of his ribs excruciating with each thump. "Do you really think I'd hand you a loaded gun?" he lied. "There's another option. A better option. The only option I'll allow you. The House cleanup crew will be here soon. They'll deliver you to the Palazzo Pitti. There you'll receive the justice that even you deserve."

Alessandro hesitantly withdrew the pistol from his mouth, threads and globs of saliva stretching from his lips to the barrel. He shivered and his eyes darkened as he released the weapon's magazine from the grip into his shaking hand. The clip wasn't empty. A single bullet remained.

The *Ruspanti* palmed the magazine back into the Walther PPK and, with a determined grunt, swung the muzzle toward Theo.

Smoke's reaction was pure reflex, an acute and brutal split-second survival response. He twisted the gun in Alessandro's grip, snapping, and ripping the finger within the trigger guard and forcing the barrel back through shattered teeth and into the depths of the *Ruspanti's* mouth, thudding his head back against the glass.

The gun's report was loud and echoing.

The 32-caliber ripped through the *Ruspanti*, shattering the back of his skull to crack and spider the broad expanse of the laminated window behind him from edge to edge. The pressure in the mirrored installation noticeably dropped, air coursing through the remnants of Alessandro's head and out the precise bullet hole drilled through the glass. The air rush escalated into a horrendous shrieking whistle, the wind shear outside the ninety-first floor gusting, sucking at the sloppy crimson gore to halo it across the outside of the building.

Chapter Forty-Eight

It was almost 4 p.m.

Sun filtered through the industrial windows of Tommy's West Village loft. The light bounced across the burnished wood floor, making the room glow and highlighting the reading nook with its hundreds of books, framing Dannii's photo-realistic painting of Theo. His eyes as blue as Tommy's. His smile as incorrigible. His hands reaching out toward the viewer. Foot, knee, and hand prints made indelible marks across the lower part of the portrait where Dannii had coaxed Theo to amble across the still-wet paint.

Andrea stretched in the warmth of the sun rays, resting bare feet on Tommy's oversized cowhide ottoman. A metal cage encircled his upper leg, stabilizing titanium rods protruding from his thigh. He added an exuberant yawn to the stretch before licking a fist full of painkillers into his mouth and swallowing them dry. Then he tossed the bottle of pills along the length of the sectional toward Tommy.

"You're a lucky guy," Andrea said. "No one could ever doubt Theo worships the ground you walk on. There's a love every boy deserves to have with his father. And Jenny and Dannii obviously adore you, too."

Tommy smiled, leaning into the cushions, his legs extended along the couch toward Andrea. He held an icepack to his chest. Another draped across his calf and ankle.

"It's a relief Lucy and Gabrielle were able to smooth out most of the bumps over the last several days," Tommy said. "Painted me as a hero in all this fucking mess, rather than the reason Theo was in danger to begin with."

Andrea gently grasped Tommy's foot and rubbed his thumb against the pads of his toes.

"Did you ever want a family, Andrea?"

The Italian's lip curled. "I have a family that I love. I have my mamma. My *fratellos*. And now I have you."

Tommy tilted his head. "I thought you said you were an orphan?"

"No. I said I was a bastard." He chuckled. "The fact of which both my mamma and I are quite proud."

"Do you know your father?"

"We have a relationship. An understanding. And as long as he keeps my mamma happy whenever she visits him in Bellagio, he knows I won't kill him."

Andrea's bluntness made Tommy smile. He wondered who his own father was. Whether he was also still alive.

"You and your family shall spend the summer with us at our estate near *Firenze*, if you wish," Andrea said. "My mamma's cooking and the countryside will help us all recuperate. The pool is decent enough for laps, and the olive groves throughout the valley are littered with trails for you and I to build our strength and agility. Our friendship and fidelity. And Theo… That young man is certain to return a foot taller and speaking fluent *Toscana*. As he should."

Tommy's cell vibrated and the doorbell camera flashed on the screen. "It's Lucy," he said, tapping the icon to buzz open the doors. He pulled on the new blue and green camouflage tank top Gabrielle had gifted him, adjusted himself, and tightened the drawstring of his pajama shorts.

"One thing before Lucy arrives, *fratello*. The House may not be aware of the extra zeros I diverted into your account." Andrea shifted his weight, grimacing, to sweep the robe across his bare hip and thigh, and half-heartedly knot the sash.

"What are you talking about?"

"I cleared the distribution of funds from Jameson's escrow account through the Palazzo. It's well earned and will secure your future, and your family's."

Tommy's mind spun as Andrea's words sank in. He stood and hobbled toward the kitchen to start the coffee percolating. It wasn't until he'd settled on a barstool, and Lucy had pushed in through the foyer doors, that he fully comprehended what Andrea had said.

Lucy dropped her satchel on the kitchen island and sat beside Tommy.

"Do you need me to leave you two alone?" Andrea asked.

Lucy shook her head. "No need. I'm sure you'll find out soon enough, anyway. Have you spoken to Nathan Lucas?" she asked Tommy.

"Nate? Yeah. Just yesterday. He'll be moving into my rental on the other side of the block."

"Do you think that's wise?"

"Yes, I do."

"Good. I'm glad. I think so too." She settled her hand on the marble island beside Tommy's, her fingers warm against his. "The House is performing all required due diligence, of course. So far, he's come up clean. I can't make any promises, but his resume is more than impressive. He may be useful."

The percolator gurgled, and Tommy circled the island and pulled down three espresso cups from the shelf. A bouquet of coffee with chocolate and caramel undertones filled the room. He poured the espressos and slid a cup toward Lucy.

"Hey," he said. "I owe you an apology. Several, I guess. Thank you for everything you've done. I'm sorry I didn't trust you when I really should have."

"I understand," she said. She brushed her fingers against his, but then stopped, glancing over her shoulder at Andrea. Then she slipped her electronic pad from her satchel.

"The local investigation is officially closed, with the coroner matching Giordano's DNA signature with the seminal fluid collected at each of the kill sites."

"I thought you had replacement samples shipping in from Europe somewhere."

"This was a cleaner solution. It tidied up the loose ends and gave them a body. Someone to blame."

Tommy wondered how the fuck they got access to Giordano's semen and then swapped the samples with his own, but he didn't ask.

Lucy's face was unreadable as she concentrated on the pad.

On the far side of the room, Andrea pressed his lips tight, his stare intent on Tommy. Also unreadable.

A thought suddenly struck Tommy. "Pirrelli and Giordano were trying to kill me. They knew I was staying with Simone at the Palace Hotel. And they had to know I was in the twins' hotel room because it had to be them who dumped Elgan in the bed next to me. Why didn't they just kill me? They had plenty of opportunity. Why play that horrific game with Nate? With Theo?"

"Why does a cat play with a mouse before ending its life?" Andrea said.

Cat and mouse—*il gatto e il topo.*

Who had said that? Was it Moretti?

Tommy shook his head. To hell with it. He didn't care. Giordano and Pirrelli were dead. Jameson was dead. The money was disbursed. Incentive no longer existed. It was over.

He let out a deep steady breath. "So, now we go back to normal."

"No," Lucy said. "You are being temporarily reassigned. A change in duty and family due to escalating and immediate threats that take precedence over your current charge. Your skills will translate to the new circumstances.

Tommy looked at Andrea, then back to Lucy. "I don't get it. Reassigned… For how long?"

"Four years. Maybe more."

"Four years?"

"This has been under consideration for several months," Lucy said. "And recent events have only confirmed the necessity and suitability of your reassignment. Especially as several in your current appointment have become, shall we say, familiar with your skillset?"

Tommy immediately thought of Eleonora. Of Rafaella. And his intimate moments with each of them.

"I'm still more than capable of carrying out my job," he said.

"Of that, I have no doubt. And neither does the Director. You are being reassigned within the Secret Service. Specifically, to the detail protecting the First Family."

Tommy carefully placed his espresso cup onto its saucer, his eyes wide.

"It will be a major drop in salary," Lucy said. "But I suspect that won't be a hardship for you considering the financial outcome of Grand Central Madison." A gentle smirk dimpled her cheeks.

Of course, she knows, Tommy thought.

"I'll ensure you have adequate time to recuperate from your injuries, but by early fall you'll report to our facility in Maryland for the required reconditioning and training. Mainly in working as part of a team. Something I've seen firsthand that you should breeze through. Honestly, I wish we could have shipped you down sooner, before this mess here in Manhattan, before the threats against the President's family had heightened to their current state."

Tommy stirred sugar into his coffee and sipped the swirling layer of crema, his thoughts racing ahead of him of what was to come.

Chapter Forty-Nine

The First Lady of the United States, Nichelle Alexander, looked out the tinted glass gymnasium window on the fortieth floor of the Four Seasons hotel. To the south, the rising sun reflected from the art déco windows of Rockefeller Center, with other less dramatic structures striking up into the golden early morning view. Her skin shone from an hour on the treadmill. Six miles. A good run.

There was hesitation in her movement and he knew she'd noticed him crouched amongst the darkest shadows of exercise machinery. She turned from the window, biting her lower lip as she clenched her fists to confront him.

Apart from the two of them, the room was empty. The entire floor was empty. The Secret Service had sealed it the night before, as well as the floors above and below. Still, he was able to bypass their security measures.

He'd waited long enough to make his move, to teach her the lesson she needed to learn.

He lunged at her. She sidestepped, but he pivoted and knocked her to the ground, both of them landing with a dull thud next to the elliptical. Gripping her around the neck, he yanked her tight against his body, the strength of his thighs holding her kicking legs securely as he wrenched her torso.

No one would hear her screams.

No one would come to her rescue.

Not this time.

Nichelle squirmed and jabbed her elbow into his ribs to little effect. She tried to bite him. Then she twisted and swung a fist down into his crotch, delivering a miscalculated and indecisive blow to his balls. He grunted and fell sideways, momentarily stunned. It was enough for her to scramble on top and straddle his prone body, to knee him in the lumbar, and adroitly yank his arm around behind his back. She pulled up, bending his wrist back at an awkward angle. Hard. For a moment, he did not move, the throbbing ache between his legs piercing right up into the depths of his gut. Dulling his senses. But then he arched, flexed, and rolled beneath her onto his back, his shorts riding up and to the side, his chest heaving beneath the sweat-drenched polo shirt from the unexpected exertion. The disconcerting retaliation from someone known mostly for walking red carpets in lavish Ralph Lauren gowns, decorating the gardens and halls of the White House for Easter Egg Hunts and State Dinners.

Aroused with the intimate contact of her comeback, he slid his groin from beneath the moist heat of her buttocks and thrust his legs up behind her. He grabbed her torso with his bare feet and ankles and slammed her down against the floor.

He didn't expect her to go for his groin again, but she did. A proven weakness in any man. Both for pain and pleasure. She shoved a hand past the meaty length of his cock to grip his balls through the flimsy cotton shorts. She squeezed tight, wrenching, digging her nails deep into the crawling skin of his scrotum. Drawing blood. The added twist made him gag, the pain radiating, burning along every nerve in his body. He involuntarily loosened his legs, and she launched herself up, to come down hard on his chest, striking both her fists against his heart, making it skip a beat. She screamed, a wild creature, as she gripped his larynx, urging her fingers deep behind the cartilage, and roughly dug a nail into the crease of his eyelid. His eyeball instantly throbbed and shot with blood. Their faces were inches apart, noses touching, both breathing deep of each other's urgent breath.

"I win this one, Special Agent Smoke," she said, dropping her gaze to the fullness of his mouth, the bite of his tongue between his teeth.

That was the distraction he'd expected. Had waited for. The lesson she still needed to learn after their months of training. Months of building her confidence. Her strength and tactics. Her agility and skill. And still he had no qualms about manhandling the First Lady of the United States for her own good.

He flipped her sideways to throw her down onto her back.

She grunted with the impact, and he rolled on top of her, pushing all the breath from her lungs and pinning her legs with his, gripping her wrists and forcing her arms out wide, her breasts flattened beneath the swell of his chest.

He had her completely immobilized.

Both their bodies firm and hot and slicked with perspiration.

Sweat dripped from his lips onto hers.

THE END

Cast

The House
Lucy O'Donnell
Gabrielle Davis
Thomas Smoke

The Palazzo Pitti
Simone Moretti
Gianetta (Simone's handler. Unseen)

The Ruspanti
Capitano Andrea Cioni
Alessandro Pirrelli (retired)
Dante Giordano (retired)
Innocenti
Sangallo
Conti
Amidei

The Family
Eleonora di Toledo
Rafaella di Toledo
Daan Stuyvesant (retired)
Angi Stuyvesant, née di Toledo (retired)

Jameson De Vries (retired)
Giulia Rossi (Jameson's wife) (retired)
Aloïs Laurent / Aloysius Laurentius (retired)
Mathéo Laurent / Matteo Laurentius (retired)
Luca De Vries (Jameson's son)
Hannah O'Donnell (Luca's bride)
Augustus (Gus) di Toledo
Felice di Toledo (Gus's husband)

Related Retirements
Elgan Glyndwr (retired)
Liz Bayer (retired)

Collateral Damage
Nate/Nathan Lucas
Jenny
Dannii
Theo

Supporting Cast
Hugh Danvers
Julianne

Introducing
Nichelle Alexander, FLOTUS

Location
New York City, NY, USA.

262

About the Author

An avid reader and researcher, novelist P.J. Parker has traveled and lived extensively around the world—intrigued by cultures and eras of historic interest and buildings of architectural significance.

P.J. currently lives and writes in the USA.

Novels by P.J. Parker

Roxelana and Suleyman

"Fascinating" "Intriguing"

America Tuwaqachi: The Saga of an American Family

"Masterful" "Unforgettable"

Fire on the Water: A Companion to Mary Shelley's *Frankenstein*

"Tremendous" "Impressive"

Origin of the Vampyre: A Companion to Doctor Polidori's *The Vampyre*

"Compelling" "Page turner"

Smoke

"Fascinating" "WOW!"

264